Memories of a life

JEWEL E. ANN

MEMORIES OF A LIFE

COLTEN & JOSIE: PART TWO

JEWEL E. ANN

CHAPTER
One

"Colten messages me hourly. Does he really think I want to know what he had for lunch? Does he need to know our dinner plans at ten in the morning? Do I care that a friend of a friend is pregnant with triplets?"

Dr. Byrd rests an ankle on his opposing knee, wearing an expression of deep thought.

I continue, "He bought new black boots for work. His mom is taking water aerobics. A funny TikTok. Detective Rains has a hangnail." I roll my eyes. "Okay, not that one, but nearly as ridiculous. He sends all these messages when what he really wants to say is, 'Are you doing okay? Have you thought about that girl, the one you think you were? Have you made an appointment with your psychiatrist? Are you still planning on marrying me? Have you told anyone else about your theory?'"

"Have you?" Dr. Byrd asks.

"Listen … it's not a theory. I haven't been wrong once since the day I woke from my near-death experience. I want to be wrong. This isn't the kind of 'right' anyone would find satisfying. But no, I haven't told anyone except the Nashville police. If I didn't have the credentials that I do, there's little doubt that I would have been committed by now."

"Do you believe in reincarnation?" he asks.

"I think I've reached the point of 'if it walks like a duck and talks like a duck.' Tomorrow the clouds could part and angels could descend from heaven. If that happens, even the most headstrong atheists will take a moment to rethink their beliefs. So … yeah. I'm inclined to believe in reincarnation since I have such inexplicable things in my head from a time way before the existence of Josephine Watts from Des Moines, Iowa."

"Tell me about the girl."

"The one I was in another life?"

He nods.

I shake my head. "I don't know. I just remember the feeling. Feeling scared. Feeling the edge of the straight blade against my scalp. It cut me. He told me to hold still."

"Who told you?"

"Winston Jeffries."

"Are you sure?"

I glance up at Dr. Byrd. "Who else would it be?"

"I don't know. I just want to know if you're sure it

was him or if you might be deducing it from the information you've gathered online coupled with the visions in your head."

"No. I mean ..." I rub my temples. "I don't know. I just want to forget. Whatever's in my head, I want to forget it. I felt a responsibility to follow through and figure it out. Now that I have, I just want to forget about it. It wasn't a premonition. I don't feel the urgency to prevent these girls from dying."

"Are you back to work?"

"Two weeks." I blow out a long breath. "I need work. I need my mind to find its place again."

"And the engagement? Are you making wedding plans?"

I laugh. "No. I haven't told my parents yet."

"Why?"

"Because ..." I shake my head. "I don't know if I can be that girl he murdered *and* be a bridezilla."

"Has Colten told his family?"

"I don't know."

"You haven't asked him?"

"He's ... I don't know. He's okay, yet not okay. Colten and I have always danced around the truth. For as long as I can remember, we've made our own reality. We've had front row seats to watching the rest of the world and acting like it doesn't affect us if we don't let it."

"How has that worked for you?"

"It's amazing, until it's catastrophically heartbreaking."

Dr. Byrd gives me a slow nod. He's clueless. I don't

mean it disrespectfully. I'm his "undetermined." Undetermined sucks.

We wind up our session with me feeling none the better. If I'm not going to let him medicate me, he's helpless. I don't think patients with near-death experiences comprise a large percentage of his clientele.

When I get home, I scroll through my emails to find the parapsychologist in Berkeley. I missed my appointment. It's time to reschedule.

CHAPTER
Two

Two students dressed in trench coats went on a shooting spree at Columbine High in Littleton, Colorado.

Colten's mom refused to let him watch the news. She wanted to protect him and his brother from such evil. We were twelve, so it wasn't out of line with good parenting.

"Let's talk about this," Dad said to me a few nights after the horrific massacre. He and Mom sat me down at the kitchen table, and we discussed the events. It's not that my parents weren't "good" parents; they just had a different definition of good parenting.

"We don't want you to be afraid to go to school," Mom said, setting a plate of cookies and a glass of milk next to me.

"I'm not."

"That's good, but if you have questions—"

"Someone said they were bullied in school, and that's why they did it," I said.

"Well, we might never know since they're no longer alive." Dad leaned back a fraction and crossed his thick arms.

"What if they weren't bullied?"

"What do you mean?" he asks.

"What if they just wanted to kill people because … they liked it?"

Rarely were my parents speechless, but that night, they had nothing. Not one word.

Finally, Mom cleared her throat. "Why do you think anyone would kill other humans for … fun?"

I shrugged. "I overheard one of my teachers talking to another teacher in the hallway. She said the boys were psychopaths. So I stopped by the library on my way home from school and looked up psychopath."

"Um … Jo, you're twelve. I don't think it's a good idea for a twelve-year-old to study psychopaths." Dad's face wrinkled. "It's a lot for your immature brain."

"Nothing is wrong with my brain. You've always said I'm too smart for my own good."

They laughed, but it was an uneasy laugh.

"If they were bullied, it would mean they hated the kids they killed. But psychopaths don't have feelings like that. They think they are better than everyone else. They don't feel bad about the things they do. They don't think about what other people are feeling when they do bad things to them. They don't have any regrets. Can you imagine doing bad things and not feeling guilty? You don't feel guilty when you shoot a deer, do you, Dad? Or if you have to shoot a bank robber, right?"

Dad coughed, bringing his fist to his mouth and easing his head side to side. "That's ... that's different, Jo. I'm not a psychopath. I would never hurt innocent people, and if I did by accident, I would feel terrible. Remorseful. Pained."

I roll my eyes. "I wasn't calling you a psychopath. I'm just saying, maybe those two boys had something wrong with them that made them not feel bad about killing other humans the way you don't feel bad about the deer. Dustin Santi told me people eat dogs in other countries the way we eat cows or chickens here. So what I think is kinda weird and gross is not weird and gross to other people. I bet those two boys who killed those kids would have eaten dogs. Don't you think?"

For the second time that night, I left my parents speechless.

While other kids at my school were lined up at the door to the guidance counselor's office to discuss how scared they were by the Columbine shooting, I was eating cookies and milk with my parents while discussing psychopaths and other cultures eating puppy dogs.

"Listen, sweetie, maybe don't talk about this with other kids ... or even other adults for that matter," Mom said.

"About psychopaths or about eating puppy dogs?" I

dipped my last bite of cookie into the milk.

My parents shared a look. "Both," Mom said.

"Why?"

"Because it's not just kids who are in shock and scared; it's adults too. Parents are having a hard time sending their kids to school because they're worried it could happen to them."

"I've been going to school. Are you worried about me?"

"We love you. And of course we'd be devastated if anything happened to you, but the chances of it happening to you at your school are really, really slim. You have a better chance of dying in a car accident," Mom said.

"Or getting hit by lightning," Dad added.

Mom shot him a scowl.

He lifted a shoulder. "What? It's true."

"I'm going to Colten's." I stood, taking my glass to the sink.

"Don't talk about it with Colten either. Okay?" Mom stressed.

I nodded, giving her a stiff smile before shoving my feet into my sneakers, pulling on a hoodie, and running across the street.

"Hey, Josie." Becca smiled, opening the front door. "Colten's upstairs, practicing piano."

I stepped inside, toeing off my shoes.

"How are you doing, hon?" she asked with an ugly, concerned look on her face.

"Fine. Why?"

"Have your parents talked with you about Columbine?"

"Uh-huh. They said not to discuss it with anyone ... and I mean anyone."

Her pink lips parted, and she gave me a single slow nod. "Of course."

"I'm going to see if Colten's about done."

"O-okay." She seemed a little off as I zipped past her, straight up the stairs.

My momentum came to a screeching halt when I reached Colten's bedroom door. His fingers played the saddest song I had ever heard. I tiptoed a little closer. His body moved with the music like the metronome on Vera's piano.

Colten was only one of three boys who I knew that played the piano. He was also the best. I wasn't the best at anything. I wasn't liked by everyone like Colten. My "uniqueness" never felt special, just different. Not Colten. He was special. He could do everything. And most days I felt certain the only reason he was my friend was because my dad was police chief. Sure, I was smart. Who really cared about that yet? No twelve-year-olds talked about honor roll or scholarships. They couldn't pronounce valedictorian let alone care about it.

"Josie, you're such a creeper," Colten mumbled without stopping his fingers.

I sighed and sat next to him on the piano bench, facing away from the keys. "Why are you playing such a sad song?"

"Why is it sad?"

"Because it's slow. It's funeral music."

"Have you been to a funeral?" He stopped playing and angled his body toward mine.

"No." I frowned. "Not yet anyway. Nobody I know will die."

His head jutted backward. "That's mean. You sound like you want someone to die so you can go to their funeral."

"I'm curious. That's all. I don't want someone to die. Not like those boys in Colorado, who killed the kids at their school."

Oops ... I may have broken my promise to my parents.

"My mom said they were sick. Not like a cold. Like something was wrong with their brains," Colten said.

"Psychopaths. I stopped by the library and looked it up. Don't worry. You're not a psychopath."

"I know I'm not. But ... how would you know?"

"Because you say sorry a lot, and you mean it. I say sorry too, but I don't always mean it. But if you died, I would be sad. So I know I'm not a psychopath either. But I've been thinking a lot about it. Do you think Richie Gregg is one? He's mean to everyone. When he gets in trouble, he doesn't care. And his dad smokes in the car when he picks Richie up from school. My dad said parents who smoke in the car with their kids don't care about their health. So if Richie's dad doesn't care about his son, he probably doesn't care about other people either, which means Richie might be like his dad."

And just like that ... I equated smoking to being a psychopath. Sure, some days I was too smart for my own good, but at twelve, I think I was, more times than not, too dumb for my own good.

"My grandpa smokes around Chad and me, but he's never killed anyone," Colten said.

"Not all psychopaths are killers. But my dad said secondhand smoke can kill you, so it's possible your grandpa could kill you by accident. I don't think they'd arrest him. My dad said a woman accidentally backed over her daughter while pulling out of the garage. The girl died, but the mom didn't get arrested because it was an accident."

"Did you finish your homework?"

I frown. "I don't have homework."

"What about your report on an American president?"

"I did it yesterday after school."

"You finished it in one day?"

I nodded. "Are you done?"

"No. I have to finish it tonight."

"I thought we'd go to the park."

"Can't. I have to finish my paper."

"I'll finish it. Who's it on?"

Colten's face soured. "You can't write my paper for me."

"Why not?"

"Because we could get in trouble."

"Who's going to know?"

Colten's lips twisted. "It's Taft."

"Taft? Why did you choose Taft? Because he was the only president to serve both as President and as Chief Justice?"

Colten blinked several times. "No. Because I like his mustache."

I snorted. "Are you serious?"

He shrugged.

"Fine. Show me your three sources. I'll write it, and then we can go to the park."

"I think this is wrong."

"Wrong is what those boys in Colorado did. This is no big deal."

"Why do you keep talking about those boys?" He opened his backpack and pulled out a black three-ring binder.

"Because it's interesting."

"It's awful."

"Awful things can be interesting. Why do you think they make us study wars in history?"

"Because they're interesting?"

I took his binder and grinned. "No. Nice try. We study bad things, so we don't repeat history. You don't listen in class, do you?"

Colten frowned. "History is boring. Nobody listens."

I listened, but I didn't have time to explain my school habits. I had a report to write so Colten could go to the park with me. There wasn't much I wouldn't do for the boy next door.

CHAPTER
Three

My future of marital bliss is off to a great start. I lied to Colten. He thinks I'm meeting with a specialist at the university. A specialist in reincarnation. If he were here to see the run-down strip mall in front of me, he'd lose his shit.

The door reads: Psychic. Walk-ins welcome. Estimated wait time is eternity.

I pull on the handle, but it's locked.

"Come in."

I glance up at a camera mounted in the corner just as the lock to the door clicks and buzzes.

Oof ...

The pungent smell of incense just about knocks me over.

"Welcome, Josephine." An older woman with witchy silver hair takes a bow. When she stands erect, her lips part into a slight smile. They're dry lips sticking to brown-stained teeth. Her cough isn't that of a smoker's. It's more of a death rattle.

"Thanks." I glance around the room. There's a black ceiling dotted in stars and moons hanging from fishing lines. Two round velvet pillows reside in the middle of the wood-floored room. White painted clouds cover the baby blue walls.

"I am Athelinda. Please remove your socks and shoes."

I glance down at my feet then at her feet. Calloused heels, bunions, crooked toes, and thick yellow nails.

"I encourage you, if it's in your zone of comfort, to remove all of your clothes and slip on a loose gown like mine." She nods to the hooks on the wall and the sheer white gowns hanging from them. "We don't want anything restricting your energy."

I can see basically everything through her gown, but I nod once anyway, shuffle my feet to the wall, and remove my clothes. Coworkers have seen me naked in the locker room at work. I'm not modest.

After I pull the gown over my head, I meet her in the middle of the room and sit on the pillow opposite her, both of us in lotus pose.

"Let's close our eyes, take a few deep breaths ... in through your nose for four seconds and out through your nose for four seconds. Keep your eyes closed as we go through a few questions."

I close my eyes, and when I do, I see the girls with

the shaved heads. The hair hanging from the tree. The cemetery.

In for four ... out for four.

I repeat this until she speaks.

"How long were you under the water?"

My eyes pop open.

"Close your eyes."

Her eyes are closed. How does she know mine are open?

"How do you know about the water?"

"Your date of birth. You were born on a Friday in October. An autumn child born on a Friday will resurrect previous lives if submerged during their final breath."

This is weird, dare I say crazy? I can see how people would bolt out of here with her logic, but I'm here because I'm struggling with my own brand of crazy.

"I don't know how long I was submerged."

"What did you see?"

"Long hair tied to tree branches in a churchyard. Then I saw girls with shaved heads being buried in existing graves."

"Who buried them? What did that person look like?"

"I don't know. I never see that person."

When I hear her wrestling around with something, I open my eyes. Her shaky twig fingers retrieve a big book from beneath her pillow as she leans to the side. It's weathered and mottled in shades of brown and says

"I AM ..." The binding whines in protest as she opens it.

"I see a lot of people with gifts. They don't feel like gifts at the time, but they are powerful privileges that come with a second chance at life." She flips through the delicate pages that look as fragile as an onion peel. "You, however, have not been granted a gift or any sort of privilege, I fear."

I frown. This was not a good idea.

She stops on a page and moves her finger beneath the lines of script, mumbling to herself.

"I know what it means. I just need help getting rid of the memories."

Athelinda glances up at me, yellow eyes narrowed into tiny slips. "What do you think it means?"

"I was one of the girls buried in the cemetery."

"Why do you think that?"

"Because I remember the feeling of fear and my head being shaved. I know where the bodies were buried."

"Was all the hair hanging from the same tree?"

I shake my head. "But all the trees were in church-yards in Tennessee."

She clears her throat. "And were all of the bodies buried in the same cemetery?"

Another headshake. "But all of the cemeteries are in Tennessee."

"So you've seen many girls and many locks of hair tied to various trees?"

"Yes."

"You've seen more than one cemetery?"

I nod.

"If you were one of the girls, how did you see more than one cemetery?"

I shrug. "Maybe I witnessed other deaths before mine. Maybe it was its own form of torture. If the killer was a psychopath, he enjoyed watching me suffer."

"I'm very sorry, Josephine. But you were not one of those girls."

"How do you know?"

"Because your element is water. You point west. Sunset. Autumn. Waning moon. Water. That's why your spirit attempted to leave when you were in the water. And where you came from is how you died in the life you resurrected. We come from the opposite of where we are now. You came from air. Your spirit in that life left this world in air, not earth. These girls were buried in *earth*. They were not hung from air. That was symbolic of something else, not the manner in which they died."

"They were dead before they were buried in earth. Their death might have been air." I don't know why I'm arguing with her. I'm not equipped with enough knowledge of elements and their symbolism.

"If they were dead before they were buried, and you were one of those girls, then you wouldn't have visions of a cemetery. Visions of previous lives are from moments when we were actually alive. I've died many times. Trust me, I know." She closes the book. "I can assure you; you weren't one of the girls."

"Then the visions don't make sense."

Her gaze drops to the book, her pointed fingernails tapping the cover. "As I was saying earlier, this is not a gift. I'm sorry this is happening to you. I wish there were more I could do."

"What is *this*? What are you referring to?"

"Vita Atonement." She brings her attention back to me.

I study her for a few moments before nodding. "Life reparation?"

Her thick brows slide up her forehead a fraction. "Exactly. This life is your chance to make up for the life you remember. Vita atonement lives are never easy. The souls trapped in a body during this kind of life cycle are often unsettled. They don't fit in well. They're often battling between *what is* and *what was* without realizing it. And it's incredibly rare to have what you have."

"What do I have?"

"Recollection. You now have the missing piece. You now know why you've struggled to find your place, to fit in, to submit to what is 'normal.' Atonement won't be easy for you, but you have a better chance than most who navigate Vita Atonement without recollection."

I shake my head. "I ... I don't have recollection if you're telling me I wasn't one of those girls."

"Josephine, you know. Your brain is trying so hard to protect you. It's why the brain blocks certain memories like trauma. It's why you don't recall the day you died, how long you were underwater, how your lungs felt when they needed oxygen but none was there to be had."

"What ..." I continue to shake my head. "What are you saying?"

"You know."

I continue to shake my head.

"You can't forget it until you let it in, atone it, and bury it for good."

"Atone what?"

"You know, Josephine. Close your eyes and let it in."

I don't want to close my eyes. I want her to stop being so cryptic. "Just tell me."

"I don't have to," she whispers. "You already know."

This is worse than the images.

This is worse than the feeling I had the night Colten unearthed the bodies.

This is ... unimaginable.

"No ..." I stumble getting to my feet.

"Let it in."

"N-no ..." I sway while my legs attempt to carry me to my clothes. Is this what it feels like to be drunk? To have no control over your body and your mind?

"You have to make this right in the universe."

"STOP IT!" I rip off the gown and grab my hair, fingers digging into my scalp. My knees buckle, sending me to the floor in a naked ball of despair. I want to pull out my hair and rip off my skin. Plunge a knife into my chest and cut out my own heart.

You weren't one of the girls ... you were Winston Jeffries.

CHAPTER
Four

"Time's up. You ready to talk yet?" Rains asks as I stare at my computer a little before ten p.m.

"What?" I glance up from my desk littered with paperwork and empty coffee cups. I've messaged Josie a dozen times and called her at least that many.

"Can we talk?"

I sigh, running a hand through my hair. "Yeah, sure. What's up?"

"I dug your ass out of trouble in Nashville. I'm still getting calls about Dr. Watts. I don't find out you were childhood friends until the two of you raid a cemetery in another state. You begged me to give you some time to 'deal' with her before explaining everything to me. Well ... times up." He sits on the edge of my desk and crosses his arms.

"We were neighbors, inseparable until I left her to

20

go into the Marines. I was messed up because my dad was an asshole. Things didn't end well with Josie. I don't see or hear from her for seventeen years, then boom! I run into her at a restaurant while she's on a date, then I see her at work. What are the chances, right?"

Rains nods slowly, brow pinched tightly.

"She hated me, still kind of hates me, but I think she loves me more. Just like I think we're getting married because I vomited some half-ass proposal to her out of nowhere. Then the shooting at the pier. Then these memories from her near-death experience. The next thing I knew, we were on a plane to Tennessee to dig up dead bodies all because she's had visions related to a serial killer who was executed over a century ago. I mean ..." I shake my head. "I couldn't make up this shit if I wanted to. Everything we told the Nashville police was true. Well, it was Josie's truth. Fuck if I know what's true right now because I don't have a better explanation for how she knew about those bodies, yet ... I can't quite swallow the idea that she was one of the victims in another life."

Rains twists his lips. "That's ..."

"Fucked-up. One hundred percent." I lean back in my chair and scrub my hands over my face. "I appreciate all your help getting the chief to dig my ass out of trouble in Nashville."

"You're lucky you still have your badge."

I nod.

"Do you believe her?"

I ask myself this question every day. "I don't know, man. I just don't know."

"She's the most intelligent, laser-focused person I know," Rains says. "She's methodical and a perfectionist when it comes to details. But even the most put-together people can lose a piece of their mind after something like what happened at the pier."

"Still doesn't explain how she knew about the bodies." I'm not trying to be argumentative with him, but there is no explanation for her knowledge of those bodies, and my mind keeps circling around to that one very important detail.

Rains nods slowly. "Sure doesn't." He inspects me with an unreadable expression. "So ... when were you going to tell me that you've been screwing the ME?"

I have no humor inside of me at the moment, yet his question pulls a chuckle from me anyway. "I'm not sure. Maybe a few days before the wedding. Josie and I have never had a normal relationship. I'm not sure why I think we can have one now. Clearly, we're off to a great start."

Rains smirks.

"She's never wanted to get married. Never wanted to have children. She's never been in the range of normal."

"So why ask her to marry you?"

Again, I chuckle, glancing at my phone, waiting for her to contact me. "I don't know. I think I want her to be with me, like really, officially be with me. And I want to tell the world that she's mine and I'm hers. God ... I sound like a pussy, but I've loved her since ... hell, I don't know. Before I really knew what I felt had a name."

"And now she sees dead people. And she doesn't want kids, but you have a daughter."

"And she's in California supposedly visiting some expert on near-death experiences, but she won't answer my calls or my texts."

"Do you follow her location?"

I shake my head.

"I'm not sure she's really going to marry you if she won't let you track her location."

"I haven't asked her."

"Why?"

I shrug a shoulder.

"You're afraid of her."

"Pfft ... I'm not afraid of her."

"She dissects dead people all day, and at night, she sees more dead people. She knows where lost bodies were buried. Fuck, man ... not gonna lie ... I'm a little afraid of her."

"You don't know her like I know her."

"Then you know she's okay. And you trust that she'll check in when she's ready. She disarmed a guy with a single shot to his leg, and she didn't take a day to even second-guess it. Did that surprise you?"

I watch the cleaning crew shuffle into the office area with their roller carts of supplies.

"Maybe she's not the same Josie you remember."

Just as I consider the truth to his words, my phone chimes.

Josie: Sorry. Busy day. I'm home.
Me: You're home? Thought you were coming home tomorrow?
Josie: I need you.

I scoot back in my chair. "I'm going home."

"That her?"

I nod while grabbing my suit jacket from the back of the chair.

"Tell her hi."

I don't answer him with more than a mumbled "okay" before taking the stairs to the exit.

I TRY to call her on the drive to her house, but she doesn't answer. I nearly forget to lock my car before running to her front door. It's unlocked, and I frown at her carelessness while opening the door and flipping the deadbolt behind me.

"Josie?" I toe off my shoes before tossing my jacket onto the back of the sofa on my way down the hall. The only light that's on in the whole house is the one to her bathroom. I ease open the door.

"I need you."

Those three words have haunted me since she sent the text and refused to answer her phone.

"Josie ..." I sigh when I see her in the bathtub filled with water and bubbles. "Why are you home early, baby?" I toss my tie onto the floor and unbutton my shirt.

When she turns her head toward me, I'm struck in the chest with the saddest smile I've ever seen. "You've never called me that," she whispers.

"Called you what?" I kneel next to the bathtub and press my lips to the side of her wet head, closing my eyes for a second to inhale her faint floral scent.

"Baby."

"Sorry. Do you not like it?" I sit back on my heels.

She tries for a genuine smile, but it's as if her face won't let her. "I do. It makes me feel..." her gaze drifts to the bubbles as she smooths the top of them with her hand "...innocent."

Innocent?

This has to be about the girl. The innocent girl she claims to have been.

As I open my mouth to ask about her trip, she abruptly stands, water and suds clinging to her naked body. "Do I look innocent?" Her voice barely a whisper.

I question if I'm hearing her exact words. My gaze roves along her body. "Baby, that's a loaded question with you standing in front of me looking like you do after weeks of not touching you like..." my gaze lifts to her "...like I want to touch you."

"Touch me," she whispers, her hands reaching for my shoulders. She snakes them around my neck.

"You're wet."

"I know." She kisses me, leaning into me, forcing me to wrap my arms around her body to keep us from falling.

Her legs wrap around my waist when I lift her from the bathtub. Her lips move against mine with urgency.

"Are you ... o-okay to do this?" I fight to get my words out between kisses. My dick is ready to break through my pants. It's hating me for questioning what's happening.

"Mosley ... just fuck me."

She wins. So does my dick. My conscience will deal with the rest later.

"W-what are you d-doing?" she murmurs against my mouth when I rest her backside on the vanity.

"I'm doing as you asked." I rip off my shirt and shove down my pants.

"Coltennn!" One of her hands flies to the edge of the sink when I plunge into her. The other hand rakes down my chest.

"Tell me you're okay," I whisper against her ear while my hands grip her ass. I want to move. I *need* to move. But I refuse to hurt her.

"Don't stop," she says on a harsh breath, her legs wrapping around my waist.

She looks like my Josephine. She *feels* like my Josephine.

Her touch.

Her voice in my ear.

The beat of her heart so close to mine.

But something is missing. Just ... something.

"Harder, Colten ..." Her fingers curl into my flesh, pulling me closer.

I drive into her over and over.

"Harder!" she demands.

"Jesus, Josie ..." I can't go any harder without breaking her. So I go faster. I grip her ass harder with one hand and grab her breast with my other hand, pinching her nipple *hard*.

"Hard—"

I kiss her, cutting her off, reaching my tongue to her fucking tonsils. Her long moan touches every inch of my skin when we find our release while every muscle contracts.

Josie wriggles out of my hold. I take a step back, breathless. She lowers to her knees and wraps her lips around my cock.

"Fuck ... J-Josie ..." I don't know what she's doing. It's ... not necessary. It's so damn unexpected. I should tell her to stop. One hand reaches for the wall while my other hand finds her head, my fingers threading through her hair. I'm going to tell her to stop in just ... a second.

Fuck me ... that feels good.

She releases me and kisses her way up my body, her hand on my cock, replacing her mouth. Her teeth tease my nipples, firmly biting each one, making my body jerk. I feel her grin against my skin while her lips ghost their way to my ear. "Fuck me again, Mosley. Only this time ... *harder.*"

CHAPTER
Five

I SLIP out of bed a little before 3:00 a.m., leaving Colten naked on his stomach and dead to the world.

The pain is numbing. I *need* to feel something real, something in this life. Something human ... something humane.

Colten could have broken every bone in my body, ripped me apart with his teeth like an animal, and it still wouldn't have been enough.

Hugging myself, I sit in the corner of the sofa and stare out the window while my fingernails dig into the flesh on the back of my arms. It's been years since I've had long nails, but I've had other things on my mind that didn't involve grooming habits.

My mind races back to California where I threw cash at Athelinda, ran out of her building, and I didn't look back. My wobbly legs picked up speed until horns honked and tires screeched. I stopped in the middle of the street while drivers swerved to keep from hitting me.

Even now, I feel breathless.

Wordless.

Lost.

Whatever life this is, I don't want it. If I am *him* ... I can't do it.

Why did Colten save me? Why couldn't he have waited just a minute longer? Maybe even ten ... twenty seconds would have made the difference between death and near death.

My poor parents. They spent my whole childhood trying to make me feel special and unique, when in reality, I was a demon in the body of their little girl. What could they have possibly done wrong to deserve me?

When the sun starts to make its way into the morning sky, I brew a cup of coffee. As soon as I take a sip, I spit it back into the cup. It's hot and tasteless. I bring my nose close to the steam and take a whiff. It has no aroma. What is wrong with me? Am I in purgatory here on Earth? Is that what Athelinda meant?

"Good morning."

I turn toward Colten's sleepy voice. His messy hair and big yawn stand a few feet behind me with a blanket tied around his waist.

"Colten ..." I whisper. "I'm so very sorry." My gaze affixes to his chest. He looks like a cat attacked him. A big, mean cat. Deep scratches. Speckled areas of dried blood. I curl my fingers and inspect my nails. They're dark with dried blood as well. When I hug my chest, I feel the rough patches on the back of my arms that probably look like a raked garden as well.

He doesn't make a single glance at his chest. Instead, he shrugs. "It's fine." He takes a step forward.

I stiffen as he kisses the corner of my mouth.

"Colten ..."

"My love," he says adoringly, almost playfully while making his own cup of coffee.

I flinch when he turns his back to me. It matches his chest. I did that. I hurt him. Marked him. And I did it all in the name of *feeling*. Only ... I didn't feel it. But I'm sure he did because he's a normal person with real feelings.

"Colten ..." I gently splay my palms and my cheek against his back. Closing my eyes, I whisper, "I'm *unwell*. You have to protect yourself ... protect your daughter."

"Hey, no." He turns, framing my face in his strong, protective, *loving* hands.

What did he do to deserve me? Wasn't having an awful dad enough?

"Baby, what are you talking about? It's a few marks. They'll heal. I'm okay. Do you hear me?" Colten shakes his head. "And what are you talking about protecting Reagan? Protect her from what?"

Me.

"Josie, what happened in California?"

I lean into his touch and close my eyes. "I have to

tell you something," I whisper. "And it's going to change *everything*. And I need you to promise me that you will walk away like you did seventeen years ago."

"Josie—"

I open my eyes. "Promise me you'll remember that your life has so much purpose and meaning. You have a beautiful daughter. And your mom and brother. A job you love. You have everything, Colten. And you had it without me."

"No." He shakes his head, eyes narrowing while his grip on my face tightens. "I'm not promising you anything of the sort. What the hell happened?"

His anger pulls a few tears from my eyes. I welcome them. I welcome any sign of human emotion. "The visions, the memories ... they're not from one of the girls."

Colten nods. "Okay."

"I was him." I bite my shaky lower lip. The ugliness of the truth burns in my chest ... in my soul. My fucking awful soul.

"Who?"

"Winston Jeffries."

Colten blinks a few times before his hands drop to his sides. In an unexpected twist, he laughs.

Laughs!

Fist at his mouth, hand over his belly laugh. "No." He snorts. "That's an interesting take on all of this, but ... no."

"I don't want to believe it either, but—"

"Good." He grabs my shoulders and lowers his face

level with mine. "Whoever put that shit in your head is mental. You absolutely should *not* believe them. Josephine Watts, you are way too smart to do anything short of what I'm doing." He laughs some more. "It's beyond ridiculous. It's laughable. You see that, right?"

I can't laugh. It's not in me. No smiles either. I find none of this amusing.

"I never see the person who did it because I'm seeing it through his eyes. I wouldn't have memories of him burying *my* dead body. I wouldn't have memories of times that he buried other bodies at different cemeteries, but I do, Colten. The *only* explanation is that I was him. A ..."

A serial killer.

I can't say the words. I don't know if I'll ever be able to say them.

Colten's head stays on an endless swivel like it's running on batteries. Back and forth. He can shake his head until it breaks from his neck. It won't change anything. God, I wish it could.

"I need you to let me be Dr. Josephine Watts, Medical Examiner. Our paths will cross with work. That's it. I can't marry you. I can't be your friend. I can't be anything to you."

His gaze shifts from me to the window, and he squints just as the sun catches his eyes. "I think we should have a small family-only ceremony in January. After the holidays. We'll take a week and honeymoon in Costa Rica or Ecuador. We'll rent a little place near a beach. Sun. Tropical food. Lazy mornings in bed. I'll book us massages and maybe a rainforest tour. It will be perfect." The only thing that's perfect is his smile. It's perfectly heartbreaking.

"Also, did I mention we found the motherlode of evidence for your favorite chainsaw killer? We had enough for an arrest, but the conviction will be a slam dunk now. He had an underground storm shelter. We must have passed it a hundred times because it was covered in brush and grass. Then Rains heard something squeak under him. I don't think we would have otherwise found it. Isn't that crazy? The saw we confiscated before the arrest wasn't on his property, but it had his prints. Before he lawyered up, he said he found it in a dumpster—he does work for a sanitation company, so it wasn't implausible. But there was blood all over it, so why would he salvage it and put it in the back of his truck?"

I wait for him to return his attention to me, and I offer a sad smile. "Colten."

He deflates when I don't take part in his distraction. Then he shrugs a shoulder, neutral expression. "It's my turn."

I chuckle, shaking my head. "Your turn to be the bossy one, huh?"

Stupid childhood promise.

"After you broke your arm, you said I could be the bossy one in approximately twenty years. It's been twenty-one years since you promised me control. It's past due."

Colten nods. He's wearing such a serious expression. It's a brave one.

"There was an asterisk with fine print. Did you read it when I made that promise to you? I think it said the agreement was null and void if it was discovered that either one of us was a murderer in another life."

"Reagan will be our flower girl." The hint of a smile pulls at his lips. "She'll be ecstatic. Katy said she loved being a flower girl at her wedding."

He has no idea how thin the thread holding me together is. I'm not sure how many more mornings I will be able to justify waking up, breathing in and out, and existing in this "Vita Atonement." I can't plan this wedding. I can't find an ounce of enthusiasm for his storm shelter discovery.

"I took little girls like Reagan, shaved their heads, and I killed them."

Colten winces. "Shut up. Just ... don't ever say that again."

"Look at you," I whisper, refocusing on his chest. "You couldn't fuck me hard enough last night. I felt nothing while shredding your skin." I slowly turn so he can see the back of my arms. "I didn't feel this either. I'm dead inside. I've always been dead inside." I turn back around. "All this time, I've been pretending. I even fooled myself into thinking that I could be a little normal, a little humane."

"I'm not walking away."

"I'm not giving you a choice." I tip my chin up, jaw set.

He grunts a laugh and pivots. "I have to work."

I don't move. Maybe I can't. Or maybe my idleness

is symbolic of standing my ground. Really shaky ground.

Minutes later, Colten emerges from the bedroom with his white shirt untucked and partially buttoned and his tie in hand. He's the sexiest man I have ever seen. I think his presence in my life is the biggest catalyst for my life reparation. I took what mattered most to other people in that other life, and in this one, I will have to give up what matters most to me.

"I love you," he says. "And I'll see you later." He bends to kiss me.

I take a step backward, averting my gaze to the floor.

He releases a soft sigh. "I'm never leaving you again."

I know this. I believe him. I will be the one to leave him.

After my front door clicks shut behind him, I pad my way to it and flip the deadbolt. Colten Mosely will not step foot in my house again unless it's to remove my lifeless body from it.

CHAPTER
Six

"I can't be your boyfriend ever again," I said the day after Josie got her cast.

She handed me a Sharpie to sign it and rolled her eyes while we sat at the kitchen table. Her mom was putting Benji down for a nap, and her dad was still at work. "Because I broke my arm?"

I signed her cast. The first signature. "No. Because your dad said I can't ever kiss you again, and what's the point of being your boyfriend if I can't kiss you?"

She snorted. "You're not seriously listening to my dad."

"I am. I am very seriously listening to your dad." I capped the marker and handed it back to her. "He's going to talk to my dad about teaching me to use a rifle."

"Your mom is never going to let you use a gun. She hates guns."

"No, she doesn't."

Josie eyes me. "Um … yeah, she does."

"How do you know that?"

"Because of Columbine. She still talks to my mom about it. And I overheard her saying to my mom that she hates guns. She used those exact words."

"Your dad is the chief of police. I think she'll let him teach me."

"She won't." Josie shrugged like her two words ended our discussion.

"I'm still asking her."

"Go ahead." She hopped off the stool and grabbed the Tupperware container of cookies, hugging it to her while peeling off the lid with her good hand before offering me one.

"I could have opened that for you."

"I'm not helpless." She wasn't. Never had been, never would be.

"If I broke my arm, I'd let you do everything for me. Do my homework. Feed me. Tie my shoes. Carry my schoolbag …"

Josie's pouty lips turned downward. I responded with a huge, chocolate-chip-cookie grin. I had no shame in my game.

"My grandma said she'd rather die than have people take care of her. She's really smart, and she thinks I'm just like her." Josie twisted her lips. "It's weird to think that death is better than letting someone help you. But if I am like her, then maybe someday I'll choose death over someone feeling sorry for me and doing stuff for me. My other grandma got sick, and she has to wear adult diapers. My grandpa helps her change them. It's really nice of him, but still ... I bet she feels embarrassed."

"He's her husband. That's probably what a good husband should do. My dad wouldn't do it for my mom, but we both know he's an asshole."

"Colten, don't say that."

"I'm going to be a better husband than him."

"You'd change your wife's adult diaper?"

My nose wrinkled. I couldn't imagine that. I had never changed a diaper before. "I mean ... maybe. If I loved her."

"Don't marry her if you don't love her." Josie rolled her eyes and laughed.

I grabbed a second cookie. "You know what I mean."

"Yeah. I know. I hope I don't need anyone's help. I want to be like my other grandma. After my grandpa died, she did everything. Mowed the lawn. Fixed a leaky toilet. She's pretty awesome."

Sometimes I wanted to be Josie. She had a great family and so much confidence.

Me?

I had an asshole dad. A stupid brother. And a mother who loved me, but she was emotionally whacked out because of my dad.

"I promised my parents I would never ask you this,

but ..." I eased into a question I'd been meaning to ask her for a long time but never got the nerve.

"Ask me what?"

She set the lid on the container of cookies, and I pressed it down before she had the chance to *not* ask me.

"Did your mom cheat on your dad?"

"What?" Her head whipped backward.

"Not recently. I mean years ago. You said your mom had sex with another guy, and that's why your skin color is a little darker. Did she cheat on him?"

"No." Her face wrinkles.

"Then why do you have a different dad?"

She stares at her cookie for several seconds. "I don't. My dad is my dad. He's not my biological dad, but he's real."

"Is that what your parents told you?"

"Yes."

"And you didn't ask any more questions?"

"Of course I did, but they said it wasn't important until I get older."

"That's weird. How old?"

"They said when I'm an adult it will make sense."

I had a million questions. My biggest question was how she could be fine with them not telling her the truth until she was an adult. I hated when my parents lied to me. Josie, however, wasn't like me or anyone else for that matter. One minute she was too curious for her own good, on the verge of getting in trouble, and the next minute, she seemed to not care about something as interesting, and maybe a little crazy, like the fact that the chief wasn't her real—*biological*—dad, yet her mom supposedly didn't have an affair.

Josephine Watts processed everything in life a little differently than other kids—and maybe most other humans.

CHAPTER
Seven

"Josie ..." My mom's eyebrows jump up her forehead after she unlocks and opens her front door. Her gaze shifts to the small suitcase at my side. "What are you doing here?" She steps aside to let me into the entry.

"I needed to get away." I slip off my shoes and set my suitcase by the stairs.

"Away from what?" She eyes me suspiciously.

"Colten."

"Trouble in paradise?" She heads into the kitchen to get food. That's how she has always greeted guests. A drink and something sweet like cookies, brownies, or lemon bars if she's feeling generous toward my dad.

I get two steps into the kitchen and stop. A six-hour drive in silence, my phone shut off to keep from hearing the chime of his texts and calls, no recollection of anything specific that I saw, heard, or thought for those six hours ... and now it hits me.

It. Hits. Me.

Tears sting my eyes while everything from my throat to the pit of my stomach seizes up into a tight knot of despair. I turn away from her and swallow hard, pinching the corners of my eyes to keep control.

I lost him ... I lost the boy next door.

"Are you still having visions and dreams?"

I clear my throat and take a deep breath while finding my way to the kitchen table before my knees give out on me. I haven't felt this hopeless and devastated since ... well, forever. "I am."

"How did your trip to California go?"

I clear my throat, fighting for every last morsel of composure. "How do you know about that?"

Mom sets a tray of brownies next to me along with a cherry-lime sparkling water. "Well, it would have been nice to have heard it from you." She gives me a little scowl. "But I had to hear it from Becca. We've been keeping in touch, and Colten told her. I guess he shares stuff with his mom."

Some stuff. Mom's not lecturing me on not telling her that I accepted his proposal a while back, so he must not have told his mom either. Smart. He sensed the wedding might not happen.

"Remember that time you and dad were in New Orleans right before you got married? You told me you had your palm read by a psychic. Dad thought it was ridiculous, but you believed her, and since then, everything has come to fruition?"

She nods, cupping her tea in her hands. "The good and the bad," she whispers.

"The good and the bad," I echo. Bad ... there was something so very bad.

There still is.

"I found a psychic of sorts who specializes in interpreting near-death experiences. She's a parapsychologist. Colten thinks I saw a 'specialist' at the university. This woman is..." I shake my head "...a very different breed."

"What did she tell you? Did she confirm that you were one of the victims?"

My head eases side to side while I pick at the brownie.

"Then what did she say?"

Again, my emotions rush to the surface, desperate to release.

I lost him.

"Will you tell me the truth?" The words squeak past my throat.

"About what, Josie?"

"I know I'm your daughter, and you're a good mom." I glance up with a shaky smile. "If I wanted to be a mom, I'd want to be you. Not grandma, even though she said I'm like her. Not Vera. Not anyone I've known or can even imagine. I'd want to be you."

Her eyes gloss over with tears, and she smiles. "Thank you, Josie. That's..." she wipes the corners of her eyes "...that's the kindest, most loving thing anyone has ever said to me."

For a breath, for the briefest of moments, I feel human. I *feel* something that's truly of this lifetime. "My point is I know you're hardwired to love me unconditionally. I know you're hardwired to see the best in me. To see nothing 'wrong' with me. But I know I've never fit into the range of normal in so many ways. Have you..." I force my gaze from my brownie back to hers "...have you ever wondered if my soul is not a good one because of my biological father?"

She winces. "No. Not once. Your soul? Are you kidding me? Josie, you are one of the kindest souls I know. You are *the* kindest soul I know. That's what makes you special, or as you have said for years, ... different."

"You've never wondered why I don't want to be a wife or a mom? You've never wondered why I brought home every dead thing I happened upon? You never wondered why I spent so much time with Roland Tompkins? You never wondered why I spent an unhealthy amount of time studying mass shootings starting with Columbine? Does my choice of profession not give you pause for a tiny second? Did you know that I'm really good at what I do? Does that all seem like something a kind person with a good soul would do?"

More tears collect in her eyes. "What did she say to you?" she whispers. "What did she do to my baby?"

I open my mouth to speak, but the thick and suffocating words lodge in my throat. All I hear is the truth. All I see is the pain in my mom's eyes. I don't want to bring it all back to her, but I am. I'm unearthing her past like I unearthed those bodies, and I can't undo it.

Then I think of Colten, and all the tears release.

Mom covers her mouth to hold back her sob as she shakes her head. "Tell me what she said."

I hate myself. I've harmed myself, but I've never truly hated myself until now. Rubbing my quivering lips together, I wipe as many tears as I can. "She said I wasn't one of the girls he killed. I was ..."

"Him," she whispers while her face contorts into anguish while her eyes fill with more tears.

I hold my breath to keep from sobbing. Clench my teeth. I don't breathe a single breath while returning a slow nod.

Mom tries to stifle her own sob, and I don't know who should be consoling who. It feels like this shared burden. Like we're carrying something heavy, and we don't know who will give out first.

Who will stumble?

Who will surrender under the weight of truth?

I feel guilty for sharing this with her, but at the same time, I feel seen. Even if I don't have a mother's love in my soul, I recognize it as the realest, most undeniably perfect part of human existence. Not all mothers are good ones, but I believe the ability to nurture without expecting anything in return is what makes women the sole reason humanity still exists.

They are the peacekeepers.

The givers of life.

The healers of hearts.

And there is me. I am an imposter. An undeserving punishment to anyone who has let me touch their life.

And ... I hate myself.

"I'm sorry," I say, wiping the tears from my face.

Mom shakes her head. "No. God no ..." She's out of her chair and wrapping her arms around me from behind my chair. "Don't you ever apologize for anything. This will not define your life. *I* am the one who is sorry that you have to experience this."

"You did n-nothing." I lay my hands over hers on my shoulders.

"I should have known," she sobs in my ear, hugging me harder.

"No, Mom." I wriggle my way out of her hold to turn toward her. Standing, I pull her into my arms.

We cry, clinging to each other until the back door opens, and my dad steps inside, removing his boots while eyeing us. "Jo, what are you doing here? What happened?"

I take a step away from my mom and wipe my eyes. "Um ..."

"She and Colten are having issues."

He rolls his eyes. "I'll call him. He should know better."

"What? No." I shake my head.

Mom grabs my hand and gives it a squeeze. "Cool your jets, Isaac. They'll work it out on their own."

We haven't talked about Colten. I don't know how

to read my mom. Does she not want my dad to know? Will he not believe me the way he didn't believe anything the psychic in New Orleans said to them years earlier?

"Have you stopped having those crazy dreams? That's probably your problem. You need to let that crap go, Jo."

Let it go.

Chin up, Jo.

Dust off your knees, Jo.

Don't you dare cry, Jo.

How would he feel if he knew and actually believed I was a man (the boy he wanted) in another life? And I didn't cry over skinned knees. I killed little girls. Would that version of me be better than the daughter who didn't live up to his expectations less than five percent of the time? And that five percent was my lack of a penis. An impossible standard at the time.

"Isaac ..." Mom wipes her face and gives him a warning.

"It was a long drive. I'm going to take a bath." I jab my thumb over my shoulder.

Dad continues to eye me. Beneath his gruff comments about my dreams, I sense his genuine concern. We've spent so much time together over the years, hunting and fishing. I count on him not only as my *real* father in life, but as a friend too. However, he can't fix this for me, and that will eat him alive. It's not that he'll believe me, just that he can't "fix" my messed-up mind.

Oh, how I wish it were as simple as weekly counseling and a magic pill.

Mom grabs her phone from the counter and holds up the screen.

Colten.

She hands it to me. I try to resist taking it, but she shoves it into my chest. "Don't shut him out."

I don't have a choice.

"Really? My mom's phone?" I answer it, climbing the stairs, feeling exhausted and full of despair.

"I'm not walking away, Josie."

"I know. That's why I'm doing it." I close the bathroom door and turn on the water to the tub. "Why did you call my mom?"

"Looking for you. I'm sitting in your living room, and you're not here. Your toothbrush is gone. I assumed; I *hoped* you went home."

"Because my parents like you and you think they'll put in a good word for you? Sorry to disappoint you, Detective Mosley, this isn't about you."

"I disagree. If it's about you, it's about me."

"I'm not marrying you."

There's a pause on the line. I grab a towel and check the water temperature. Have I upset him? Hurt him? It's not a lie. This isn't about him.

"I'll take you however I can have you."

I put him on speaker and set it on the counter while I undress. "Maybe you can have me in another life. But not this one."

"What if I'm not asking?"

"Then you don't know me at all." I move the phone to the ledge of the tub and step into the water.

"What's that sound?"

"The bathtub. I'm five seconds from ending this call. I'd appreciate it if you'd leave my house."

"Josephine ..." He sighs as I slide into the water and close my eyes. "Do you have any idea how many times you kept me from drowning? How many times your hand reached for mine like a goddamn lifeline? When everything around me felt so heavy and impossibly ugly, there you were. When I pushed you away, you kept running back to me over and over again. Even when you knew you couldn't solve my problems ... You. Held. My. Hand. Something so simple as the delicate hand of a friend is what carried me through some really tough times. Did you know that? Did you know that you carried me with one fucking hand?"

I blink, letting my tears disappear into the water. I hug my fisted hands to my heart while my body shakes with silent sobs. This is different. He had a terrible father. *I* was a killer. I killed little girls.

"So that's one ... one life saved by Josephine Watts. I know you're counting. You're thinking about the lives taken by *him*. Don't let him win. He's not here, but you are. Make it right. Do good. Be kind. Love unconditionally. If this is true, if we get more than one life, then this is your chance to be everything he wasn't."

My eyes continue to burn with endless tears. Not a single word can squeak past the emotion in my throat. It's not that Colten says the right thing at the right time. It's that he believes me, or at least, he believes *in* me. My ride-or-die. It's gut-wrenching to be loved like this and not feel worthy.

It would be so easy to take his proffered hand and pull him under with me, but it's not just him. He has Reagan. And for her, I press *End*.

CHAPTER

Eight

"Daddy!" Reagan runs into my arms as Katy follows her up my driveway, carrying her bag.

"What's your magic potion?" Katy asks, giving me a half grin. "She's never this excited to see me after spending time with you."

I kiss Reagan's cheek and set her down. She runs into the house. "I need a snack," she says.

"I have good snacks. That's my secret."

"Junk food." Katy rolls her eyes and hands me Reagan's bag.

"Raisins."

"Covered in chocolate?"

"Is there any other way?" I smirk.

"Colten ..." Katy shakes her head and turns, taking a few steps.

"Have fun."

She laughs. "It's a conference. I'm certain that's the definition of anti-fun. Oh ..." Turning back toward me, she twists her lips for a second. "Is it safe for me to ask about Josie?"

"Safe?"

"Reagan's mentioned her name several times. She said Josie got hurt, but she's doing better. She said Josie read her a bedtime story, and she's your friend from a long time ago. Am I being too nosey asking about her?"

"I've known Josie since the fourth grade. We were neighbors. She's an assistant medical examiner, so our professions cross occasionally. Before I moved here, it had been seventeen years since I'd seen her. There. Now you know about Josie."

"So ... she read our daughter a bedtime story. Is she *more* than an old friend?"

I press my lips together, contemplating my answer. "Since you're a happily married newlywed, can I be honest with you?"

"Yeah ..." she says slowly.

"Josie is the reason we never got married."

Katy grunts a laugh. "And here I thought me saying no was the reason we never got married."

I slide my hands into my front pockets. "You said no because I hesitated when you asked if I loved you. I hesitated because you weren't ..." I take a deep breath. It hurts to talk about her when I feel like I'm losing her.

"I wasn't Josie," she murmurs.

I nod.

Katy stares out at the street. "Well, I certainly hope you don't let her get away this time if she's the only woman you're capable of loving." She continues toward her car.

"Did you really love me?"

Katy rests her chin on her shoulder, her gaze not quite finding me. "Yeah. I loved you. And I love Sean. I guess my heart's bigger than yours." She gets into her car and pulls out of my driveway.

I turn, slowly shaking my head. Maybe she does have a bigger heart or maybe Josephine Watts is larger than life.

"Are you eating all the chocolate raisins, Button?" I nuzzle my face into Reagan's neck.

She giggles. "No."

I eat the one pinched between her two fingers.

"Daddy!"

This girl ... she's the only thing keeping me from losing my mind while Josie tries to distance herself from me. I'm not letting her go again. I won't abandon her. And I'm not giving her a choice in the matter. I will save her.

"Is Josie coming over?"

I sit next to her at the table and grab a handful of raisins from the box. "You won't see Josie this time. Sorry."

"Is she still sick?"

"She's better, but she's not here. She went back to Iowa to visit her parents."

Reagan shrugs. "Okay."

I smile. It is okay. Everything will be okay. It has to be.

CHAPTER
Nine

Shortly after Josie turned seventeen, she did a genealogy project for history. I asked her to a movie with me and some other friends, but she needed to work on her project by asking her mom about her biological dad.

Six of us went to the movie without Josie. Less than an hour into it, an employee interrupted the movie, calling my name. I was a little embarrassed and a little freaked out. It had to be an emergency.

Did something happen to my mom or Chad?

Funny ... I didn't spare a thought for my dad.

I followed the employee to the entrance where Josie stood. Her eyes looked like red spider webs. She'd been crying.

"Josie, what happened?"

She hugged me and started crying again. I didn't

know what to do, so I held her for what seemed like forever.

"Let's get out of here, okay?" I said, shifting my body so she was hugged to my side.

We climbed into my old truck, and everything went silent. Josie no longer cried. She stared out the window, holding completely still. Eerily still.

I did the only thing I knew to do ... the thing I knew she'd do. I reached my hand across the console and laced my fingers together with hers. It drew a shaky breath from her. And it scared me. I had never seen Josie like that.

"My father," she whispered. "My biological father ... he..." she swallowed hard "...raped my mother. She was on her way to her car. It was late and dark after her class. My dad was waiting for her at home. It was their anniversary, and he had a candlelit dinner waiting for her. But she never came home that night. One of his officer friends came to the house and told him someone found her on the ground next to her car. They called for help. She was at the hospital. Battered ... but not broken."

I squeezed her hand, at a loss for words.

She laughed, but it was far from a happy laugh. "Want to know why they kept me instead of aborting me?"

All I had was a slow nod.

"Because it was their anniversary, and they didn't want it to forever be a reminder of something awful. So now ... it's the anniversary of ..." She laughed a little more. That time it sounded slightly maniacal. "My conception. My fucking conception. How messed up is that?"

It was all very messed up.

"I have half the DNA of a rapist. Didn't expect to find that out when I sat down to discuss my project with my mom. I have evil running through my veins, and there is nothing I can do about it."

I squeezed her hand again, and she squeezed mine back while turning her head toward me.

"I didn't ask her, but I kinda read between the lines. If it had been a day earlier or a day later, I might not exist."

Clearing the thickness from my throat, I found my voice. "Well, that would be tragic."

She smiled. It made me feel like a king. I liked doing or saying anything to make Josie smile. It was the most tangible thing I never held in my hands, but god ... I felt it everywhere.

"Drive, Colten."

"Where are we going?"

She fastened her seat belt and stared out her window, releasing a soft sigh. "Anywhere."

We drove out of town until we hit no other option but gravel roads and miles of corn fields. I pulled to a stop when the road I chose dead ended at a dirt circle drive, an old barn, and the remnants of a silo.

"I have a blanket in the back seat. We could get in the bed of the truck."

Josie nodded. "Yeah." She opened her door while I retrieved the blanket.

Before I made it to the back, she had the tailgate down and hopped into the bed. I jumped in behind her and spread out the blanket. When I sat with my back to the window, she nestled between my bent knees with her back to my chest. I hugged her to me, inhaling her sweet shampoo, absorbing her warmth, and imagining how awful life would be without her ... fighting with feeling oddly thankful that someone raped her mom. It was confusing.

"Where do you think we'll be in ten years?" she asked. "Together, right?"

My arms hugged her tighter. I liked that plan, not that it was much of a plan. "Yeah."

"Or at least friends. You might want things I don't want. A wife. Children. A normal life." She laughed. "You're going to be the best dad. Nothing like your dad. And you're going to let your kids do and be whatever they want. And you're never going to cheat on your wife. You're never going to rape a stranger and leave her on the ground in a parking lot."

I grunted a painful laugh. "Uh ... I certainly hope I'm not a rapist. Maybe we should elevate my life's goals to something greater than the simple lack of being a rapist and a cheater."

"I said you'd have a wife and kids. That's good, right? I mean ... you want that, don't you?"

I wanted *her* ... however I could have her. That seemed like a long shot at best. My life was slowly unraveling. My grades. My desire to be anything more than "not my dad."

It didn't matter how Josie came into the world; she was going to do great things and make it a better place. Josie made everything better.

"What do you want?" I asked without answering her question.

She rested her head back onto my shoulder, staring at the starry sky while the screeching of crickets and katydids filled the air. "I think I want to be a doctor. I don't know what area of specialty, but something that's ... I don't know. Something hard or something that most doctors don't want to do."

"Like a butt doctor?"

Josie giggled. "A proctologist? Maybe. Or maybe a podiatrist. Stare at feet all day."

"At least a gynecologist gets to see babies."

Again, she giggled. "Yeah, nothing good comes out of the butt or hides between toes. And when I'm not doing gross stuff, I'll come watch you play baseball. Maybe I'll be best friends with your wife."

I had no answer to that. It was hard to imagine that our sneaking around, hiding our relationship from friends and her parents, was going to end in just ... friendship.

"But you don't have a wife yet." She turned her head and grinned at me.

"Not that I know of." I grinned back at her.

"Do you still want to kiss me now that you know I have evil in my blood?"

"You have evil in your blood. I have asshole in mine. Maybe we were made for each other."

Her smile swelled. "Maybe," she whispered.

I kissed her. After a while, we repositioned, lying on the blanket.

Kissing.

Our legs scissored.

And our future uncertain at best.

CHAPTER
Ten

"I WAS A TERRIBLE DAUGHTER," I said to my mom after my dad left for work. We sat on the deck in our robes, sipping coffee, watching pedestrians pass on the trail that used to be dirt. It's now a beautiful green space, and my tree is still there.

"What are you talking about?"

I blow at the steam. "My junior year, when you told me about the rape, I was so self-absorbed, thinking only about myself. I felt so angry and betrayed. And just ... lost. I felt sorry for myself. For *myself.* And you were the one who was raped." I shake my head. "That was really terrible of me. But that's who I am. I'm a terrible person."

"Stop it." She reaches over, resting her hand on my leg and squeezing it. "Look at me."

I lift my gaze to hers. The same question swirls in my head.

What did she ever do to deserve me?

"If I told you dandelions are taking over the neighborhood, and you took a walk, all you'd focus on are the dandelions. It wouldn't matter if there were ten or ten million. That's all your eyes would see because I planted the idea in your mind. It's a distorted reality. You never thought you had bad blood before I told you about the night you were conceived. You never thought you were a serial killer until some psychic told you. The fact is you were a child conceived from rape. And maybe … just maybe your soul carries a piece of a man who did awful things over a hundred years ago. But that's not who you are."

I don't know who I am. My mind won't shut off and let me go back to the woman I was before the shooting. It took years for me to accept what happened to my mom and what that meant for me.

"Sometimes, I feel like it's too much. It's exhausting waking up every morning with a hangover from my dreams. My head hurts, and the anxiety is like nothing I have ever experienced. I don't want to eat pills for the rest of my life to keep from *feeling*. I don't want to spend every waking hour second-guessing my choices, wondering if I've just had a bad day or if I'm in a bad mood because I'm a bad person. And I can't un-read what I've already read. If reincarnation is a real thing, then it explains why a five-year-old can sit down at a piano and play Mozart without having ever taken a lesson or without having ever heard Mozart. So then the question I have is ... what happens when I do something without realizing what or why I'm doing it?"

What happens when I do something bad because in another life I was a psychopath? What if that's my hidden talent?

It would explain why I'm so good at what I do.

Clinical.

Precise.

Emotionless.

"Don't answer that." I stand. "I'm going to head home. I just needed to tell you. I guess I needed someone to share the burden with me. And ..." I puff my cheeks before blowing out a long breath. "Once again, I'm a terrible daughter. I've handed you an impossible situation to solve. And I know by nature, you feel the need to solve all of my problems."

She stands, setting her coffee on the side table. "You're right. I wish I could solve all your problems. While I'm at it, I'd like to solve all the world's problems. But I can't. And I know this." She presses her hands to my cheeks. "But it's not going to stop me from trying. I love you as much as one human can possibly love another human." She bites her lips together for a beat as emotions fill her eyes. "It was my choice to bring you into this world. You are *not* allowed to leave it while I'm still alive. Do you hear me?"

My jaw clenches as if not breathing, not blinking, not moving will keep me from falling apart. I nod. No mother should have to say those words to her child. It's a fucking suicide speech. And I showed up less than twenty-four hours ago, laying out all the reasons my mom might need to convince me it's not okay to exit this world yet.

"Josephine, do. You. Hear. Me?"

I nod.

"Now, go make things right with Colten."

I can't. I just … can't.

WHEN I GET HOME, there's a note on my pillow.

All those girls I kissed when we were kids … I closed my eyes and thought of you.

I hold the note to my chest and close my eyes … and I think of Colten.

After a restless night of more images of dead girls' bodies, I wake at four and start making notes of the number of bodies at each location and the names on the headstones. I don't think this is Vita Atonement, but I feel like it's the only visible road to take right now.

I snap a photo of my notes and send it to the lead detective who interrogated me in Nashville.

I meet with my physical therapist a final time before going back to work. Then I stop by the grocery store. When I get home, I put my groceries away and decide it's time to get back on my stationary bike per my therapist's suggestion. When I go into the bedroom and toss my shirt onto my bed, there's another note.

Detective Mosley is a trespasser.

I loved it when you sat next to me while I played the piano ... but I loved it more when you'd lie on my bed, making my pillow smell like you. Before I left this note, I rubbed myself all over your pillow. I hope you like it. I hope you like me.

Without thinking, I find myself hugging that note too, against my chest, closing my eyes ... and thinking of Colten.

Over the next two weeks, Colten dabbles in breaking and entering every time I leave my house. I'm not sure how he gets any work done. Chicago has way too much crime for him to leave daily notes on my pillow.

Remember that time you found a dead frog by your favorite tree? I found him near the pond by the batting cages, and I left him by your tree as a gift to you. I'll never forget how excited you were. I'll never forget how I felt like nobody knew you like I did. I'm still loving knowing that no other human will ever know you like I do.

Colten gave me a dead frog. It makes me laugh out loud. I remember that day, but he never said a word, never let on that it was him.

Another day ...

The week I mowed your lawn while your family went on vacation, I spent hours under the tree in the front yard, lying in the grass in your favorite reading spot. I liked the world through your eyes. I still do.

Another day ...

The last time Reagan stayed with me, I told her about Artemis. Then I told her you were my Artemis.

Another day …

The greatest day of my life, aside from the birth of Reagan: the day Jo Watts turned out to be the neighbor girl instead of the neighbor boy.

"You're with me today, Dr. Watts," Dr. Cornwell says the second I walk into the conference room on my first day back to work.

My colleagues give me a few smiles and kind "welcome backs." They're not looking at me like someone who got shot in the line of duty. I'm not sure how to read their expressions.

"You're quite the local celebrity." Cornwell holds up a physical newspaper.

I snatch it from him.

Assistant medical examiner believes she was a murder victim from over a century ago. Helps officials find victims' bodies in Nashville.

"Is it true?" Cornwell asks.

"Which part?" I hand the newspaper back to him without reading past the headline.

"Any of it? All of it?"

I glance around the room, all eyes on me. "Listen, I'm just going to tell you what I've told everyone else. I had a near-death experience after the shooting. Since then, I've had visions and dreams about Winston Jeffries's victims. Everyone in the room knows me well enough to know that I don't believe in this kind of lunacy. Yet, here I am, experiencing it firsthand. I have no explanation."

That's not totally true anymore, but it was for a while, so it's all they're getting. I have no plans of telling the police that I was wrong about my role.

"And why am I with you today?" I shoot Cornwell a look.

"My, my ... aren't you a little chippy today. Anyone else would find it an honor to be with me for the day."

"I feel like you don't trust me. Like you're demoting me."

"I'm observing you for one day. Just one short day, Dr. Watts. It's the responsible thing to do. I need to make sure you're physically and emotionally up to the task."

"You're just observing?"

He nods, holding up his hands. "I won't touch a thing."

I take a seat at the table and remain obediently quiet while Dr. Cornwell goes over the cases for the day.

When I get to the autopsy suite, Alicia has my first case on the table waiting for me. "Josie, good to see you back."

"Thanks."

Alicia eyes Dr. Cornwell. I ignore every ounce of skepticism in the room, which is hard to do because it's thick today.

Will I stumble?

Hesitate?

Miss something?

Mess something up?

Will Dr. Cornwell have to jump in and save the day? Save my ass?

Not a chance.

My brain is good at multitasking. It can be fucked ten ways to Sunday from the near-death experience yet not miss a step or a shred of evidence over the next two hours. I don't give Dr. Cornwell a single glance nor do I acknowledge the other critics who should be focused on their own cases.

"Next," I say, leaving Alicia to close up while I take a restroom break, strutting out of the autopsy suite with confidence. I rip off my PPE and speed walk down one long hallway and then another, finding refuge on the other side of a vending machine.

On a gasp, I hunch over, resting my hands on my thighs.

Breathe ... breathe ... breathe ...

I'm a killer. I don't deserve the trust of these victim's families or Dr. Cornwell or all of Cook County. I am a fraud. An imposter. And I can't fucking find a breath.

A hand touches my shoulder, making me jump. The second my gaze lifts, I see him.

Colten.

He says nothing. Nothing is exactly what I need because I can't breathe or talk. I'm scared that I might start crying if I'm forced to do either.

I need a minute. A minute of silence.

I slowly stand up, and he pulls me to him, my face

against his chest while his hand cups the back of my head.

Weeks of breaking into my house.

Weeks of leaving me notes.

Weeks of silence from me.

And he says nothing.

God ... I love this man.

When I feel a vibration, I step back. Colten pulls his phone from the inside pocket of his jacket and answers it. "Mosley."

My gaze affixes to his chest because now things feel awkward. The silence no longer fits. I glance at my hand while he takes it in his.

When I look up at him with his phone to his ear, he gives me a tiny smile that says all that it's always said.

I've got you. You're not alone. This will pass.

He squeezes my hand before releasing it, turning, and pushing through the door to the stairway. I get my butt into the locker room, use the toilet, and gown-up for my next case.

CHAPTER
Eleven

"This is unprofessional," Dr. Byrd says, taking a seat across from me at a Mediterranean restaurant a few blocks from his office. "You're my patient."

"I'm not, Terrance." I take a sip of water. "I'm just an old friend buying you dinner."

"I'm married." He gives me a lifted eyebrow while placing his napkin on his lap.

"Good thing I'm okay with buying you dinner without the promise of sex."

"I'm ordering the most expensive thing on the menu *and* dessert. Maybe even a few drinks. You'll also pay for my cab home, correct?" He gives me a challenging expression. "I feel like this 'friends having dinner' is just your way of not paying for my services."

"Or ... I want to talk to you in an environment where you can leave your professionalism at the door and be completely honest with me." I draw lines in the condensation on my water glass.

"What makes you think I've been anything less than honest with you?"

"Because I can tell you're out of your comfort zone with my issues. And when I tell you what I found out in California, you're going to want to tell me I'm batshit crazy. I need your *honest* expertise. Nothing sugar-coated. Not like when I tell a family their loved one probably didn't suffer, but I know that probability is slim at best."

Terrance eyes me just before the waiter takes our order. As soon as it's just us again, he blows out a long breath. "Tell me. And I'll give you my honest opinion."

I glance around the restaurant to see how close the nearest table and set of ears are to us. "I saw a psychic who knows a lot about near-death experiences."

"You lost me at psychic. I'm already silently judging you."

I chuckle. "I'm judging me too. And that's not accurate. She's a parapsychologist. Just hear me out. She said I wasn't one of the victims."

"Never mind. I like her after all."

"Wow. You won't let me finish. You must really have to force yourself to hold back your reaction when you're on the clock."

He smirks. "You have no idea."

I give him the stink eye. "As I was saying ... she pointed out all the reasons I wasn't one of the girls he killed. And it made sense, well, most of it. Then she nudged me until my brain stretched just far enough to see what I had been missing."

Terrance presses his lips together, biting his tongue, I'm sure.

"I was Winston Jeffries."

He doesn't let anything leak. No reaction whatsoever.

Running my hands through my hair, I frown. "I killed thirty-seven little girls in another life. I was a psychopath. And while I didn't want to believe it; now, I see it's the only thing that fits. God ... it fits so many parts of my life before the shooting."

He blinks once, maybe twice.

"You can speak now."

Nodding slowly, he scratches his chin. "You're batshit crazy."

I nod several times. "I know. Except ... I'm not. Not really. I know what I see. And I've sent other locations to the Nashville police, and they've found more bodies right where I told them they would be. One girl ... one girl that he killed wouldn't know all the locations of thirty-seven bodies. Did you not see today's paper?"

"I don't believe everything that gets printed."

"Well, believe it. Open your mouth. Chew it up. Then swallow it. After you digest it, tell me what it means if it doesn't mean that I was Winston Jeffries."

Resting one arm and his opposing elbow on the table, he props his chin on his fist in a thinker's pose. "Out-of-body or near-death experiences are not well studied for obvious reasons, but I'm sure you already know this. Death is not a specific moment, even if a qualified professional marks a time of death. It's a potentially reversible process. Not everyone who goes into cardiac arrest dies. Again, you know this. So the question is, what happens in that small space of time when the heart, lungs, and brain cease to function? Understanding of the human brain is still in its infancy despite great strides over the years. I think there are some brilliant minds who are making good guesses at what these NDEs mean. I'm just not one of them. And I don't know who your psychic friend is, but I'd be happy to refer you to a professor I know. He's written a few papers on neurophenomenology of near-death experiences. I know he's worked with other doctors using high-density ECG during an induced NDE-like state, but to my knowledge they've had little success. However, if I'm being completely honest, Josie, I'm inclined to ask what your endgame is with this? Let's take liberty and just say you are right. You were Winston Jeffries. Now what? You can't undo the past. You can't be held accountable for something that happened over a century ago. You're not a serial killer in this life. What is the endgame? Do you just need someone to say they believe you? If that's the case, I'll do that. I have no explanation for the bodies. The bodies sell it for me."

"I don't need to be believed. Or right. Or anything ego-driven. I need to forget it. All of it. It's poison in my brain. Imagine waking up every day after a long night of seeing dead children in your dreams. Then imagine feeling responsible for their deaths. This is what I'm living with right now. And it's not just when I sleep. Right now, I can see the graves. The dead girls. There's not a pill strong enough to get rid of these visions. And it makes me question my entire existence. I don't understand what my purpose is. And I'm so scared of some switch getting flipped and losing it. I don't trust myself."

"You're afraid you're going to hurt someone or yourself?"

I nod.

"Which one?"

"Both," I whisper as our food arrives.

After we eat for a few minutes without speaking, Terrance glances up at me, wiping his mouth. "How are you and Colten?"

"Over."

"Why?"

I give him a look. He can't be that stupid.

"Did he end it, or did you?"

"I ended it."

"Why?"

"Terry, you can't really be asking me this."

"I am. You've always talked fondly of Colten. The love of your life. Your best friend since the fourth grade. I wouldn't normally advocate anyone using another person to give them purpose or reason for their existence. But in your case, I'm inclined to make an exception. Maybe instead of distancing yourself, you should..." he twists his lips "...lean in a bit."

"Lean in a bit?" I narrow my eyes. "That's your brilliant, a-decade-of-medical-school advice to me. Lean in?"

He offers a half shrug before taking a bite of his food. "Let him help you through this. You trust him. He might be the perfect person to get you through the rough patch."

"The rough patch? You are definitely not getting dessert out of this. I think about dead girls all day and all night. It's not a rough patch. It's unimaginable mental anguish."

"Maybe consider changing your profession or taking more time off. Give yourself more opportunities to not see or think about the deceased. Memories, real or not, are imperfect. They fade whether we want them to or not. Time is your friend."

"I'm not changing professions. I love my job."

"Then lean into that. Are you back to work?"

I nod. "Today was my first day back."

"And it went well?"

My gaze shifts to my plate. "It went ... fine."

"What's that pause about?"

On a sigh, I glance up at him. "The chief ME hovered over me all day, making sure I was okay to be back at work. And I was. I did everything right. I didn't need any help. But ..."

"But?"

"Mid-morning, I had a mini breakdown or panic attack. I couldn't get Winston Jeffries out of my mind. And then I started questioning if I should be back at work yet ... or ever. I started to feel like a fraud. What would people think of me if they knew my secret?"

"This doesn't have to be something you're hiding. That implies you have accountability. This is something you're working through. It's nobody's business but yours. No accountability. No need to feel like a fraud."

I consider his words.

At the same time, I see naked girls, heads shaved, in a pile awaiting burial.

I was one sick fuck ...

After dinner, I get Terry a cab, but I can't go home.

How did I survive seventeen years without *him*?

When life hits an impasse, when the air gets too thick, when I can't find my way, I navigate to *him*.

CHAPTER
Twelve

Josie's car is in my driveway when I get home just before ten-thirty at night. I make a slow trek to the door, wondering what's brought her here. It's been a long fucking day thinking about our silent interaction at the county medical examiner's office. I was a little surprised to see her during my quick visit with one of the other MEs. I thought she had one more week before returning to work.

Has she read my notes? Kept them? Ripped them apart? Lit them on fire?

The door opens to silence. There's a light on over the kitchen sink, but she's nowhere in sight. When I reach the top of the stairs while loosening my tie, I see her curled into a ball on my bed, hugging my pillow.

I skipped dinner, and now I'm starving. I could use a shower, and my teeth need to be brushed and flossed.

But I can't make it past the bed. The floor creaks beneath me when I take a step closer, and Josie jumps.

Her tired eyes blink open after she sits up and rubs them several times. "Hi," she whispers.

"Hi." I sit on the edge of the bed, angling slightly toward her.

"My uh ... psychiatrist ..." She crawls toward me.

I grab her hips as she straddles my lap, dark hair stuck to her face that she doesn't bother to address. She's so fucking beautiful it hurts to look at her when I know she's not well.

"He told me to lean in."

I nod slowly. "Lean in, huh?"

"Yeah," she whispers, brushing her hands over the back of mine and interlacing our fingers while bringing my palms to her face. "Can I lean into you?" Her head tips to the side, *leaning in* to my touch.

My lips find hers, kissing her slowly. Her hands slide to my tie, removing it and letting it drop to the floor before working the buttons to my shirt. Our kiss grows stronger as she pushes my shirt over my shoulders.

One by one, our clothes get tossed aside until it's just us, the sheets, and the rest of the night.

She leans into me.

And I lean into her.

This isn't the body of a serial killer. My hands, followed by my lips, trace every soft curve. She makes the sexiest sound when I slide my tongue between her spread legs. Her fingers dig into my back, finding old scars and making new ones while I move inside of her.

The bedsprings offer a slight protest, syncing with our labored breaths and the occasional whisper of my name ... of her name ... of a god whose existence feels less likely every day.

I wish we could stay like this forever because it feels like the *us* we've been searching for since the day we met. When she collapses on top of me, gasping for her next breath, I roll us to the side. Pulling the sheets over our naked, entwined bodies, I drift off to sleep with the first girl who felt like the sun. The air. Gravity. And my whole world and reason for existing.

My alarm goes off at five.

No Josie.

But my sheets smell like flowers and spring rain ... and maybe a hint of formaldehyde, so it's a damn good morning.

I hope.

I slip on jogging shorts and a hoodie and grab my tennis shoes before heading downstairs. Josie's not in the family room or the kitchen, but there's a note by my coffeemaker.

Pilates. Shower. Breakfast. Work. Thanks for letting me lean in. XO ~J

CHAPTER
Thirteen

"I can go," Dr. Cornwell says at the morning meeting.

"If you don't quit coddling me, I'm going to lose it." It's too late. I can't walk back those words. *Lose it like Winston Jeffries?* I sigh. "I did fine yesterday."

Not counting the breakdown by the vending machine.

"It was my case. I wrote the report. I can testify in court. I'm fine. Really."

He slides his reading glasses up his nose. "Very well then. Off you go." He gives me a shooing motion with his hand.

After I get to the courthouse, wait forever to get through security, use the restroom, and make my way toward the courtroom, I run into Dylan Paine.

"I'm surprised to see you here," she says, applying lip gloss before going into the courtroom.

"I'm testifying."

"I know." She pauses her motions and gives her lips a light tap together. "I'm just surprised."

"Why? Because you don't think I'm a real doctor?"

Dylan grins. "I've never said that. I just think you're young, not as experienced as Dr. Cornwell."

"Funny ... I have a long list of people who I think are more experienced than you, but I don't feel the need to remind you."

She draws her head back a few inches. I'm a little punchy today. Just as she starts to speak, the elevator dings, and the doors open.

Dylan smiles, and I glance over my shoulder at Colten. Chicago's too big, and so is this courthouse to find myself stuck in this same threesome again. It has to be part of my atonement.

"Detective Mosely. It's always nice to see you." Dylan bats her fake eyelashes.

Maybe she and her husband have an open marriage, but I doubt it. I think she's nothing more than a disingenuous whore.

Wow, Josie ... who are you?

Colten gives her a tiny smile and walks toward me, stopping with a good three feet between us. "Morning," he says.

Just as Dylan opens her mouth to speak, I take two steps closer to him. Way closer than colleagues or even friends would stand. Through the corner of my eye, I see her mouth clamp shut, choking on her unspoken words. I couldn't care less about her. She needs to get her ass into the courtroom and start making her case before the DA puts me on the stand to obliterate every shred of evidence she thinks she has to exonerate her client.

"You look..." the corner of Colten's mouth curls a fraction "...pretty today."

My grin doesn't hold back, especially when Dylan makes a tiny huffing noise and clicks her heels into the courtroom. "Do you remember the first time you called me pretty?"

Colten presses his lips together for a few seconds. "That's a hard one because I thought it so many times. When did I get the nerve to say it?"

"The first time you saw me trying on fly fishing waders in the garage. You weren't saying it as a compliment."

His barely detectable smirk morphs into a full-on shit-eating grin. "Yes, I was absolutely complimenting you. I hid most of my compliments behind sarcasm because it was the only way I could say them to you without you making fun of me."

I roll my eyes. "So your game was to make fun of me before I made fun of you?"

"My game was to give you the *illusion* that I was making fun of you, when in reality, I was a lovesick boy."

I wet my lips because they are not glossed like Dylan's—and because I want Colten to kiss me.

"I'm still that same lovesick boy," he whispers before answering my silent request with a soft kiss.

I grin against his lips. "When are we going to talk about you breaking into my house?"

He stands erect. "Says the woman who broke into mine last night."

"I used the key," I cup my hands at my mouth and whisper yell, "under your planter."

"Well, I used the key on my keychain." He pulls his keys out of his pocket and shows me a key, presumably my house key.

"Where did you get that?"

"Your dad made me a copy shortly after the shooting."

"My dad has a key to my house?"

"So it would seem." He pockets his keys.

"And he's making copies and giving them out to ... just anyone?"

"Just anyone? Is that my new rank?"

I start to return a snarky reply, but it dies on my tongue. I'm all out of snark this morning. "Listen, last night—"

"Don't." He shakes his head. "I don't want to be another burden in that mind of yours. I'm not a problem you need to figure out and solve. I'm not giving up on you or on us. Nor am I pushing you for anything you're not ready to give."

"What if I'm never ready?"

He shrugs. "Maybe lovesick boy is my destiny."

Ouch ...

"Destiny can suck."

"Tell me about it." He winks before bending forward and pressing his lips next to my ear.

It makes me shiver every time.

"I love you, Josephine Watts," he whispers.

"That sucks for you too," I mumble.

Colten deposits the lightest kiss to my cheek.

Another shiver.

"You're mine. Not his." He sidesteps me and makes his way to the courtroom past me without one glance back.

When I'm called in to testify, I state the facts. I'm then subjected to a slew of ridiculous what-ifs from Dylan Paine.

She ends her questioning with the most ridiculous one. "How often do you conclude an undetermined cause of death?"

"As often as the cause is unable to be determined."

She frowns at me squashing her attempt to make me look incompetent in front of the jury.

"Would you say more often than your superiors?"

"Objection," the DA says. "Irrelevant."

"Sustained," Judge Adelman says. He knows I'm extremely qualified to be on this stand and often superior to my superiors.

"Doctor Watts, were you recently injured in the line of duty?"

"Objection," Dan, the DA, is not happy with Mrs. Paine In The Ass. "Irrelevant."

"Sustained."

"Is it true that you had a near-death experience, and now you see dead people?"

"Objection! Badgering the witness."

"Sustained. Counsel, approach the bench."

I watch both attorneys approach the bench; then I scan the jury. Dylan needs to discredit me because she's losing her case. And I'll hand it to the douchebag, she's managed to sow a little doubt into their minds. I can tell from the looks on some of their faces.

The attorneys leave the bench.

"No further questions, Your Honor," Dylan says with her back to the judge.

Dan faces me. "Doctor Watts, did you graduate at the top of your class in medical school?"

"Yes."

"Did the chief medical examiner himself pursue you, encourage you to leave general surgery, and make the glowing recommendation for your forensic pathology fellowship?"

"Yes."

"Have you published nearly forty peer-reviewed papers?"

"Yes."

"Have you had hands-on teaching with medical students?"

"Yes."

"Have you been cleared to work since you took a bullet in the line of duty?"

"Yes."

"No further questions, Your Honor."

The judge dismisses me. When I walk past Dylan's table, I give her a wink. It's a good luck wink. She's going to need it.

When I exit the courtroom, Detective Mosley's leaning against the opposing wall with his head bowed to his phone. He glances up, and much like yesterday, he says exactly what I need to hear without saying anything. Pushing off the wall, he slips his phone into his pocket with one hand while taking my hand in his other. We wordlessly make our way out of the court-house and down the stairs where we stop, and he turns toward me.

I grab his lapels, staring at his chest while taking in a deep breath. I wasn't expecting Dylan to cross that line. I was angry, but I didn't show it. Still, I imagined shaving her long blond locks from her head, and that's messed-up. So messed-up.

"Lean in," Colten says, interrupting my thoughts.

I don't look up at him; I tighten my grip on his lapels ... and lean in, resting my forehead on his shirt over his heart. I *hate* feeling so unworthy of him. It's uniquely hollowing.

I am a bad person loved by a good man.

"I believe you," he says. "I just don't know how to fight demons that lived in another century. And as much as I want to crawl into your head and occupy every inch of space in your brain, I can't. I also can't let you walk away. I *trust* you, Josie. You have to let that be enough."

Tipping my chin up to look him in the eyes, I give him a sad smile. "What if I don't trust myself?"

Colten inches his head side to side and repeats himself from earlier. "You're mine. Not his."

Colten's, not Winston's.

I can't separate it quite like that.

CHAPTER
Fourteen

"I HEARD my parents talking about your mom," Josie said as we were biking to the pool the summer before sixth grade.

"What were they saying?"

"That your mom is ... hmm, what was the word? Struggling? Yeah, I think that was the word. They said she needs to get help."

"Help doing what?"

"I think it's because she cries a lot, and my mom said she's sometimes in her robe all day. She gets the mail in her robe, and she takes you to piano lessons in her robe."

"She's sad because my dad's living in a trailer."

"If it were me, I'd be sad because my husband cheated on me. No ... not sad. I'd be mad. I'd probably hurt him."

I laughed as we locked our bikes to the rack by the pool entrance. "What would you do?"

"Blunt trauma to his testicles."

"What?" I didn't hear her right. Did I?

"My mom said I should never kick a boy in the testicles because it can cause serious damage. I looked it up. Pain. Swelling. Even a rupture with lots of blood in your scrotum."

"My what?"

"Scrotum. It's the part of you that looks like a turkey and holds your testicles, letting them hang low from your body to keep cool. If they get too warm, your sperm die."

"Shh ..." My cheeks filled with hot embarrassment when the teenaged girl checking our pool passes gave us a weird look. She must have heard Josie say testicles *and* sperm.

I veered right near the boys' locker rooms, and Josie went left toward the girls'. Meeting on the other side, we searched for a place to keep our towels and bags.

"If I had a husband, and he cheated on me, I'd kick him hard in the balls with my boots. My mom said it could cause a guy to not be able to make children someday. And that seems like a fair punishment for cheating, don't you think?"

I'd been kicked in the balls on more than one occasion, usually an accident. Just talking about it made my stomach hurt. "I don't think my mom will kick my dad in the nuts. She says she still loves him."

"I'd kick him in the testicles, but I think my parents would ground me."

"Don't call them testicles." I dropped my bag next to the fence.

"That's what they're called."

"You sound like a doctor."

"Maybe someday I'll be a doctor, so it's a good idea for me to keep calling them testicles instead of nuts or balls."

I never thought she had a loud voice until we were in public talking about testicles. Then it felt like she was using a megaphone, and everyone could hear her.

"The one exception to kicking someone in the testicles ..."

Here we go again.

"... is if someone is trying to kidnap you or touch your genitals. A kidnapper or a pedophile. Or it could be the same person, right?"

I had no idea what a pedophile was, and I wasn't going to ask her until we were someplace private for fear that she'd use the word *genitals* ten times in her loudest voice.

"If a pedophile kidnapped you, they could tie you up and touch you whenever they wanted to. I suppose that would be easier than stalking kids outside of schools. Right?"

I gathered that a pedophile was a pervert. That's what my mom called adults who touched kids' privates. I felt certain Josie's dad talked with her a lot about pedophiles or perverts. Josie was eleven going on thirty.

"Do you want a grape ice pop?" I asked her, desperately wanting to change the subject.

"Orange."

I nodded, escaping to the concession stand before she could talk about ... anything. The second I returned with the ice pop, she started up again.

"I think I'm going to start spending time with your mom like when you're at baseball practice. Chad spends all of his time playing video games. And you guys don't have a dog or any other family pet, so I'll spend time with her. Then maybe she'll not be so sad. Maybe she'll get dressed."

Even at eleven, I knew there was something special about Josephine Watts. She wasn't trying to be anything more than the girl who treated other people the way she wanted to be treated. Of course, I didn't tell her that, but maybe I should have.

"You can be our pet." I laughed at my own joke.

Josie attempted to give me a sneer, but she started giggling. "I won't even pee on the carpet. My dad said we can't get a dog because they pee on the carpet, and then you have to pay a carpet cleaner to suck up the mess, and they charge you a whole bunch of money for every visit. He said we can't afford a dog because they can barely afford Benji and me. I know they really mean him, not me, because the only time they call the carpet cleaner is when Benji makes a mess."

"We had a dog in Texas, but my dad ran him over with the car."

Josie's nose wrinkles. "Did he die right away?"

"No. His back legs were broken, and he was going to need a cart with little wheels. And something was wrong with his insides too. We were going to have to push on his belly to help him go pee. So my dad had the vet kill him."

"Put him down." Josie rolled her eyes. "Not kill him."

"The vet gave him something so his heart would stop beating. He killed him."

Josie finished the last of her ice pop and nodded. "Yeah, I think so too." Then she shrugged. "My dad and I kill animals. Maybe I should be a vet someday."

We tossed our wrappers into the trash and headed straight to the line for the waterslide. From that day on, Josie made a point to visit my mom almost every day until my dad moved back home. Josie was a lot of things, but first and foremost, she was a good person.

CHAPTER
Fifteen

I WAKE from a restless sleep with a gasp, jackknifing to sitting. Heart racing. Chest burning. Sweat beading along my brow and trickling down my back. He took the girls from family gatherings. *I* took the girls from family gatherings.

After a 2 a.m. shower, I pull on a pair of black sweatpants and a white tank top and gulp down a glass of water. It clinks when I set it in the sink while closing my eyes. Young girls with long hair, ribbons, and giggles of innocence.

For hours, I stare out the window, nestled under a blanket on the sofa, waiting for sleep. I manage two hours of no dreams and wake when I hear the alarm in my bedroom. While shuffling my feet down the hall-way, there's a knock at my door. I continue to the bedroom to shut off my alarm first. As I get closer to the door, the deadbolt turns. I jump to the side, squatting down and retrieving my gun from my purse on the floor. When Colten's head peeks around the corner, I blow out a sigh with the gun still aimed at him.

"Morning," he says with his eyebrows raised, and his gaze glued to my gun.

"You have to stop breaking into my house." I lower my gun and return it to my purse.

He holds up his key. "Remember? I'm not breaking into your house."

I stand. "What are you doing here? It's five o'clock."

"I got called just after midnight. A woman's body was found in a suitcase at the airport. I was on my way home and decided I needed to see you."

"I know where you live. My house isn't between the airport and your house. Nor is it between the police station and your house."

"I didn't say *you* were on my way home. I said I was on my way home and wanted to see you."

"I'm not much of a sight at the moment."

"You didn't sleep well?"

I yawn. "I haven't slept well since you made the terrible decision to save me."

Colten follows me to my bathroom. "It wasn't a decision or a choice. It's instinctual. I need you in this life."

"Liar." I comb through my slightly damp hair.

He frowns at my reflection. "Remember that period when you visited with my mom nearly every day until my dad moved back home?"

I give him a single nod.

"It was the nicest thing I had ever seen anyone do for another human. At the time, I couldn't figure out why you would do it. She wasn't your mom. And nobody told you to do it. I was too immature to see it."

"See what?" I pull my hair into a tight bun.

"See that you were a good person. It's who you are. You don't have to try. No one tells you to be a good person. It's *who* you are."

I squeeze a glob of toothpaste onto my toothbrush and eye him in the mirror.

"I trust you." His hands find my waist while his lips press to the back of my neck.

I spit and rinse. "I abducted the girls from big events like weddings and funerals. Anywhere there was a crowd of people who were too distracted to properly watch the kids. Good people don't do that." I turn toward him, resting my hands on the edge of the sink. "It's only a matter of time before I see how they died. And I don't know if I'm emotionally equipped to deal with that. I've seen some truly grotesque things. I've dealt with liquid human remains. I've autopsied decapitated heads, no bodies. I've seen children who have been violently raped before being killed. I've put unborn babies in jars. It's a job. It's what I do, not who I am. But those girls ..."

Colten's hands slide around my neck, his thumbs brushing my cheeks. "What can I do?"

I deflate. I was ready for him to scold me for saying *I* instead of *he.* I was ready for him to give me part two of the you're-a-good-person pep talk. "Just be you," I whisper, snaking my arms around his waist.

"Who am I?"

I close my eyes, feeling exhausted. "Everything."

"Call in. Don't go to work today," he says.

I peer up at him. My gut reaction is to roll my eyes at the ridiculous suggestion. I don't skip work. That's not me. I also don't ignore my gut reactions. For some reason, I find myself nodding.

"I'm tired. Can we crawl into your bed and sleep until noon? I have to write up some reports, but I can do that later."

Again, I nod. Then I text Dr. Cornwell before sliding into bed next to Colten. He pulls me to his warm body and kisses my forehead.

Maybe it's Colten's embrace or maybe it's sheer exhaustion, but I sleep until eleven-thirty without a single vision or dream. I wake before him, but I don't move. His face is so close to mine; I can't help but inspect every tiny detail from the little scar by his eyebrow to the gray working its way into his five o'clock shadow. Long eyelashes. Full, downturned lips.

God ... it's always been him.

Colten's Josie *is* kind. Colten's Josie wouldn't harm anyone. Colten's Josie is confident and smart. Colten's Josie doesn't run from fear. I like Colten's Josie.

As if the spinning thoughts in my head are making actual sounds, Colten blinks open his eyes.

"I'm going to need help because self-doubt is a pernicious bitch. Your job is to get me there. Get the job done. And remind me every day that I'm your Artemis. Okay?"

Colten blinks slowly. "What did I miss?" he asks in a sleepy voice. "Get you where? Get what job done?"

"Get me to the altar. Make sure I'm wearing white, but I don't look ridiculous. Don't take no for an answer. Then just ... hold on to me."

It takes a few seconds for things to register, but when they do, his grin swells, engulfing his entire face.

It's a glorious smile. Spectacular. Just like him.

I give him my best smile as well, but it hurts. Everything inside my chest hurts. It hurts to stay. It hurts to walk away. Life hurts. I just think it could hurt a little less with Colten in it. And ... I hurt because I'm scared out of my mind that this is a terrible idea. But ... he trusts me. And ... I trust him.

CHAPTER
Sixteen

"Want to talk about it?" Dr. Cornwell asks when I arrive in the conference room.

"About?" I fill a cup with coffee while everyone else takes a seat at the table.

Dr. Cornwell pours a generous dose of creamer into his coffee. "You took a personal day yesterday."

"And?"

"It's your first personal day."

I smile. "Well, that's not true. I took a lot of days off after I died."

Stirring his coffee, he eyes me. I half expect him to laugh, but he doesn't. Not even a smile. "I can only imagine what you must be going through. Has it gotten any better?"

Better? He thinks I believe I was a young girl

murdered by Winston Jeffries. I can only imagine what he would think if he knew the truth.

The truth ...

Is it true?

Truth is ascribed to things representing reality. I've never felt so out of touch with reality. How could I possibly know what's true?

"I'm getting married." That's my brilliant answer. If I just believe hard enough, marrying the boy I've loved for as long as I can remember might be the answer to ... something.

Dr. Cornwell's bushy, gray eyebrows jump up his forehead. "I didn't know you were seeing anyone."

Gotta hand it to Alicia, she keeps our talks a secret.

"Colten Mosley."

Those bushy brows take a dive into a sharp V of confusion.

"Detective Mosley."

"Oh. How am I just now hearing about this?"

"The engagement?"

"All of it. I had no idea he was courting you."

For a second time, he makes me smile. It feels like something a normal human would do. I've never felt perfectly normal, but it was far better than not feeling human.

"How long has this courting been taking place?"

I chuckle. Now he's doing it to get a reaction from me. "Since we were nine."

"Oh good lord ... that's some stamina."

I can't help myself. "Yes. Colten has a lot of stamina." I smirk.

Dr. Cornwell glances down at his coffee mug; then his gaze jumps back up to mine. He just got it. "Well..." he clears his throat, and I swear he's blushing a bit "...I suppose congratulations are in order."

"Thanks." I really need to call my parents. They should have found out before my boss. I glance past him to the rest of the MEs at the table. "Can we keep it between us for a few days? I haven't told all of my family."

Any. I haven't told anyone.

He makes a lock and key motion at his lips.

I take a seat at the table, and Dr. Cornwell introduces the cases for the day. He only gets a few words in before the most cringe-worthy sound blasts from my phone at full volume.

First, I silence my phone in the morning before I shower.

Second, I don't have songs for ringtones.

Third, I'm going to kill Colten.

It's his name on my screen with a goofy picture of his face, like a mug shot, that I did not take. And he has the ringtone set to The Dixie Cups' "Chapel of Love."

Fumbling with my phone, I mute the call and send it to voicemail.

"I guess the cat's out of the bag now." Cornwell grins.

Heat fills my cheeks, all eyes on me ... the blushing bride.

As an early wedding gift, Cornwell gives me the

five-year-old girl who was found dead in her family's swimming pool. He leads the students around the autopsy suite, spending extra time at my table. I ignore the look in his eyes, the test he's given me.

Am I okay with a drowning victim?

Am I okay with a young girl?

Am *I* okay?

"What is the mechanism in acute drownings?" Cornwell asks.

"Hypoxemia and irreversible cerebral anoxia," one of the students says as I make my Y incision.

"Good. What are the five stages of drowning?"

"Water infiltrates the airway—"

"Nope. Anyone else?" Cornwell prods.

His abrupt interruption of the first student keeps everyone else silent.

"Surprise and panic," I say. "Then water enters the lungs. You involuntarily hold your breath. Next ... lights out. In as little as thirty seconds, you're uncon-scious. Respiratory arrest. You start to sink. Turn blue. Possible convulsions. Cerebral hypoxia and ... death."

"I don't think everyone counts the last one," one of the students says. "Because when you're dead, you're no longer drowning."

I glance up at her. "What if you're not dead?"

Her gaze darts around at the other students, but no one jumps in to save her.

After a few seconds, she clears her throat and eyes me again. "You mean if you're not biologically dead?"

I nod, pausing my scalpel.

"You have three minutes."

"Then what?"

"Well, your brain cells die, and your chances are kinda ... non-existent."

"Dr. Watts drowned with a gunshot wound to her abdomen," Dr. Cornwell announces. "But she's a freak of nature. We don't know how long she was submerged, but it seems likely it was longer than three minutes. We'll never know. Anyway ... here she is with enough living brain cells to do her job flawlessly."

He emphasizes the "flawlessly". It's his nod of approval. Another test I've managed to pass.

"TOUCH MY PHONE AGAIN, and I will remove both of your hands, Mosley."

Colten glances up from his desk, a little before seven. There are only a few people left on the floor. He pushes back in his chair and stands while wearing a champion's grin. "You won't."

I set my bag on his desk and let him pull me into his body. "Try me." I tilt my head back to look at him.

"You like what my hands do to you. I'd only have my tongue, and while we both enjoy what I can do with it, I think you'd miss these magical digits." He holds up his hands and wiggles his fingers.

I glance around to see if anyone's paying attention to us. "Everyone at work knows, yet ... I haven't told my parents."

"They're thrilled. Your mom screamed, and your dad did his long 'hmm' as if he wasn't sure, but then he said I was the only man for you."

"You told my parents!" I grab his shirt and jerk it.

"I'm making it happen, baby. You told me to get you to the altar. Step one: tell our family."

Our family.

Not families.

We have a village. My parents love him, and his mom loves me. We are one family. My fingers release his shirt, and I press my hands flat to his chest. "Were they really happy?" All anger disappears.

Something about his expression softens. "You're okay with me telling them?"

I shrug before lifting onto my toes and brushing my lips over his. "Get me to the altar, and I'll say I do." I kiss him.

His hands cup my face. When the kiss ends, he narrows his eyes a fraction, and he takes a seat in his chair, scratching his chin. I ease my backside onto the edge of his desk.

"I fucking love you so much."

I smile, unsure of what to say back to him. All of my emotions clog my throat. I love him too. But it doesn't take away my fear. Trusting him is all I can do.

Resting his elbows on the chair's arms, he rubs his lips together before grinning. "I didn't tell your parents. I just wanted to get you worked up, but you only gave me ten seconds of satisfaction."

With a slight eye roll, I shake my head. "My parents

adore you. Really, you could have told them."

"My par—" Colten pauses. "My mom adores you, but you know that."

"You were going to say parents."

His brow furrows while he gives me a slow nod. "My dad liked you." He lowers his gaze.

"Why do you make it sound like that was a bad thing?"

"Because it was," he mumbles.

"I don't understand." I nudge his leg with mine, forcing his gaze back to me.

He frowns. "I was on my way to your house to tell your dad about us. To tell him that I loved you. And I wanted to go wherever you went after graduation."

I slowly shake my head.

"Just as I was walking out the door, my dad came home. He made some snide remark about me secretly pining for the chief's daughter. I said it wasn't going to be a secret much longer." Colten rubs his forehead. "Then my dad said you were the smartest decision I had ever made. And he was amazed I hadn't screwed it up yet. He thought your good work ethic would rub off on me. And ... well ... that rubbed me the wrong way. It triggered my toxic need to do the exact opposite of what he wanted." He shakes his head. "I ... I was so damn self-destructive. I didn't want to please him. I didn't want to *be* him. So I didn't tell your dad that I loved you. I did the opposite. And when your dad suggested the Marines, I knew my dad would hate that idea. So ..."

He glances up at me again.

I don't know what to say. This hurts.

Colten rakes his hands through his hair, leaving it a mess. "Have you ever wanted so badly to not become something or someone, that you're willing to destroy your own world to prevent it? You're willing to destroy everyone around you too?"

After a few breaths, I get misty eyed, and recognition flickers in Colten's eyes. I start to speak, but I can't, so I swallow back some of the suffocating emotion.

On a slow exhale, he closes his eyes for a beat. "Of course you know," he whispers.

I let seventeen years pass. I held a grudge for *seventeen years*. I hated Colten Mosley because ... I *loved* Colten Mosley. That wasn't hate. I had no idea what true hate felt like until Athelinda shattered my existence into so many unrecognizable pieces that I can't imagine ever feeling whole again. Still, I'm trying.

My job.

My family.

My friends.

Colten.

They're pieces I recognize. They belong to Josephine Watts. I need all the pieces of her I can get.

I wipe the corner of my eyes. "Did you tell your mom?"

"Not yet, but she'll be elated." He leans forward in his chair and takes my hands, brushing his thumbs along my knuckles. "I think we should set a date."

This fear is borderline paralyzing. I still have the

urge to go hide. Sometimes I have the urge to inflict pain upon myself. The guilt ... it fills my lungs like I'm in a constant second stage of drowning. Then there's the other shoe waiting to drop, the next horrific, century-old vision.

How did I murder those girls?

"Bring up a calendar." I smile despite the knots in my stomach. I never thought the day would come that I'd have to psych myself up just to be a functioning human being.

Colten's whole face comes to life. "Yeah?"

I give him the why-not shrug.

He releases my hands and snatches his phone from his desk. "I was originally thinking right after the holidays. I know they're right around the corner, but ..." Giving me a quick glance, his nose wrinkles a bit. He's bracing for me to object or return some sort of apprehension.

"Perfect," I say, feigning my best calm confidence. My pulse has to be close to one-forty. Maybe January is too far away. Maybe we should elope immediately. Will it really happen if we wait for me to go out of my mind?

"How about the seventh?"

"The seventh it is." I have to remind myself not to grit my teeth or clench my fists. I'm getting married on January seventh. Normal, non-serial killers do that sort of stuff. *Josephine Watts* deserves this. I really, really want to be her.

He taps his phone screen, adding an event to his calendar on that date:

Marrying the girl of my dreams.

"Listen," he says, head still bowed to his phone screen. "When we tell my mom and she asks about your engagement ring, tell her it's being sized."

"I don't have an engagement ring, probably because I proposed to you."

"Whoa ... what?" His head snaps up. "Not true. Not true at all. I proposed to you at the donut shop."

"Oh? Was that really a proposal?" My lips twist to the side. "Maybe, but I broke off our engagement after I got back from California. Two nights ago, I proposed to you."

Tiny wrinkles line his forehead. "You thought 'Get me to the altar. Make sure I'm wearing white but I don't look ridiculous. Don't take no for an answer. Then just ... hold on to me,' was a proposal?"

Pushing off his desk, I step between his legs and lace my hands through his hair while his hands grip the back of my legs. "It was an epic proposal. The kind only one's soulmate would give. It wasn't predictable. It wasn't a cliche. It was all heart. It was twenty-six years of friendship finally taking that next ... beautiful ... step."

Colten's gaze locks with mine. It, too, is beautiful. "Just to be really clear, in case you missed it a few minutes earlier ... I fucking love you so much."

I make the slow descent to his mouth. "You, my future husband, are something to behold. And I fucking love you so much too."

CHAPTER
Seventeen

My parents react to our engagement news just as Colten predicts: he's perfect, I'm perfect, we are even more perfect together.

Becca will find out soon. It's been a week since telling my parents and swearing them to secrecy. My mom is dying to plan this wedding with Becca. I've booked another session with Dr. Byrd. I'm not sure if that makes me responsible, proactive with my mental health, or if I'm admitting that I'm mentally slipping.

"I'll stay in the car," I say when Colten pulls up to Katy's house to pick up Reagan for the big surprise.

"You should meet Katy. She'll want to meet you since you're now a big part of Reagan's life."

I'm a thirty-five-year-old woman who dissects dead bodies. I'm marrying the love of my life despite not caring about marriage. I don't want kids of my own. Oh

... and I was a serial killer in a past life. Just the kind of person a mother would want to be a *big* part of her daughter's life.

Colten struts his way to the front door of the white with red brick two-story while I lag three steps behind him.

When he reaches the steps to the stoop, he glances back at me and holds out his hand. "Come here."

I take it and drag my feet up the stairs.

"Is she hot?" I ask before he knocks on the door.

"What?" He gives me a funny look.

I shrug. "You always went for the hottest girls in school. I'm just curious if you continued that trend."

It takes him a second to speak or even blink. "You're right." He smirks. "I went for you, Josie, and you were by far the hottest girl in school."

I scoff. "I was not. And you know what I'm talking about. We were never officially anything."

"You're right again." He squeezes my hand while his other hand knocks on the storm door. "We were everything."

The door opens.

Yep. Katy is a hottie.

"Hey! Reagan is finishing her snack. Come in." Katy smiles at me; then her gaze goes to my hand in Colten's.

"Katy, this is Josie Watts. Josie, this is Katy."

"Nice to meet you." Katy smiles. I think it's genuine, but I've always struggled to read hot girls correctly.

"You as well," I say.

"What time does your mom's flight get in?" Katy asks Colten.

"In an hour."

"Well, I haven't told Reagan since you said it's a surprise. Is she coming for anything special or just a visit?"

"Josie's mom is coming tomorrow, and the four of them are going to go wedding dress shopping."

Katy's eyes widen. "Oh ... is your mom getting remarried?"

Colten chuckles. "No."

Katy's attention shifts to me.

"January seventh." I grin, and I fear it looks as goofy as it feels. "Mark your calendar." *Well, shit. Did I just invite Colten's baby mama to our wedding?*

"Wow! Congratulations." Katy shakes her head at Colten. "Never thought I'd live to see the day."

Me neither.

"Reagan?" Colten calls her name. His thumb rubs my finger, a little fidgety and anxious to get out of here.

"Daddy!" She tears around the corner and flies into his arms, forcing him to release my hand.

"What's this?" He kisses her cheek, and she squeals when he licks something from the corner of her mouth. "Mmm ... strawberries." He sets her down. "Grab your bag. We have to get going. I have a surprise for you."

Katy eyes me again after Reagan runs upstairs. Was I supposed to give Reagan a big hug and exuberant greeting as well? I didn't even say hi.

What's wrong with me? I helped watch Benji. I even changed a few diapers. I should have a few motherly instincts or nurturing tendencies embedded in me somewhere.

"Is this your first marriage," Katy asks.

"Yes."

"Kids?"

I shake my head and offer a stiff grin.

"Oh, well, I guess it's a race to see who gives Reagan a sibling first," she says.

Colten laughs. It's a nervous laugh, and his equally nervous thumb is about to wear through the skin on my finger.

"You'll win. We're never having kids," I say with confidence.

"Oh." Katy looks at Colten for confirmation.

No confirmation needed. There is a zero percent chance of us having kids.

"Well..." Colten shoots me a sidelong glance "... never is a long time. Anything could happen."

Nope. Not anything.

"Ready!" Reagan barrels down the stairs, dragging her duffel bag behind her.

Colten takes the bag and Reagan's hand. "See you Wednesday."

"Bye." Katy leans down and kisses Reagan's head. "Love you, sweetie."

Reagan talks our ears off on the way to the airport.

"See the plane?" Colten points to the sky as we exit toward the terminal.

"Are we going in an airplane?" she asks, bursting with excitement.

I hope Becca can live up to the high expectation of a trip on a plane.

"No, Button. It's something else."

We park and head toward the gate. By the time we get there, Becca's coming down the elevator.

"Grandma!" Reagan races toward her.

Apparently, Grandma is better than airplanes.

Colten steps behind me and wraps his arms around my waist, kissing my head. While Reagan has Becca preoccupied fifteen feet away from us, I turn in his arms because I have to get this off of my chest.

"I had a tubal ligation before I started med school. No babies."

He frowns. "You had your tubes tied?"

"Yes."

"Why?"

"Because I don't want children."

He shakes his head slowly. "But how could you know for certain at such a young age?"

"Colten, I've known this for as long as I can recall. I told you this when we were kids."

"But that's just it; we were kids."

"And now I'm in my mid-thirties, and I still don't want kids."

I can't read his expression, but it doesn't give me a good feeling.

"Before we tell your mom and Reagan, you need to

decide right now if Reagan is it for you. I will not be giving you a child. Not ever."

"I choose you." No hesitation. He says it so quickly, so confidently, it punches a hole in my gut. He's giving me the kind of love most women only dream of. And I feel unworthy. "It's you. No question."

I nod just as he glances over my shoulder.

"What are you two up to?" Becca says, holding her arms out for Colten.

He hugs her before picking up Reagan, hiking her onto his hip. "I asked Josie to marry me, and she said yes."

Incorrect. But I don't squabble over the details.

Becca's eyes fill with tears while she pulls me in for a hug. "Finally," she whispers.

"I want to be the flower girl!" Reagan claps her hands together several times.

"Of course, Button."

When Becca releases me, her palms press to my cheeks. "You've always been my daughter. I can't believe my boy is finally making it official."

I smile. "My mom's coming tomorrow. How do you feel about shopping for a wedding dress?"

"Ah, perfect!" Her hands drop from my face and go straight to my left hand. "Where's your ring?"

"It's being fitted," Colten says before I have a chance to answer. "Let's get going. Parking is expensive."

CHAPTER
Eighteen

MY MOM ARRIVES Saturday morning in time for the four of us girls to have lunch before shopping for dresses. While my mom chatters nonstop, Becca sips her post lunch coffee and strokes the back of Regan's long, dark hair while she plays on her iPad.

I'm mesmerized by it, fixating on it. I can see it hanging from a tree in a cemetery. The silky strands whipping in the breeze. I can imagine what she'd look like without her hair. I know exactly what she would look like without a pulse. Without a breath. No reflexes. No pupillary constriction. Her skin would sag, making her prominent joints become pronounced. Her sphincters would relax, passing feces and urine. All the blood would drain from smaller veins. She'd be pallid. Pallor mortis. As hours pass, her body temperature would drop to the air temperature around it. Without a heartbeat, blood would pool from gravity. Livor mortis. More time would pass, and her muscles might stiffen. Children don't always follow the same pattern as adults. Rigor mortis might spread from her jaw and neck to her chest, abdomen, and extremities. A lifeless body. The end of innocence.

"Where are you?" Mom rests her hand on my arm, tearing my gaze away from Reagan.

I feel warm. Too warm. And my heart's racing fast. Too fast. "No ... nowhere. I ... um ..." I scoot back in my chair. "I need to use the restroom. Please excuse me." When I get to the ladies' room, I splash water on my face and press several hand towels to it. Using the same towels, I shove them inside of my blouse and blot the sweat from my cleavage and armpits.

"She's fine," I whisper. "She's fine." I didn't hurt Reagan. I would never hurt Reagan.

Right?

While I run my fingers through my hair, I curl them into fists and tug ... tug more ... harder ... harder ...

The door opens to my right, letting the chattering from the restaurant seep inside. I release my hair and fix it while a lady closes the stall door behind me.

"Everything okay?" Becca asks when I return to the table.

"Absolutely." I smile, sitting in my chair just as the waitress sets the bill on the table. I grab it before anyone else can.

"No. I've got this, Josie." Mom tries to argue with me.

I shove my credit card into the black check presenter, and the waitress scoops it up two seconds later.

"Sorry. Too late." I wink at her. I've gone from trying to pull my hair out of my head to a version of chipper that makes me cringe.

In the cool fall air, we stroll down the busy street toward the bridal boutique and pass a hair salon.

"Mind if we stop in here to see if they have an opening?" I ask.

Mom and Becca share looks of confusion.

"I've been so busy with work that I've totally neglected my hair. And I'd love to have it looking nice before I try on gowns."

They nod and offer agreeable smiles.

"Great. Uh ..." I gesture to the opposite side of the street. "There's a toy store if you want to walk around it with Reagan until I'm done."

Again, they return slow nods. "Text me when you're done?" Mom asks.

"Sounds good."

I'm in luck. They have an opening.

An hour later, I meet them outside of the toy store. The door opens, and they emerge, glancing around for me. They look right past me the first time.

"There she is!" Reagan spots me.

I smile, making my way to them. Mom's and Becca's jaws drop.

"Do you like it?" I wrinkle my nose and rub my hand over the back of my head and my short pixie cut.

"I like it," Reagan finally says when my mom and Becca don't answer.

"D-do you like it?" My mom breaks her silence.

"Yeah. It will be way better for work. I can sleep in later because it will take me two seconds to do my hair. Less drying time after I shower. And on my wedding day, I won't have to fuss over flyaways."

"Flyaways," my mom whispers, losing some color from her cheeks.

"It's refreshing." Becca smiles. "Shall we try on dresses?"

"Let's do it." I take Reagan's hand. With a new bounce in my step, feeling so much lighter, I lead them to the bridal boutique.

For the nearly two hours we're here, trying on dresses, my mom keeps looking at me. She looks brokenhearted.

When I try on dress number fifteen, I smile at her in the mirror. "It's just hair, Mom."

With a forced smile, she nods.

"This is the one," I declare, turning in a slow circle. It's a simple, long-sleeved off-the-shoulder, white dress. An elegant sheath dress. Perfect for a January wedding in the Midwest.

"It's stunning," Mom says, seeming to snap out of her shock. Finally.

"Colten is going to bawl his eyes out," Becca says.

Everyone laughs.

I don't see Colten crying on our wedding day.

Four dress orders later, we head to Colten's house, grabbing pizza on the way.

"Looks like he's home," Becca says when she sees his car.

Reagan sprints into the house. "Daddy! We got dresses!" Seconds later, she trots down the stairs just as we're shutting the door behind us, carrying the pizza and drinks to the kitchen. "He said he needs a shower."

"Well, we'll start eating. He won't care," Becca says, opening the pizza boxes on the table.

My mom sits in a chair and sighs. "Oh my achy feet."

"Right?" Becca plops down and passes a plate to my mom.

"I'll be right back," I mumble, but I don't think they hear me over their aching moans and rumbling stomachs.

As I ascend the stairs, I run a hand through my short hair. From the moment I told the guy at the salon to chop it off, right up until this very moment, I felt confident and empowered. I clearly have hair issues. I thought this would help. Now, I don't know.

I can't stop thinking about Colten's reaction. He loves (loved) my hair. Running his hands through it. Burying his nose into it before taking a long inhale. Stroking it after sex.

I open the door to his bedroom then the door to his bathroom. His naked backside is to me as he washes his hair in the shower, the glass covered in condensation. When the door clicks shut behind me, he glances over his shoulder, wiping suds from his face.

I fold my hands behind me and lean against the door. I've never felt so naked.

He pushes open the glass door, eyeing me with an unreadable expression. Maybe it's the steam or maybe it's the memories of what I survived today and how out of control I felt this afternoon, but I can't look him in the eye.

"Rough day, baby?"

I nod slowly, keeping my gaze on the deep blue bathmat.

Wet feet step out onto it. Another step. And another step. His hands cup my face, forcing me to look at him as he drips water all around us, on my blouse and jeans. "You look pretty." He grins. "Like ... really pretty."

All the emotions from the day pool in my eyes a breath before his mouth covers mine. He reaches behind me and locks the door before his hands make quick work of unbuttoning my blouse, removing my bra, and ridding me of everything from the waist down. Then he kisses me again, guiding me into the shower, closing the door behind us.

His hands caress my scalp like they did before I cut my hair, like he's running his fingers through invisible locks. I draw a low groan from his chest when my hand wraps around his cock.

I used to love that Colten Mosley saw everything about me. He had X-ray vision to my emotions. Now, it's painfully embarrassing. After seventeen years, I reappear in his life only to completely fall apart. Who signs up for this?

His lips brush along my neck while his hand cups my breast. "Stop thinking so hard, Watts." I feel his grin along my skin. "I love you. You love me. Don't complicate it." He kisses my shoulder. "Let us be the one part of your life that's easy."

My eyes drift shut, and my head lulls back slowly with every inch he journeys down my body.

"Colten ..." I whisper, one hand flat on the tile to my side, my other hand in his hair while his tongue flicks between my legs.

"Hmm?" he hums, making my next breath stumble from my chest.

"Why do you love me?"

He doesn't answer right away. Maybe he didn't hear me over the water. Maybe he didn't hear me because my words came out as nothing more than a mumble. With his mouth between my legs and his hands on my ass, I manage to stay solely in this moment. My mind likes this moment ... so much.

I love you. You love me. Don't complicate it.

My orgasm rips through every cell in my body until I think I might pass out. Colten kisses his way back up my body.

My breasts.

My neck.

My ear.

And he whispers, "I love you because I'm incapable

of *not* loving you. It's involuntary. It's a deeply woven thread in my fucking soul." His right hand grabs my leg, pulling it up as he pushes into me.

I suck in a breath, each thrust harder than the one before. He takes me all the way up again, blows my mind, and catches me when I start to fall, when my knees give out, when I just want to let him carry me forever. His hand moves from my breast to my hand on the tile wall, and his fingers lace with mine, squeezing hard.

"I love you ..." I whisper while my lips brush his cheek. "I love you more than life."

We kiss, our lips the only thing moving while the loop of pleasure spins out of control, his release warm inside of me ... everything's warm, yet a little shivery, like we're floating. This cocktail of sensations holds my mind completely captive in this moment.

When I find my legs again, we share nothing but smiles, the kind we used to share as two mischievous kids. Then we quickly dress and head toward the stairs.

"Oh, wait." Colten turns around, retreating to his bedroom.

I follow him, poking my head around the corner while he disappears into the closet for a few seconds, returning with something in his hand.

"It's been *resized*." He winks, holding a ring pinched between his finger and thumb. "Can you pretend that you're not seeing it for the first time? Can you pretend that I had this the day I proposed to you in the donut shop? Can you pretend that you said yes in that very moment?"

It's not a diamond. I don't think. It has fern-like specks in the stone.

"It's dendritic quartz. In honor of Artemis. A reminder of the forest she loved." He slides the stone set in platinum onto my ring finger.

It's a perfect fit. I don't know how he did it.

"I'm glad it's back." I lift my gaze from the ring to him. "I missed it."

Colten returns a slow nod, his expression a little more serious. "I know the feeling."

Me ...

He means me.

He wraps me in his arms, presses his hand to the back of my head, lowers his nose, and inhales like nothing has changed.

CHAPTER
Nineteen

Two weeks before I turned eleven, I decided to trim my hair since my mom was too busy with Benji to take me to get my hair cut. Having no patience to wait until my dad could take me or watch Benji, I decided to figure it out on my own with my mom's sewing scissors. My bangs were too long, so I cut them. They were crooked, so I cut them more ... and more, and suddenly they were way too short. So I cut the rest of my hair, hoping it would even out the look, make it so my bangs didn't look so short. Every cut led to another cut to even and straighten, but I had no luck getting anything to look even or straight ... just butchered all to hell. And bangs about six millimeters long.

"Oh my god, Josephine Eleanor Watts!" My mom gasped after putting Benji down for his nap.

I stared at her reflection in the mirror. She

surveyed the pile of hair in the bathroom sink and all over the floor before returning her attention to my reflection.

"It got away from me," I mumbled.

With one hand cupped over her mouth, she nodded. "I told you I'd take you next week," she said, her hand drifting from her mouth to my hair, barely touching it like it could break.

"I know." I frowned.

"Sweetie, your bangs ..." Her fingertips grazed the spiky ends of my barely existent bangs. The stubble on my dad's face after three days was longer than my bangs.

"I can't go to school." Tears filled my eyes. "They won't let me wear a hat. And everyone will make fun of me. I can't. I won't."

"Shh ..." she hugged me and caressed my butchered hair. "We'll figure something out."

Something indeed.

After working her magic on what was left of my hair, I ended up with a layered bob that reached no farther than my earlobes, and my new best friend was a headband. Mom combed hair forward from the crown of my head and secured it with a headband. Viola! Fake bangs.

"They're gonna know," I murmured the next morning at breakfast.

"Not if you leave your headband in place."

"They'll make fun of the headband because I never wear a headband."

"You have a new hairstyle. They'll clearly see that it's short, so the headband will just be part of your new, shorter hairstyle." She set a glass of orange juice by my bowl of cereal.

"Ugh!" I grumbled. "I'm not even hungry." Pushing back my chair, I ran upstairs and spent the next ten minutes staring at my teary-eyed reflection in the mirror before I had to catch the bus.

"Wait up!" Colten called.

"Go away. Not today," I said, but he couldn't hear me.

"Did you get your hair cut?"

"Duh," I said halting at the bus stop.

He jumped in front of me, inspecting me.

I kept glancing away. "Could you stop staring so much?"

"What? Don't you like it?"

I laughed. "Of course, I like it."

I hated it.

"Don't you?" I forced myself to look him in the eye.

Colten nodded slowly. "You look pretty. Like ... really pretty."

I hadn't known him all that long, but I'd known him long enough to know he meant it. Colten Mosley thought I looked pretty.

At school, several teachers complimented me on my new hairdo. None of my friends said much, but that was okay. I wasn't keeping it that way for long. The sooner it grew back out, the better.

Nearly making it through my first fake-bangs day,

the last recess came along to ruin it. Toby Tyler, meanest boy in school, thought it would be funny to steal my headband and run to the ball diamond with it.

"TOBY!" I pressed my palm to my super short bangs and chased him. "STOP!" Catching up to him, I jumped for my headband while he held it just out of reach.

"Oh my gosh, you freak. What happened to your hair?" Toby laughed and so did two of his buddies.

In the process of trying to get the headband, I revealed my spiky bangs. A putting green.

Tears filled my eyes, but there was no way I was letting a single one go, not in front of Toby.

"Give it back, Toby."

I glanced behind me at Colten strutting his way toward us.

"She's a freak, Colten. Your little girlfriend is a freak," Toby taunted.

Colten grabbed Toby's shirt and shoved him onto the ground.

"What the heck?" Toby had the audacity to look shocked, but Colten had two inches on him, and everyone knew it was no competition.

"Get out of here, and don't touch her again." Colten grabbed my headband.

Toby growled something before stomping away with his friends.

I turned my back to Colten and quickly blotted my eyes before facing him again. "Thanks," I murmured, taking the headband and tipping my chin while trying to put it back on my head with the fake bangs pulled forward.

"What happened?" Colten asked.

"Toby took my headband because he's a jerk."

"No. I mean, what happened to your hair in front?"

"I cut it too short. And now I can't fix it." I ripped the headband back off my head and threw it on the ground.

Colten picked it up and shook the dirt from it.

"My mom took hair from back here and pulled it forward, so it looked like bangs, but ..." Again, I got emotional and had to fight the tears.

Colten slipped the headband onto my head and pulled it forward while tucking hair from the back of my head toward my forehead under the band, just like my mom had done. "There. It's fine. I'll tell Toby to keep his mouth shut, or I'll punch him in the face."

"Don't do that." I glanced up at Colten, patting my head to check my hair.

"I won't. I'm just going to tell him that so he doesn't tell everyone that ..." He wrinkled his nose, gaze inspecting my hair again.

"That I'm ugly?"

"No. You're not ugly. I told you this morning that you look pretty ... very pretty."

I didn't need or want a Prince Charming, but had I been in search of one, it would have been Colten Mosley.

CHAPTER
Twenty

"I DIDN'T THINK I'd see you again," Dr. Byrd says.

"That makes two of us."

"Nice haircut, by the way. I bet it's a breeze to do in the morning."

I walk around his office, inspecting his succulents while he remains at his desk. "Tell me how you really feel about my hair? Ask me why I did it?"

"Why did you do it?"

I turn. "I don't know. You tell me. You're the expert."

Pressing his lips together, Terrance lifts his chin and dips it into a sharp nod.

"Oh, and I'm engaged again. You said to lean in, so I'm leaning all in." I touch one of the thick leaves, and it snaps off. Figures. I'm not to be trusted.

"Are you angry?"

"What makes you say that?" I toss the broken leaf onto his desk and plop into the chair.

"You didn't answer my question," he says.

"You didn't answer mine."

He grins. "Okay. I sense you're angry because you paced my office for ten minutes before sitting down. You announced your engagement with no enthusiasm. And you're picking a hole in the arm of that chair."

I stop my fidgeting and frown at the tiny hole I made. "I had lunch with my mom, Colten's mom, and his daughter. And while Colten's mom stroked his daughter's long hair, I imagined what she would look like without that hair. Then, I imagined what she would look like dead. So yeah ... that has me a little agitated."

"And that's the reason for the new hairdo?"

My lips twist. "No. I did that because I tried to pull my hair out while I was in the bathroom failing miserably at composing myself."

"Are you having more visions or dreams?"

"Yes."

"Do you want to share them?"

"Last night, I woke up after seeing one of the girls foaming at the mouth. I poisoned the girls."

He squints. "Are you sure?"

"Sure? No. I'm clearly not sure about anything. But it fits. I was a chemist. That's what I found on the internet. Most poisons come from soil, and the parapsychologist insists the girls died from earth."

"What if we keep a separation? Refer to him as Winston Jeffries instead of you."

"Now, you sound like Colten."

"I'm trying to keep things straight because we are discussing two lives. Winston Jeffries and Josephine Watts. I need to know that when you're saying I, you're referring to something in this life. That's all. Okay?"

I nod, folding my hands on my lap so they don't destroy anything else today.

"Cyanide?" he asks.

"Perhaps. Or Strychnine."

"It's another piece to the puzzle you can share with the authorities."

"I'm sure they're working hard on this century-old crime." I roll my eyes.

"Then let's address your fears."

"What am I afraid of?"

"Maybe hurting someone? Hurting Colten's daughter? But you must remember that thoughts are just that ... thoughts. You imagined things about her, but did you actively want those things to happen to her?"

"What? Of course not."

"Then let's talk about ways for you to practice self-awareness and mindfulness. You've already identified your negative thoughts. Now let's work on replacing them with something that is true or realistic. What makes you feel good?"

"Sex with Colten."

Terrance gives me a small nod but averts his gaze to his notebook.

"When these awful thoughts come into my head, I should replace them with thoughts about having sex with Colten?"

"Sure." He clears his throat. "If it's appropriate. If you're with friends or family or at work, it might not be the appropriate redirect. Maybe think of your favorite food."

"Colten's cock."

Terrance eyes me.

I return a toothy grin. "Kidding."

"Fuck you, Josie."

I bark a laugh. This laugh alone is worth every penny of our session. "Are you allowed to say that to a patient?"

He pours himself a glass of water. "Every case is different. Sometimes I have to be unconventional."

"And there's nothing conventional about me?"

He sips his water. "You already know the answer to that."

"Okay. So think happy thoughts. That's what you've got for me today?"

"Replace negative thoughts. I'm not saying you have to think happy thoughts all day. We have thousands of thoughts go through our mind every day; most of them are neither happy nor sad. Think of all the thoughts we have about mundane tasks that we do. I also don't want you thought-stopping."

"What's that?"

"It's looking for negative thoughts so you can stop them. It means you're subjecting yourself to anxiety by anticipating negative thoughts. Deal with them only when they happen. Don't anticipate them happening. But when they do, redirect your thinking to—"

"Sex with Colten. Got it."

Terrance blows a breath out of his nose. No smile. "The goal is to make this automatic. And eventually, you might notice less and less of these negative thoughts. You can also try guided meditation at night. Or you can take a dopamine blocker."

"I'm not taking antipsychotic drugs again."

He nods. "I understand." He glances at his watch. "Time's up."

ON MY WAY HOME, Colten calls me.

"How was therapy?"

"How did you know I was at therapy?"

"I'm tracking your phone. I set that up when I set up your ringtone. I can't get you to the altar if I can't find you."

"Mmm ... I don't know if I buy that."

"So what did Dr. Birdie say?"

"Dr. Byrd. And he said I need to have more sex and think about it as often as possible. I realize you have a demanding job, so I might have to recruit some help."

"I'm not laughing."

"Me neither. I hate those dating apps, but if I just stick to random hookups and don't fret over meeting for dinner first, it will be easier."

"Still not laughing."

"Really? That one was a little funny. Where are you?"

"I just got home."

"Helping your mom make dinner?"

"My mom took Reagan to a movie."

"My mom left this morning."

"Uh-huh." He seems a little distracted.

"You're not inviting me over?"

"I'm working on my car."

"Which one?"

"Samantha."

I laugh. "Samantha?"

"I named my cars after the first woman I fucked in them."

What the hell?

"How original." I skip my exit. "Well, I'll see you around."

"Okay. Night." He disconnects the call.

I floor it, speeding past my exit. Who says that to their fiancée? I have no desire to get into any of his cars ever again. Who the hell did he fuck in my dad's Chevelle? He's a grown adult. Why is he screwing women in his cars?

As soon as I pull into his driveway, I march to his garage, opening the access door and slamming it behind me.

"Watts," he says from the pit under his car, country music blaring from the speaker. He peeks his head out, his blue tee clinging to his chest, grease on his face and arms. "Didn't think I'd be seeing you tonight."

"What's the Chevelle's name? What's your work car's name? Do you have names for each of the rooms in your house?" I park my hands on my hips.

He hops out of the pit and grabs a towel, wiping his hands. "Are you hooking up on dating apps?"

I roll my eyes. "Of course not."

"You're losing your edge. Not gonna lie ... I'm a little disappointed." Tossing the towel aside, he takes a swig of cola from the can on his workbench.

"Are you bullshitting me? Did you *lie* to me about naming your cars after skanks?"

"Skanks?" He coughs after taking a swig. "Why do the women I date have to be skanks?"

"If grown women are fucking you in your cars, then they're skanks."

"I love you, Josephine Watts. I've loved you for as long as I can remember." He saunters toward me. "But if you joke about hooking up with men from your stupid little dating apps, then I'm going to get even. Now, we're even." His black boots hit the toes of my white sneakers.

"Your Corvette's name isn't Samantha." It's not a question. It's ... a confession of my gullibility.

He smirks.

I nod slowly, looking just past his shoulder as I unbutton my jeans.

"What are you doing?"

After toeing off my shoes, I shimmy out of the jeans

and shrug off my tee, standing in front of him in my bra and panties. "I want you to name her Josie."

Excitement spreads along his face as his smirk explodes into a full, ear-reaching smile. "Which one?"

My hands twist behind my back to unhook my bra. "All of them."

"You're a temptress. The devil in disguise." He leans down to kiss me.

"You're the devil! Murderer!"

I lean to the side, holding my hand up to stop him while pinching my eyes shut.

"What is it?" he asks.

I shake my head. "It's …"

A voice. It's the first time I've heard a voice in my head. So clear. So close. No vision. Just a voice. A girl screaming those words. A young girl.

"You're the devil! Murderer!"

It's so loud I can't hear Colten. His lips move, but I can't hear him. Again, I close my eyes. My hands press to the side of my head over my ears.

He cuffs my wrists, pulling my hands away from my face. "Josie!"

And then it's silent in my head.

"Baby, look at me." It's barely an echo, but I hear Colten. "Tell me what's happening."

I shake my head.

"No. Don't do that. Tell. Me. Tell me what you saw."

I continue to shake my head. "I … I didn't see. I … I heard a voice."

"Whose voice?"

My gaze flits around the garage; I can't focus. It's nauseating. The voice. The young girl. What she screamed ... it's all nauseating.

"A girl," I whisper, fisting my hands and hugging them to my chest so he doesn't see me shaking.

Colten kisses my forehead. "It's okay. Everything's okay." He retrieves my clothes from the floor and proceeds to dress me. I feel like a child. "What did the girl say?"

"S-she ..." I shake my head. "She screamed. She called ... she ... she called me the devil." Forcing my gaze to stay on his, I choke on my next words. "She called me a murderer."

Colten's brows draw tight, a smudge of grease on his cheek, pain in his eyes. "Him. Not you."

I blink.

"Him. Not you," he repeats.

I think of Dr. Byrd asking me not to say "I" when referring to him. But ... it's getting harder to separate the two in my mind since that life wants to infiltrate this one.

"Do you hear me?"

I nod.

"Him. Not you."

I start to turn, but he hooks his arm around my waist, pulling my back to his chest while he buries his face into my neck. My bare neck ... because I had my hair chopped off ... because I'm slowly losing touch with reality.

"We'll figure this out," he whispers. "But you're not

alone." His right hand slides from my stomach to my chest, his palm over my heart.

I cover his hand with mine. "I'm scared," I whisper.

He hugs me so tightly I swear my bones bend. "Not on my watch ... not ever again." His words settle along my skin, slowly sinking beneath the surface. Does he feel guilty that I got shot on his watch? And how can he protect me from ... myself?

CHAPTER
Twenty-One

I CAN'T LOSE her again.

The problem is ... I have no fucking clue what to do.

Josie sits on my workbench while I finish messing with my car for the night. She's wearing a brave face as if I'm the one who needs reassurance.

"I think I'm going to go back to California," she says.

"Negatory."

"Negatory? What do you mean by that?"

I chuckle. "Well, the last time you went to California, you tried to dump me."

"Let you go."

"When we were seniors, did you feel dumped or let go?"

"Fine, dumped. But—"

"I'll go with you," I say, reaching for my socket wrench and glancing up at her.

Her lips twist. "Um ... no. Not a good idea."

"Well, then you aren't going either." I crank the socket a few times and poke my head out of the pit. "Why is it not a good idea for me to go with you?"

"Because I don't want to deal with your reaction to Athelinda."

"Ath what?"

"Athelinda. She's the *specialist*."

I refocus on the bolt. "And what reaction will I have? She's a doctor. I'm sure she knows more than I do about this stuff."

"She's not a doctor."

"Professor ... whatever."

"She's not a professor."

"You said she works at the university. If she's not a doctor or a professor, what is she?"

She remains silent.

Again, I poke my head out. "Josie?"

Her nose wrinkles. "I stretched the truth a bit."

"You lied?"

"That sounds so bad."

"How should it sound?"

"I don't know." She hugs her arms to herself and shrugs. I hate seeing her like this. The girl I knew ... the woman I heard behind me at the restaurant ... the doctor in her element ... is not this Josephine Watts. The shorthaired woman before me has a fragility I never imagined possible. Since the accident, I've only had tiny glimpses of her where I haven't seen deep worry in her dark eyes.

Will the day come when my mind fully wraps around this? I wake every morning thinking *this* will be the day Josie realizes she wasn't a serial killer. I go to sleep every night praying for a simple explanation.

There is none.

"There's nothing you can't tell me," I say, climbing out of the pit and wiping my hands. "You know that, right?"

Her gaze lifts from her lap to meet my gaze. "I saw a parapsychologist. And she wasn't at the university."

I nod, continuing to work the grease off my hands.

"Her name means one who guards and is immortal. She's a little eccentric. And she's died a few times too."

I cough, tossing the towel aside. "A few times? How is that even possible?" I don't mean to sound skeptical, but surviving one death is statistically very unlikely, but a few?

Another shrug from her. "How did I know about the buried bodies? And by all means, I'm genuinely asking you because I'd happily jump at another explanation."

Wedging myself between her dangling legs, I rest my hands on her thighs. "Why do you want to see her again? Because you heard a voice?"

"Because she gave me the impression that she felt sorry for me like a stage four cancer diagnosis. I want to know how to get rid of the visions and the voices. There has to be something."

"You didn't ask her about this the first time?"

She shakes her head. "When I realized that I wasn't one of the victims, I had to get out of there."

I nod slowly.

"Daddy! We're back!" Reagan flies through the garage door.

"I'm greasy, Button. Easy. How was the movie?"

"Reagan!" My mom reaches the garage door, breathless. "Oh, thank god."

With narrowed eyes, I inspect my mom and her visible relief.

She presses her hand to her chest. "I was worried you two were ... well ... I just wanted to make sure everyone was *decent*."

I press my lips together and nod once, taking Reagan's shoulders and pointing her toward my mom.

Josie hops off the workbench and manages to force a smile for my mom and Reagan.

"Let's head into the house," I say as Reagan skips toward the door and my mom nods in relief.

"I'm going to head home," Josie says behind me.

"Come inside, just for a little bit." I take her hand, and she doesn't argue. "I'm going to grab a quick shower. Mom made brownies earlier. Go eat one, and wait for me."

Mom and Reagan head straight to the kitchen, probably for brownies.

"I'll be upstairs if you need me. I'll hurry." I drop a quick kiss on her lips. "Will you be okay?"

Josie blinks a few times as if she's deep in thought before nodding once.

I take the fastest shower I have ever taken. No shaving. I'm not sure I got off all the grease. If Josie has another *moment*, I don't want it to be when she's alone with my mom and Reagan. When I get to the kitchen, Mom's putting the lid on the brownie pan, Reagan's at the kitchen table coloring, and Josie's standing behind her, braiding her hair.

It's normal. I think. I've never seen Josie braid hair, but clearly she can. It seems a little motherly of her, but she's not the motherly type. Maybe Reagan asked her to, but I kind of doubt it. When my gaze shifts from Josie's hands in my daughter's hair to Josie's face, she's eyeing me with more focus than she's had in the past hour.

I smile. It feels real, but maybe I'm missing the mark. She frowns and slowly undoes the braid before clearing her throat. "Thanks for the brownie. I need to get home."

"Well, give me a hug in case I don't see you again before my flight." Mom hugs Josie, and Josie lightly rests her hands on my mom's arms. Even her hug is off.

"Bye, Reagan." Josie's hand starts to move toward Reagan's head like she's going to rest it there while saying goodbye, but she stops inches from the crown of her head and balls her hand into a fist, returning it to her side.

"Colten, I'm ... unwell. You have to protect yourself ... protect your daughter."

Reagan mumbles a soft goodbye.

I follow Josie to the front door. "Stay," I whisper just as she reaches for the handle.

She turns. "You looked mortified when you saw me braiding her hair."

I shake my head. "I didn't know you could braid hair. That's all."

With a headshake, she frowns. "That wasn't a look of wonder or surprise. That was the look of a protective father."

Again, my head eases side to side. "You're wrong."

"I have to work in the morning. I don't have anything here."

"Stay anyway."

She attempts a smile. "We have the rest of our lives, right?"

"I'm more of a seize the moment kind of guy."

Opening the door, she chuckles. "No. You're not. Seventeen years ago, you could have seized the moment, but you didn't. And since then, you've had roughly one hundred forty-eight thousand, nine hundred and twenty hours to seize the moment. To find me. You didn't. And Reagan is one of the reasons. That's okay. You are now and always will be a father first." The corner of her mouth curls a little. "When I went hunting with my dad, he once told me that he didn't know what kind of man he was until he became a father. You're a good father, Colten, and a good man."

I let her get two steps out the door before I follow

her to her car. "Wait until you see what kind of husband I'm going to be."

At the driver's door, she turns, hands sliding up my chest and around my neck. She's right; Reagan is my world. I can't change that nor would I ever want to. But Josephine Watts owns some serious real estate behind my ribcage.

"Everything has fine print," she says, staring at my chest while her fingers play along the nape of my neck. "Reagan is your fine print. If we don't make it to the altar, she's the fine print. I know it. You know it. Don't pretend we don't."

"That little firecracker in there? I'm still trying to figure her out. It's only been five years. But you ... I know you. The best parts. And I laid claim to them many years ago. I don't need fine print."

I'm ready, completely anticipating a rebuttal.

Nothing.

She lifts onto her toes and pulls me toward her, giving me a slow kiss. Despite the air of melancholy around us, I kiss her, wrapping my future in my arms. Fuck the fine print or what she thought I was thinking earlier. I am *not* losing her again.

CHAPTER
Twenty-Two

"Don't interrupt. Just listen. And don't judge. She'll be wearing a very thin gown, and you'll see everything beneath it. I'll change into a gown as well, just be cool. And if by some chance she asks you to wear one, take off all your clothes and just do it. No questions asked," I say to Colten before we get out of the rental car parked in a spot out front of Athelinda's.

"I feel blindsided and a little pre-violated. You had two weeks and a four-hour flight to tell me this, but I'm just now being told?"

When I don't respond to his humor, he reaches for my hand and squeezes it. "Josie, I feel like aliens landed, and I didn't believe in them, but now they're here and there's no denying it. I'm trying to figure out how to adjust my thoughts to include aliens."

I nod several times while opening the door. "You

should have let me die. Living with aliens sucks." Before he can open his mouth, I get out of the car and take long strides toward the door.

"Josie—"

I hold up my hand to stop him from saying another word while I wait for Athelinda to buzz us in.

"Peace to you, beautiful friends. Please, take everything off and slip on a gown. We have much work to do." Athelinda presses her palms together at her chest and takes a small bow.

"This is Colten. He's my—"

"Yes, of course, my dear Josephine. No time for formalities. Clothes off."

After removing my socks and shoes, I head over to the wall with the gowns on hooks, unbuttoning my blouse on the way.

Jeans.

Bra.

Panties.

After I slip on the gown, I turn. Colten offers me a look that I can't decipher.

His face softens. "Josie," he whispers. He's still bothered by our last discussion.

"Put on a gown," I say.

He glances over his shoulder at Athelinda perched on her pillow, yellowish eyes on us. When he returns his attention to me, I give him one look. No words. Not even a blink.

Keeping his gaze on me, he shrugs off his shirt. He pauses for a few seconds before tugging the button to his jeans. When those have been removed, he partakes in another short stare off before glancing back at Athelinda again. She watches him with a straight face as well.

On a long inhale, he removes his briefs and stands straight with every ounce of confidence in his body.

I hand him a gown and brush past him toward Athelinda. When I sit on a pillow, she leans toward me and presses her cold hands to my face.

"You're exhausted." She frowns.

I swallow hard because she sees me, really sees me, and it has nothing to do with my threadbare gown.

Colten takes a seat on the pillow between us as we sit at 12:00, 3:00, and 6:00. He pulls his legs into a criss-cross and folds his hands over his junk.

"What do you see?" she asks me.

"I poisoned them. They foamed at the mouth."

Athelinda nods, pressing her dry lips together. She's okay with me referring to *him* as *I*.

I feel Colten's gaze on me. I didn't tell him that part. "I want to know how to get rid of the memories. I don't need to solve anything else. I don't need to recollect the moment I killed them or how they resisted when I tried to abduct them. I don't want to know if I did depraved things to them. I just want to forget everything before it gets worse. Or before I ..."

Colten stiffens. He's focused on a marriage; I'm focused on not taking my own life every time I see or hear something in my head. Cake samples would be so much easier.

"I'm afraid you will have to live with this," she says.

"Well, I wasn't living with it before the shooting."

She nods. "Perhaps you'll get some form of dementia as you age."

"Dementia? That's my best hope? What about a brain injury?" I'm being sarcastic.

Athelinda lifts a bony shoulder into a small shrug. "That could do it too."

"Jesus ..." Colten scrubs his hands over his face.

"How do I make things right?"

"That's a discovery you'll encounter on your life's journey. I can't say because no two are ever the same."

"And what am I supposed to do when I'm at a low point? When Colten's watching me stroke his daughter's hair, and I know what he's thinking—"

"I wasn't thinking anything," he says.

I ignore him, keeping my expectant gaze on Athelinda.

"You think WWJD."

"What if I don't believe in Jesus?"

She smirks. "That would be tragic. Jesus is one of my favorites. Long hair. Abs for days. Water into wine. Feeding five thousand. Healing a paralyzed man. The blind. The deaf. The resurrection? Seriously, the resurrection! Has there ever been a more perfect man?"

Colten readjusts on his pillow.

"What Would Josie Do?" she corrects. "When you feel overwhelmed. When you wake from these visions or hear voices in your head, think about Josephine Watts. What would she do?"

My head eases side to side. "I ... I don't know anymore. I've spent too much time analyzing my personality, my interests, my choices in life and comparing them to those of a psychopath." I stare at the floor between us. "My mom was raped. I am the child of rape. The perfect portal for evil. Oh my god ... think about it. JW. WJ. Josephine Watts. Winston Jeffries. That means something, right?"

"Josie ..." Colten rests his hand on my leg.

It feels like the temperature of the room drops ten degrees. Athelinda offers me a sad smile and nods. "Maybe."

My gaze lifts to the ceiling, focusing on stars.

"This life is a blink. And you know without a doubt, now, that we don't end when our hearts stop beating. If you weren't in this life..." she glances over at Colten "...you'd be missed. Your absence would leave emotional holes. But those holes are nothing compared to what you're experiencing now ... or what you'll experience as these visions multiply. Only you know. Only you can see your purpose. Only you can choose your direction. Only you will know if it becomes too much."

"What?" Colten shakes his head. "What the fuck are you talking about? Are you ... are you giving her permission to die? To kill herself? What the fuck is wrong with you?"

I don't feel his anger and rage. I feel empowered.

"Get up. Get dressed. We're leaving." Colten grabs my arm while he stands.

I shake my head.

He squats beside me. "Look at me." His hands frame my face. "I will not let anything happen to you. We are stronger than this. Do you hear me?" His words bleed with desperation, and it's heartbreaking.

"You have to make peace with her decision, whatever it may be," Athelinda says.

Colten ignores her, keeping his gaze on me. "She doesn't know you. *I* know you. I love you. We will get through this."

"How?" I whisper.

He swallows hard while lines dig into his forehead. "Together."

Oh, Colten ...

I let him help me to my feet. Athelinda's sad smile makes an encore performance. I mirror her expression. Colten can be sympathetic. Agreeable. Sacrificial. He can be a million things, but he can't be me. He can't truly understand what this is like for me.

He tears off his gown, no longer caring about Athelinda's eyes on him. I dress a little slower.

"There is one ..."

My gaze slides to her as she starts to speak.

Her teeth scrape along her dry lower lip. "One other possibility."

"Let's go." Colten ties his shoes.

"What?" I ask.

She leans to the side and retrieves her *I AM ...* book. While flipping through the pages, she hums. "The odds would not be in your favor." Her finger traces with lines of script on the page. "They'd be so much not in your favor that I'm not sure I'd even call them odds."

"Just tell me."

Lifting her head slowly, she draws in a quick breath and releases it with one big whoosh. "If you have another near-death experience, it could erase these memories."

"No. Fuck no. Let's go, Josie." Colten's hand encircles my wrist, but I pull against his tug.

"It can't be worse than the other option," I say, opting to not say the actual words.

Suicide. Taking my own life. Checking out.

"Actually, it could. Dying instead of coming back to life is the least of my concerns for you." She glances down at the book again. "You could experience something just as bad or worse. It's foolish to assume this is only your second life. You could have brain damage. You could be in a coma, on a ventilator, which would mean your loved ones would have to make an awful decision."

"Or it could work," I whisper.

"Josephine, I am a rare exception to any rule. Most people don't come back from death once, let alone more than once. Your chances of winning the lottery might be better."

I shake my head. "My heart stops and we start it back up. I'll take those chances over the lottery."

"Jesus, Josie ..." Colten tugs on my wrist again. "No. We're leaving."

"No. That's not how it works," Athelinda says. "For you to have even a remote chance of losing the past-life memories, your heart has to stop beating for longer than it did last time. When it's not beating, your soul shifts through its many lifecycles. It won't release the one in your head until its time has expired. For that to happen, it has to be longer."

Colten grabs my purse and my shoes. "We're out of here."

This time, I don't fight him. My gaze locks with Athelinda's while he pulls me to the door.

She presses her palms together again and bows. "May you find your way in this life ... or another life."

When we get into the rental car, Colten doesn't start it. He grips the steering wheel and stares straight ahead. "Thanksgiving is next week. Christmas is the following month. Then we're getting married. I need..." He clears his throat.

I ease my head to the side. His eyes are red, jaw set.

"I *need* you to be there. I..." he pinches the bridge of his nose "...I need you to be in my life."

If I died, he'd grieve. My family would mourn my death. Then everyone would slowly move on. That's how it works in life. There's a process that follows death. Maybe not everyone follows the process in a particular order or at the same pace, but there's a process.

This is worse. It's limbo. This level of uncertainty is torture.

As long as I'm alive with Winston Jeffries in my

head, it's going to feel impossible for Colten to ... live. He'll always wonder if I'm okay. He'll not sleep well ever again. He'll never fully concentrate at work. He'll live in this limbo and pretend that everything's okay because I'm alive and in his life.

I don't want to be in his life like this. However, I don't know that I'm ready to leave. Instead, I have to trust that I'll know. When the time comes, I'll just ... know.

My hand slides across the console to his leg. "I'm here. I'll make turkey. I'll find the perfect tree. I'll meet you at the altar."

That's it. That's as far as I can go, but he doesn't need to know that. The relief on his face means too much. It means everything right now.

"I fucking love you. You know that, right?" He takes my hand and kisses it over and over before pressing it to his cheek, closing his eyes for a brief second.

"I know," I whisper. "I ... know."

CHAPTER
Twenty-Three

Chad didn't mean to start the neighbor's house on fire, but he did.

"Is Dad taking us to watch the fireworks?" he asked Mom the morning of July fourth. Our first Fourth of July since our parents separated.

I didn't care if he came home to take us to watch fireworks. I didn't care if he ever came home.

"Sorry, hon. He has other plans." Mom offered us a sad smile while she served us patriotic pancakes. Blueberries, strawberries, and bananas.

"What other plans?"

"I don't know."

"Well, call him," Chad insisted.

"It's none of my business, hon."

"You're not divorced. Call him." Chad was relentless. He was either fixated on his games and oblivious to the rest of the world or fixated on something else and relentless to the person whom he thought was responsible for granting his new wish. There was absolutely no in-between with him.

"Josie's dad said you could do better." I wasn't sure if anyone wanted my two cents, but I gave it anyway.

Mom stood up straight, set the spatula on the counter like it was a bomb ready to explode. Taking a deep breath, she turned toward the table and wiped her hands on a towel. "He is your father. And you need a father. Despite what Isaac said, I'm not looking for a replacement. I'm not looking to do better. I'm simply trying to raise two boys, take care of a house on my own, and keep myself from crying all day long. Maybe ... maybe your father doesn't deserve me. Maybe I can do better. But I still love him. Even if I'm angry with him. Even if some days I feel like I hate him for what he did to our family ... I still love him. Falling in love is the biggest risk your heart will ever take. You can't fall in love if your heart is not available, and the only way to make it available is by allowing it to be vulnerable. I hope you never have your hearts broken, but not taking the risk would be far more tragic."

Only in hindsight did I realize what an epic speech my mom gave to two clueless boys. Only in hindsight did I realize how honest and *vulnerable* she allowed her heart to be just to give us a peek into the world of relationships and heartbreak.

Sadly, neither Chad nor I had the emotional maturity to gain a single ounce of wisdom from that speech.

"If you're not going to call Dad, then I'm going to do it." Good old Chad. Dog with a bone.

"You will eat your breakfast. Brush your teeth. And help me with the dishes I need to make to take over to the Watts's house later."

"No. I won't." Chad poked the bear so hard I couldn't help but cringe.

Mom was patient, but she wasn't Jesus. "GO. TO. YOUR. ROOM!" She jabbed a finger in the direction of the stairs.

Chad, being the stubborn and belligerent little fuck that he was, threw a pancake at my mom, smacking her in the face. Her whole head turned red like the strawberries while syrup and whipped topping dripped from her jaw.

She stomped toward him. I had never seen her look so feral. Apparently, neither had Chad because he jolted out of his chair and sprinted up the stairs. When she turned back toward me, I tucked my chin and shoveled down my breakfast. Then, I cleaned up the kitchen without being asked and checked in on my mom. She was face down on her bed crying.

"Come on, twerp," Chad said, poking his head in the bathroom while I brushed my teeth.

"Where?" I asked.

"To get fireworks."

"They're illegal."

"They're in the garage."

I squinted at him before spitting.

"Dad bought them in Missouri the summer that we

moved. But then he found out that we lived next door to the chief of police, so he never set them off."

I jogged down the stairs behind Chad. "We still live across the street from the chief of police."

"He just pulled out of his driveway. We can set a few off before he gets back."

"I don't think it's a good idea. Mom doesn't even let me use a lighter for candles."

"Listen, pussy, sometimes you have to do fun stuff because it's fun, not because your mommy says it's okay." Chad pulled out the ladder and set it up right in the middle of the stall where Dad used to park. Retrieving a box from the boards along the rafters, Chad dropped it to the ground with a big *thunk*.

I lifted one of the flaps like something might jump out at me.

"Right there. Let's set off that rocket." Chad grabbed the big one from the top. "Now ..." he glanced around the garage. "Where's a lighter?"

I knew there was a lighter in the top drawer of dad's tool bench. He had very few tools, but he had a tool bench. He bought it after we moved to Des Moines. I think it happened shortly after Chief Watts asked him if he had a certain tool because the chief couldn't find his. My dad had a hammer and maybe two screw-drivers. I think it embarrassed him because, two days later, he bought the tool bench and several hundred dollars' worth of tools.

"It might be in the top drawer," I murmured. I

wasn't going to get it. This was all on Chad. At the same time, I was a little curious about the rocket.

Chad opened the top drawer, and sure enough, it was there. He plucked it from its spot. His fingerprints, not mine.

"Come on ..." He scuffed his sneakers along the ground to the backyard.

"What if you catch a tree on fire?" I asked.

"The trees are too green to catch on fire. God ... you're so stupid."

He was right. I was stupid. I was stupid to worry about the trees instead of the houses around us.

"Are you sure this is a good idea?" I asked as he set the rocket on the pad of concrete, literally feet from our house.

"Colten, shut up. You're such a baby." He lit the fuse, and we skittered back a few more feet as the flame quickly worked its way to the rocket.

Whoosh!

There it went. I had a full two seconds of retreat. For those two seconds, I felt like a baby. A mama's boy who was too afraid to have a little fun. After all, wasn't that what boys did? Break a few rules all in the name of fun?

Then ... it crashed into the neighbor's window. The Burmeisters. It was the first time I said the word "fuck" aloud.

"Go! Go! Go!" Chad shoved me toward the garage, and I ran as fast as I could.

"There's no phone in here!" I said in a panic.

"Shh!" Chad grabbed the box of fireworks and nearly fell off the ladder trying to heave them back into their spot.

"Chad! Their house is on fire! We have to call 9-1-1."

"So we get into trouble?" He glanced down at me like I was crazy. "Let them call. What's it matter?"

"What if they're not home? Mrs. Burmeister is really old. What if she can't get out of the house? What if the rocket hit her? Oh my god! She could be dead!"

"Shh!" He jumped off the ladder.

"I'm not being quiet. I'm calling for help." I started toward the door, but Chad grabbed the back of my shirt.

"You can't."

Something snapped. This urgency filled my veins, and my fists pounded against my brother until he released me. Then I sprinted inside and called 9-1-1. "Our neighbor's house is on fire. Come quick!"

"What's going on?" Mom ran down the stairs.

"Chad set the neighbor's house on fire! I have to see if Josie's dad is back home." I dropped the phone while the 9-1-1 operator was still talking to me.

Just as I crossed the street, Chief Watts pulled into their driveway. He opened his door and stepped out, holding two bags of ice. "Hey, Colten. What's—"

"The Burmeister's house is on fire. I ... I called 9-1-1."

He dropped the bags of ice and jogged across the street, past our driveway and through our backyard, hopping the short fence into the Burmeister's yard as smoke billowed from the broken window.

Chief Watts tried the handle. Then, he broke the window next to the door, kicked the jagged shards of glass with his boot, and slipped into the house. Minutes later, he emerged, coughing a little, and carrying Humphrey, their white cat, just as firetrucks arrived.

"They're gone."

My hand covered my mouth.

We killed the Burmeisters. I didn't do it, but I knew I would get blamed along with Chad. What would happen to us? Did they send young kids to prison?

Chief rested his hand on my shoulder for a second. He must have read my expression. "They're out of town for the holiday. Josie's supposed to be feeding their cat."

I nodded several times. I thought Josie did mention that, but I'd forgotten.

"Take the cat to my house." He handed Humphrey to me and headed around to the front of the house toward the firetrucks.

"Whoa! What happened?" As I turned around, Josie ran up behind me, mouth agape, eyes on the smoke coming from the window.

I handed her the cat. "Take him. I have to do something."

"Colten?"

I ignored her as I ran into the garage.

"What is wrong with you?" Mom screamed at

Chad. The garage door was open. He was sitting in the driver's seat of her car. "Why would you do this? Tell me why?" She stopped screaming and fell to her knees with her head on his lap.

He stared straight ahead, tears streaming down his face.

"I love you," she whispered. "No matter what ... I. Love. You."

CHAPTER
Twenty-Four

WE STAY the night in California. Josie doesn't eat a bite of her dinner, and when I talk, she plasters on the fakest smile and nods.

"Would you like to take this to go?" the waiter asks her while depositing the bill onto the table.

She shakes her head.

"My dad killed himself."

Josie glances up at me, a hint of confusion in her expression.

"Two weeks after my parents separated, my mom took a whole bottle of pills."

Josie's expression falls flat. She didn't know that.

My gaze wanders around the restaurant. "We were at school. Luckily, my dad came home late that morning to pack up a few more of his belongings. I remember my mom being in the hospital for several days. Dad told us she had kidney stones."

Josie nods and whispers, "I remember that."

"Do you remember when Chad set the neighbor's house on fire on the Fourth of July?"

She nods again.

I let my gaze land on hers and stay there. "My mom found my brother in the garage. In her car. The car was running."

More confusion lines her face.

I tap the table a few times. "The garage doors were down."

Josie flinches. "Colten ..."

I chuckle and shake my head. "People in my life try to kill themselves." Reaching across the table, I take her hand. "I'd like it to stop."

Her gaze falls to her lap, chin down. When I squeeze her hand, tears race down her cheeks. She releases a quick sob and holds her breath. I'm not trying to hurt her or guilt her. I'm trying to save her, and I'm trying to stop this epic streak of tragedy in my life.

I place money on the table, slide out of the booth, and tuck her next to me as we exit the restaurant.

When we get to the hotel, she doesn't say a word and neither do I. We kiss. Discard our clothes. And make love like it's the last time we're ever going to do it.

"WHY DIDN'T you ever tell me about your brother?" she whispers, her back spooned to my chest a little after midnight.

"It took me a while to figure it out. And when I did, when I overheard my parents talking months later, discussing Chad's punishment and his therapy ... I got the nerve to ask my mom what they were talking about. My dad told her not to tell me, but she did anyway. And she made me promise not to tell anyone, even you. And for some reason, that felt like a secret I needed to keep because she cried the whole time she told me about Chad. I still have that image of them in the garage."

I kiss her head. "I wanted to tell you. I wanted to tell you when you told me about your mom being raped. I felt guilty for keeping something from you when you told me everything. But I didn't think Chad's attempted suicide was going to brighten your day after the news your parents gave you."

Josie laughs a little, her foot stroking mine. After a few minutes of silence, she maneuvers her body so that she's facing me. "I feel like I have cancer, and I need to promise everyone that I'm not going to die. At the same time, I feel like the cancer is spreading, and I can't stop it." Her fingertips ghost along my lips, tracing them. "I feel like I need to tell adult Colten that I'm going to be fine. But ... I think I could have told seventeen-year-old Colten that I'm really fucking scared of the cancer. And I feel like I'm going to disappoint everyone around."

I kiss the pads of her fingers. "For the record, seventeen-year-old Colten wanted to save you from the unfair and cruel things in his life. He was just too stupid and scared to figure out how to do it."

"And now?" she whispers.

"And now ..." I close my eyes as if I can hide from the truth.

"Say it, Colten. Saying it doesn't make it any more real. It doesn't make you a coward. It shows your strength. Don't ever run from the truth. The truth *always* wins."

I open my eyes. "I'm terrified. I feel responsible. I feel out of control. So damn helpless."

"Responsible? For the shooting?"

I think about that. "Maybe," I murmur.

"Or do you feel responsible for saving me?"

This is so messed-up. Why should one feel guilty for saving another life? Maybe because I feel like she blames me.

"What would you have done? Had it been me?"

She blinks several times before giggling and rolling onto her back, tossing an arm over her face to hide it. "I would have saved you. I would have done absolutely anything to save you. Risked my own life. Cut the beating heart out of an innocent bystander to give it to you. I would have slayed all the dragons and lit the whole world on fire to save you."

I can't help my grin. "And if it were me experiencing what you're experiencing, what would you do? WWJD?"

"I don't know," she whispers. "I've never known

how to let you go. But you ..." She rolls back toward me. All the laughter has died. Vanished smiles. "You let me go—"

"Josie—"

"Shh ..." She presses her finger to my lips. "I know why you did it. The point is you did it. And you survived. I hope I don't have to ever ask you to live without me, but you *can*."

She's so wrong. Maybe then, but not now. For seventeen years, I had hope, even if only a sliver. Living without her—truly without her—without even a sliver of hope, it would kill me.

"Are you going to catch a wild turkey for Thanksgiving?"

It takes a few seconds, but she grins. "Well, we know *you're* not going to catch one. And you don't catch them. They can actually run quite fast. I'd suggest a shotgun, muzzleloader, or if you're feeling really confident, you can use a bow."

This grin on my face feels good. I like our new conversation, and I like having a glimpse of my childhood friend again. So filled with facts about random things.

"Why do you have that smile on your face?"

"Because." I peck at her lips.

"Because isn't an answer. I just told you I feel like I have an incurable cancer and you're grinning?"

"This is it, baby. All we have is now. This very moment. And in this very moment, you are with me.

We are gloriously naked. And we're discussing the best ways to hunt wild turkeys."

"But in the next moment, I could—"

"Nope." I kiss her again, biting her bottom lip and giving it a playful tug. "This moment. Not the one before, not the one after. Be present with me."

"This moment," she echoes.

I roll so she's under me, so I'm nestled between her sexy legs. So I'm inside her. My eyes close while my lips press to her shoulder. "This one right here ... it might be the very best moment."

Josie kisses my ear and teases the nape of my neck.

Fuck cancer ...

CHAPTER
Twenty-Five

ONCOLOGISTS GIVE CANCER PATIENTS AN IDEA, a possible timeline for the progression of their cancer. Odds of survival with treatment versus without treatment. Even the foremost experts in the field acknowledge there are so many variables that can change that timeline. Change *everything*.

I have no timeline. I'm not sure if it's a blessing or a curse.

We celebrate Thanksgiving with my parents in Des Moines and make plans to spend Christmas with Becca and Reagan here in Chicago so he can have Reagan Christmas Eve at his house. Plans are good. I like plans.

I work.

Colten works.

We put a *For Sale* sign in my yard. It makes more sense for me to live with him since Reagan has a room there with a fantastic white cat mural.

The images continue to flesh out in my dreams. More voices. More everything. The cancer is spreading.

I give Colten his moments, the good ones. And I swallow the bad ones. I suffer in silence as much as possible.

Like cancer patients, I have my good days and my bad days.

Today is a flat-out awful day.

"She was a cancer patient," Cornwell says as I glance at my tablet and my first case of the morning. "The dad said he found her dead in bed. Her oncologist isn't as confident in that explanation."

I nod, reading through notes from law enforcement at the scene.

"Dr. Watts?"

I glance up at Cornwell. "I can take her," he says.

I shake my head, eyes narrowed. "Why?"

"She's eleven. And she has no hair from chemo."

My gaze returns to the tablet, but my eyes no longer follow the words. "So?"

"Josephine, look at me."

Taking in a slow, controlled breath, I lift my gaze to his.

"It's been months since your accident, and while you're doing your job well, I've noticed you take a little longer to do it. You take a little longer to respond to questions from me. You take longer to write up your reports."

"Is it a race? Is it affecting anyone else?"

"No, but I worry about you. Are you still in therapy?"

"No."

"Do you think it might help?"

"Help what?"

He frowns.

I roll my eyes. "Fine. I'm still not sleeping well. It might be affecting my speed, but that's it. And I can handle a cancer patient. Hair or no hair. Now, anything else?"

He inspects me for several seconds over his glasses before shaking his head.

Forty-five minutes later, I'm in full PPE, staring at the girl with no hair.

"Dr. Watts?"

I close my eyes.

"If you don't hold still, I'm going to rip every lock of hair from your head."

"It hurts!"

"Then you should have taken better care of yourself. I have to deal with your sister's hair; I shouldn't be bothered with yours as well. I feel like I have two daughters."

"Ouch!"

"ENOUGH! Sit. Down! Don't move. I'm going to take care of this once and for all."

"Don't ... p-please ... what are you d-doing? I'm s-sorry ... Please stop!"

"Dr. Watts? Josephine!"

I open my eyes.

Alicia offers me a sad smile. "Are you okay?"

I nod.

"Are you sure?"

Glancing around the autopsy suite, I search for anyone else eyeing me. "I'm sure."

It takes me an hour longer than it should to complete the autopsy.

"Let's talk," Cornwell says, stepping into my office and shutting the door behind him.

I glance up for a quick second before finishing the last line on my report. "*You're* coming to my office *and* shutting the door behind you. Should I be worried?"

He takes a seat in the chair opposite me, crossing his legs and folding his hands on his lap. "I'm not one to invoke unnecessary worry. However, I think a little worry might be appropriate. You're not you. You're doing an admirable job of pretending to be you. However, as admirable as it is, it's painful for me to watch you struggle. It's painful to see a feigned confidence instead of the real deal. When I'm in the same room as you, I swear I can feel your demons, but I can't see them, and I don't know what they're saying."

Leaning back in my chair, I study him for a few seconds. I've always thought I could confide in him. Not because I think he's experienced what I'm experiencing, it's because he's seen so much in his life. He's dissected the unimaginable. He's given a voice to the dead. And right now, I feel like I am *a* voice of the dead.

"Do you want the whole story?"

Cornwell's eyes narrow for a beat before he nods. While I proceed to tell him everything, he doesn't move, aside from the occasional blink. Not a nod. Not a smile. Not a grimace. The words fly out of my mouth while I have the courage to say them. And when I finish, he still says nothing.

"Dr. Cornwell?"

This time when he blinks, his gaze falls to his lap. "Josie ..."

He never calls me Josie. I don't like the way he says it.

"I think you are talented beyond words. I've never worked with someone like you. But you know this." He returns his attention to me, something quite grave in his eyes. "I feel honored that you trusted me enough to share this with me. However, as your superior, I must make decisions based on what's right for the job in which you've been appointed to do. I'm going to recommend that you take a leave of absence, your return contingent on a psychiatric evaluation and completion of any recommended treatment."

I'm ... blindsided.

How did I get this wrong?

"I had an evaluation after the accident."

"You need another one."

"I'm seeing a psychiatrist." My voice escalates.

"For an evaluation or to talk through your issues?"

"Talk through my issues. I already had—"

"So you're admitting you have issues?"

"Goddammit, Cornwell!" I stand resting my fists on my desk. "I took off more time for my injury than you did for your double hernia repair. I've seen two psychiatrists. I'm back to work. Who gives a flying fuck if I'm a little slower? I'm just as sharp. I'm completing my tasks, writing up reports, testifying in court. I died! What the hell do you expect? I'm still better at my job than every other ME in this building ... including you and your old ass. When you die and come back to life, then we'll have this conversation. When you figure out the mysteries of the universe and become a foremost expert on near-death experiences, then we'll have this conversation. But until then, I am not going to let you fucking fire me!"

He won't even look at me. Instead, he presses his hands to the arms of the chair and stands. "Take the leave of absence and get your shit together or empty your desk. I'm sorry." Turning, like the coward he is, he exits my office.

OUT OF ALL THE nights I wish Reagan were with her mom, it's this one. I'm not that lucky today.

Colten: Could you pick Reagan up on your way home?

He must not have checked my location because I'm already home. At my house.

I pedal faster on my stationary bike, staring at his

message. I barely made it home without running my car into a tree; I don't think transporting children is a good idea.

Avoiding the actual messenger app so he won't know that I saw his message, I turn off my location. I need time to figure out what I'm doing and if it's even worth doing ... if anything in this life is still worth doing.

After cycling, I do Pilates. Drink a half gallon of water. Clean every inch of my house with music blaring. And finally take a shower.

"Why the hell did you turn off your location?"

I shut off the water and pivot toward Colten. Eyeing him without a reply, I retrieve my towel and dry my body.

"Are you going to answer me? Did you see my text? I had to pick up Reagan and take her to work with me and have someone watch her while I interrogated a suspect."

I wrap my towel around my body. "She's not my responsibility. Sorry."

"Yes, I realize that. I thought we were getting married, and you knew she was part of the deal. You picked her up the week after Thanksgiving."

"And you're welcome, but as a rule, I'd say ... don't count on me for ... anything." I step out of the shower and rub the hand towel over the steamy mirror.

"What's wrong?"

I drop my head and stare at the sink. "I lost my job."

"You what?"

"I SAID—"

Colten cups his hand over my mouth. "Reagan is sitting on the sofa in your living room, just down the hallway."

I jerk my head away from his hold and take a seat on the toilet, pressing a hand to my head and fisting what little hair I can. "Go home. Take your daughter home. I just ..." My hand drops to my leg. "I need space. If I'm truly losing my fucking mind, I don't want to do it in front of Reagan."

Colten hunches in front of me, resting his hands on my legs. He looks like he's had a long day too. His hair is nearly as messy as mine. Tie loose and crooked. Tired eyes. "Why were you fired?"

Any other man would leave. They'd either give me the middle finger and find someone less messed-up ... or they'd stick their tail between their legs and skitter off. Sometimes I wish Colten would be that man. Instead, he ignores all boundaries and climbs all the walls I build. We have too much history. He helped write the book on Josephine Watts.

"I told Cornwell."

"Told him what?"

"Everything."

"Why?"

"Because I needed to tell someone."

"You have me."

I shake my head. "It's not the same. You've said it yourself. You're hardwired to love me. So are my parents. My therapist is trained to…" I shrug "…I don't even know. Alicia is my friend. But Cornwell has always pushed me. He's been a mentor. He has a lot of insight and years of experience. I feel like he's probably heard everything by this point in his career and his life in general. I thought he'd give me perspective in a way that no one else has been able to do."

Colten bows his head and mumbles, "But he didn't."

"No. He did. He not so gently reminded me that if this were happening to anyone else and I were an outsider looking in, I'd think that person was crazy. He didn't say those words, but that's what I took from it. And he's not wrong. He said to get help or clean out my desk."

"And what did you do?"

"No one can help me. So I cleaned out my …" I haven't cried since I left work. I've been too angry. But now … I'm just incredibly sad and hopeless. So with a blink, my tears break free. "I c-cleaned out my d-desk," I whisper past the lump in my throat.

Being a medical examiner is my life. It's the reason I've been single with no kids. I know my love for the man before me is indescribable, but he can't be my job. It's not a void that a person can fill. Losing my job— and my mind—feels like my soul has been stripped and is no longer recognizable. I don't recognize my reflection in the mirror.

I've lost my identity, and I don't know if I will ever find it again.

Colten catches my tears. He's caught so many tears, he could have his own personal Josephine Watts Ocean. "We've got this."

Damn you, Colten ...

We. Ride or die.

Only, he can't die. He has a beautiful little girl. And I know he loves her more than he has loved anyone, including me. And that makes me love him even more. It also makes me hate myself for allowing him back into my life. Maybe seventeen years ago he had it right. We should have ended our story on a sad note—on a moonlight sonata. I fear all that's left of our story is a tragic ending. I can't slow it down. I can't change its course. I think the ending has already been written. It was written the day I came into this world as Josephine Watts, another innocent victim of Winston Jeffries' wrath.

"Take Reagan home," I say, just above a whisper.

He rests his forehead against mine, easing it side to side. "I can't. I won't leave you. The night I fell down the stairs at that party, you got me home. You stayed with me because you wanted to make sure I was okay. That I wasn't going to ..."

Die.

I stayed with him to make sure he didn't stop breathing, that he didn't die from a concussion.

"Go."

He cups my face, forcing me to look at him. "Tell me you're not going to take your life."

Jesus ...

It's jarring. I don't know why it is. It just is. He's not saying anything that hasn't passed through my mind more than once a day, every day, since the accident. Spoken words give life and meaning. They take thoughts and ignite them, sending them into the world to burn. They can fizzle out. Or they can destroy everything.

You can only dance around the truth if it's unspoken. The elephant can't stay in the room once it's been acknowledged. And Colten can't turn back time and unsay those words.

"Say it," he says, teeth gritted, emotion choking his words. "Promise me on my life, on Reagan's life, on your family's life ... promise me you will crawl into bed and fight every last nightmare, wake up in the morning, and continue to fight because you are stronger than this. You are so much fucking stronger than *him*."

I blink more tears.

"And if you can't promise me that..." he kisses every inch of my cheeks "...then I can't leave you."

When he looks at me, I search for words. For answers. For promises.

Before I can speak, he stands, opens the door, and heads straight to my closet.

"What are you doing?" I say at the threshold while he shoves clothes into a bag.

"You hesitated. You've lectured me on hesitation. The truth lies in those painful breaths of silence. So..." he pulls the towel from my body and proceeds to dress me in sweats and a hoodie "...you're coming with me. I'll arrange for my mom to fly in tomorrow, and I'll ask your parents to drive here first thing in the morning." He zips my bag and pulls the hood onto my wet head. For a second, he pauses.

Maybe he's daring me to protest, cross my arms, stomp my feet, beg him to trust me.

I. Have. Nothing.

No job.

No purpose.

No identity.

A hollow body filled with horrible visions.

He doesn't need to call anyone. He needs to drop me off at the hospital and admit me to the psych ward. If I tell them the truth, every last gruesome bit of it, they will conclude that I am unwell. And maybe Colten needs to have someone tell him that so he can save himself, so he can have permission to walk away and focus on what matters most.

Taking my hand, he leads me toward the front door. "Let's go, Button. Josie's feeling a little under the weather, so we'll get her put into bed, and I'll read you all the books you want."

I can't even look at Reagan, so I keep my chin tucked and let Colten lead us to his car, drive us to his house, and guide me upstairs while sending Reagan into the bathroom to brush her teeth for bed.

Just as he gets me settled under the covers, Reagan pokes her head into the room. "I'm ready."

"Grab your books and bring them here."

Christ ... he's afraid to cross the hall to her room and leave me alone.

"These!" She jumps onto the bed, letting her books scatter at the foot of it while crawling toward me. Colten looks in on us from his bathroom while brushing his teeth. "Josie, I'm sorry you're sick. Maybe you'll feel better tomorrow." She kisses my forehead. "Nope. No fever."

The already suffocating lump in my throat doubles as my eyes burn with more tears. I close them before any escape.

"Okay, Button, let Josie sleep. Get on my side and pick your first story," Colten mumbles over his toothbrush.

That's all I remember because I'm so very tired. Everything goes dark behind my eyelids. Quiet. Peaceful. And then ...

I hear a voice.

"Little girls. Little girls everywhere. Oh ... what's that? You lost your hair? Well, that's what you get for being better than your brother. That's what you get for making him look bad. Just ask sweet little Beth with her strawberry locks ... oh ... that's right. She's dead."

"NOOOOO! I KILLED HER. I KILLEDHER. IKILLEDHER!" I jackknife to sitting.

"Daddy ..." Reagan's voice. She's crying. "W-what's wrong with J-josie?"

"Shh ... I've got you," his voice fades, and the door shuts.

Her cries muffle. His footsteps fade. The door to her room clicks shut. And I'm alone with a cold sweat along my brow, a pounding heart, and the realization that I, Winston Jeffries, killed my sister Bethany. I poisoned her. I shaved her head. And I buried her body in a cemetery. Then I cried. I grieved. I did all the things my parents expected me to do while everyone searched for her. They searched for her until my mom took her own life with the same straight blade she used to shave my head. Then my dad drank himself into a coma every evening, waking up in the middle of the night to puke and do things to me that no dad should do to his son. I can smell the mix of putrid stomach contents laced with alcohol.

I can smell it from over a century ago. And that is why … Josephine Watts has never consumed a drop of alcohol.

Puzzles start out slow, but as more pieces are found, it comes together faster and faster. This puzzle is coming together in bigger chunks. Not a piece at a time anymore. Ten pieces. Twenty pieces. And the picture it's creating just keeps getting more unbearable.

Throwing off the covers, I find my feet under shaky legs. When my heart starts to slow, I can hear Reagan's soft sobs. How does a five-year-old, who was once afraid of the boogieman, process someone leaping out of their sleep and screaming, "I KILLED HER!"

Dizzy with the faint residual echo of his voice in my head, I ease open the bedroom door and navigate the stairs by gripping the railing to steady my swaying gait.

I shove my feet into my sneakers at the entry and stumble into the cold December air, light flurries peppering the night skies, blurring my vision, and making me even more dizzy while my faltering steps take me toward the street.

"Josie!"

I walk down the middle of the street.

"JOSIE!"

I mentally go through my own autopsy. Blunt force trauma.

When people get hit by cars, it shatters their skeletons and their organs rupture. It can be unsightly. And it's usually not autopsied. But sometimes bodies are found after a hit and run, and we have to determine if a vehicle ran over a dead body or if it was the cause of death.

"STOP!" Colten wraps his arms around my whole body, like he could tackle me to the ground, only we don't fall. He drags me to the sidewalk as a horn screeches in our ears and taillights beam bright red in the distance a few seconds later.

He scoops me up in his arms like a child and carries me to the house.

"You have to stop saving me," I whisper.

When he gets me back into bed, Reagan comes into the room and crawls in next to me under the covers. "I have bad dreams too," she whispers. "Daddy will keep you safe. He keeps me safe."

Colten shuts off the light and slides in next to me so that I'm sandwiched between them. His arms snake around my waist, and his lips press to my ear while he whispers, "I'll stop saving you when you stop trying to die. But I'll never stop loving you, *needing you*, so tough luck, Mr. Duck."

CHAPTER
Twenty-Six

"THIS ISN'T YOUR REGULAR TIME," Dr. Byrd says, when I have a seat by the window, this time opting for the rocking chair. He has a solid mix of seating choices.

"I lost my job, so my schedule suddenly opened up. And since I've been entertaining the idea of suicide, I thought a quick check-in might be a good idea. You know ... before I check out."

He eyes me without sharing my jovial sense of humor, probably because it's hard to figure out where the humor lies in my current situation.

"How often are you having these thoughts?"

"Daily."

"These thoughts ... how intense are they ... on a scale of one to ten?"

"Eight. Nine must be actively acquiring a weapon, drugs, rope, or unfastening my seat belt while approaching a tree at ninety miles per hour. Correct? And ten means dead or a failed attempt? Eight. I'm going with eight."

"How serious are you about following through?"

"Is this a checklist of questions you learned in school? It is. Isn't it? Next are you going to ask me if I've given any thought as to how I would do it?"

"Have you?"

"I'm a medical examiner. I know all the ways to die. It doesn't require much thought."

He nods. He's having self-doubt. No amount of training can prepare one to talk another human down from the ledge.

"Maybe we can talk about my job."

Dr. Byrd nods again. "What happened?"

"I was fired."

He frowns.

"Well, that's not fair. I wasn't outright fired. It was more of an ultimatum. Get a psychiatric evaluation. Get help. Or clean out my desk. I cleaned out my desk."

"Why?"

"Why are you asking questions you know the answers to? This isn't PTSD. This isn't going away. If I let you medicate me to the point that I no longer recall my past life, then I'll be close to comatose and unable to do my job anyway."

"Why did your superior give you the ultimatum? What tipped him off?"

"I'm a little slower than I used to be. Still capable. Still doing solid work. Just slower."

And I told him I was a murderer.

"Why are you slower?"

"Do you have kids, Terry?"

"Two."

I nod. "Imagine trying to do your job with your kids here. Chattering. Getting into trouble. Shaving each other's heads. Threatening to kill someone. Just ... stuff like that. Would you run behind? Would it take you longer to do your job?"

"Of course."

I shrug. "Well, now you know. I have to cut through the voices, the images, the reminders of that life while trying to do my job, and sometimes it slows me down. But I do, in fact, get my job done. Well, not anymore because I don't have a job. And that's what brings me here. Without my job, I have nothing."

"You have family. Friends. You're getting married."

"Let me rephrase. Without my job, I *am* nothing. No purpose. No identity."

Dr. Byrd stares out the window for a second. It's unusual for him. I'm used to his laser focus. "Sometimes, our identities and purpose in life change."

"Terry, I won't make it. I won't make it another forty ... sixty years with Winston Jeffries in my head. I don't know if I'll make it four to six months. Four to six weeks. You know this is a torture, not so different than ways that POWs are treated. And now I don't have a purpose. *Wife* is not my purpose, even if it becomes part of my identity. I don't believe it's my purpose."

Dr. Byrd stares out the window again. Even the "expert" has no solution.

And so ... we're done.

When I exit his office, Mom smiles at me. Mom, my babysitter for the day. Mom, my driver. I'm never alone.

"Would you be up for some shopping?" she asks. "I have a few gifts left to get."

"Sure." I search for a smile and find one that seems to appease her.

Over the next two hours, we file in and out of stores.

"What are you getting for Reagan?" she asks.

"I don't know. What do young girls like?"

Mom chuckles while flipping through a rack of men's shirts. "Need I remind you that you were once a five-year-old girl?"

"Need I remind you that I wasn't a normal five-year-old girl? And now we know why. I doubt Reagan is into dead things, but I suppose we can see if there's a zombie Barbie or a mortician Barbie." I laugh. Then I laugh some more. "Mortician Barbie comes with a casket and a dead body."

"Shh ..." Mom glances around the store.

I press my lips together to compose myself, but in the next breath, I have a memory, but it's not Winston's life.

"I had Barbies and a few other dolls."

Mom moves to another rack, but she doesn't look at me.

"I cut off their hair. All of it."

She ignores me.

"Mom, I cut off their hair. You knew this, but you didn't remind me?"

"What would have been the point? I think your dad would like this one. Red is his color. What do you think?"

"I think when I'm dead, everyone will look back at so many things in my life and find it to be a goddamn miracle that I made it as long as I did."

"Josephine Eleanor Watts ..."

We have a silent standoff. What does she expect me to say?

"I'm getting your dad this shirt." She turns and heads toward the checkout.

When we get in the car, she exhales and glances over at me. "I've talked with Colten. And we're both in similar situations with you."

"How so?" I stare out my window at the throng of people loaded down with gifts, congesting the sidewalks and gazing at the storefront displays.

"I chose to have you instead of aborting you. He chose to save you. You are so loved. And we hate what you're experiencing. Even if we try to imagine, I'm sure it doesn't even come close. I try to imagine what it would be like to relive the rape repeatedly. Or imagine what it would be like to watch him do the same thing to other women. And even if I could fathom that, I know it doesn't come close to what you're experiencing." She reaches for my hand and squeezes it.

I glance at our hands before lifting my gaze to hers filled with tears. "I can't undo your life," she says. "I can't undo my choice to bring you into this world. And I can't unlove you. Neither can Colten, your dad, your brother, your friends. We can't imagine this life without you. And maybe it's selfish on our part if you are miserable every day and every night..." she wipes several tears that spring free "...but you can't ask us to let you die." With her next blink, all the tears escape.

I'm not a mother. I never will be a mother. So I can't really understand how she's feeling. But I remember how I felt when I lost Colten. I remember that feeling led to self-harm, compelled to cut myself by the debilitating pain.

And he wasn't really gone.

He wasn't gone, yet I thought about him every day for seventeen years. What if that day he broke up with me was the day he died? What if one of the times he felt his world crumbling around him, he would have decided to end his life, like his father did years later?

What would have happened to me? Would I have grieved him and moved on, knowing he wasn't in the world? Would the absence of hope have been the closure I needed? Or would I have spiraled out of control and taken my own life? Romeo and Juliet.

"Reagan loves books. I'm going to get her books. Maybe a Kindle. Maybe a fun reading light or a cute book bag to take to the library. Katy dropped her off, a few weeks ago, with some new library books in a plastic grocery bag." I nod ahead. "Let's stop by the bookstore on the way home. I know a good one."

Mom wipes the rest of her tears and sniffles. Then she nods.

Books.

All I can give her is books.

She seems content with that.

After we get a slew of gifts for Reagan at the bookstore, she drives me to Colten's. His car is in the driveway. My parents are staying at my house, and his mom is staying with him. Everyone is here for me ... and Christmas, but mostly me.

Suicide watch is a full-time job.

"Want me to take Reagan's gifts to your house and wrap them so she doesn't see them?"

"She's at Katy's, but yeah, that would be great. Thanks." I open the door.

"I love you, Josephine."

I glance back at her before climbing completely out of the car. "I love you too, Mom. That will never change."

She nods slowly, but I see sadness resurrecting in her eyes. I see the pain and worry over the promise I can't make. "Night."

"Night." I close the door, but she doesn't pull out until I'm at Colten's door and he's in her line of sight.

Nobody trusts me.

"Good day?" he asks.

"Sure." I hug him.

His arms wrap around my waist. Lately, he's been hugging me a little tighter, a little longer, and I let him because I need it too. The world is a livable place when I'm in his arms. I can breathe a little easier, and hope doesn't feel like a dream out of reach.

When he does release me, he takes my coat and hangs it in the entry closet.

"Where's your mom?" I ask.

"In her bedroom. She had a slight headache, so she went to bed shortly after I got home."

I follow him to the kitchen.

"Hungry?"

I shrug. "We had a late lunch, so I'm not starving."

Colten opens a drawer by the fridge. "I'll give you half if you show me your tits." He tears open a Twix.

I don't look at the candy bar; I look at him and smile. "I saw you. Sometimes when I glanced at your window, I saw you looking at me. But you jumped behind the curtain. You always made me feel interesting in a good way. You always made me feel special. Sometimes I wondered ... if we wouldn't have been neighbors, would you have given me a second look? The time of day?" I reach for his proffered candy bar. "Half of your Twix?"

He takes a bite of his candy bar and scoots a chair close to mine so, when he sits, my knees are between his. "Probably not because you intimidated the hell out of me."

I roll my eyes.

He shrugs, taking another bite of his Twix. "True story."

"Why?"

"Because you were so smart and confident. And pretty ... god you were so pretty. And your dad wouldn't have been the neighbor who took me under his wing. He simply would have been the police chief, and you would have been the police chief's daughter aka off-limits."

I break off a piece of the Twix, stretching the caramel until it breaks then popping it into my mouth.

"When I was in the shower this morning, I thought back to the times when my dad would let me jump off his fishing boat into the lake. I'd go under and hold my breath until I just couldn't go another second. Until my cheeks hurt from holding the air in them, until my lungs burned. Once, my dad jumped in after me because he thought something had happened to me." I chuckle. "He was so mad. I just liked seeing how long I could hold my breath. Then I thought about Winston Jeffries, and I remembered something."

"What was that?"

I shake my head, setting the rest of my uneaten candy bar on the table. "I think someone tried to drown him or strangle him. I just remember so clearly the feeling of not being able to breathe, like someone was holding me under water or wrapping their hands around my neck."

Colten rests his hands on my knees.

"And then this afternoon, I remembered something I did to my Barbie dolls ... all of my dolls."

"You tried to drown them?" he says jokingly.

"No. I cut off all of their hair."

Colten's grin falls off his face.

"People can have tics and not know it until someone brings it to their attention. I dated a guy in college who would finish his sentence and then repeat the last few words of the sentence in a whisper, like an echo. He had no idea he did it until I mentioned it. To his knowledge, he didn't have a condition that would cause it. Maybe it was stress or sleep deprivation, or maybe it was genetic. It's just interesting that one can do something like that and not realize it. That's how I feel. I feel like I've had something that I didn't recognize until now. And the pieces now fit where they didn't fit before. Winston Jeffries has been popping into my life for ... well, maybe forever. And I'm only now starting to make the connections."

"You're not him, Josie. And you're not the only person who has cut their baby doll's or Barbie's hair. You're not the first person to see how long you can hold your breath underwater. You're not the only person who has been curious about death. And while I will concede that you have been and always will be a unique person, it has nothing to do with Winston Jeffries."

What do I say when he says all the right things? I wish I could love my way through this. Why can't love be enough? Why can't love conquer all? Standing, I yawn and stretch my arms over my head. "I'm going to bed."

Colten nods, gaze on my empty chair. "I'll be up in a few minutes." He forces his gaze to mine. "Will you be okay?"

I nod, not hesitating for a single second. I hate that he feels like I can't be left alone. I feel like a temperamental plant that is always on the verge of dying if it's watered too little or too much, if you change its location in the house or forget to talk to it. I am the exact opposite of independent.

"Good." He reaches for my hand and squeezes it. There's a lot of hand squeezing lately. Colten looks exhausted.

Loving me isn't easy. I can't help but wonder if he ever regrets moving to Chicago. I wouldn't blame him.

CHAPTER
Twenty-Seven

Nᴇᴡ ᴏʙsᴇʀᴠᴀᴛɪᴏɴ: The less worthy one feels, the less they *feel* anything.

My parents leave Christmas Eve day after lunch to visit Benji. We'll see them again at the wedding in a few weeks. Becca returns to Texas to be with Chad and his partner for Christmas. It's just Colten, Reagan, and me until Katy picks her up to be with her and Sean on Christmas morning.

"Josie!" Colten grabs the hot pad and takes the pan from me as I hold its searing hot handle. Only, it's not searing to me. "Baby, oh shit ..." He runs my hand under cool water.

I don't feel that either.

"Daddy said a bad word," Reagan observes from her post as present watcher by the tree.

I stare at my hand, red and white. Like Christmas.

"Josie?" Colten presses his chest to my back while keeping my hand under the stream of water. "Say something. How bad is it?"

"I'm ... I'm sorry."

"No." He kisses my head over and over. "Don't apologize. But, baby ... you didn't drop the pan or scream or so much as flinch."

"I'm sorry."

"Stop. No." He wets a towel and wraps it around my hand, turning me to face him. "I think we should get it looked at."

I ease my head side to side, lifting my unfocused gaze to meet his concerned face. "It's ... fine," I whisper.

"Daddy, it's time to open gifts."

"After dinner, Button," he says while continuing to scrutinize me.

"Let's eat." I hug my hand to my chest and turn toward the plates of food.

"Just sit down. I'll finish dishing up the food and bring it to the table."

Reagan hops into her chair. Instead of taking a seat, I stand behind her, stroking her hair with my good hand. "You'd look adorable in short hair."

"Like yours?" she asks, twisting her body to see me.

I smile and nod.

"Reagan, your mom would not approve of cutting your hair," Colten says, setting two of the plates on the table and eyeing me—eyeing my hand stroking her hair. A tiny line forms along the bridge of his nose.

"Baby, have a seat." He nods to the chair across from Reagan.

Every time I touch her hair, he gets that look.

Can he love me and not trust me?

After dinner, Reagan bolts to the tree. "Presents!"

"Give me five minutes. I'm going to get bandages for Josie's hand."

"Hurry up!" She shakes one of the boxes.

"It's fine," I say.

He removes the towel. It's not fine. It's pretty bad. Still, I somehow don't feel it. I felt the look he gave me over Reagan's hair, but not this burn.

"It's not fine. Come with me."

I follow him to his bedroom, taking a seat on the edge of the bed as he grabs first-aid supplies out of the bathroom.

While applying burn cream and gauze bandages, he glances up at me. "You're a little off tonight."

I look at him and nod several times.

"What's up? You're not getting cold feet, are you?"

"About what?"

He grins. "Um ... the wedding. You should have received an invite. I'd love it if you could make it."

"Do you not trust me with Reagan?"

"What are you talking about?" He knows that answer. That's why he's not looking at me.

"Does it make you nervous when I touch her hair?"

He shakes his head, still not looking at me. "No. It makes me nervous when you talk about cutting her hair. I don't want to deal with Katy on that."

"Tonight ... *tonight* I said she'd look cute in short hair. But I've touched her hair other times, and you always give me the same look."

Colten tapes the end of the gauze bandage. "What look is that?"

"Self-doubt."

He grunts a laugh. "Self-doubt about what?"

Before I can answer, he returns the supplies to the bathroom.

"I think it gives you pause. Even if only for a few seconds, you wonder if Winston Jeffries is really dead."

"Nope," he says from the bathroom. "I know he's dead. But..." shutting off the light to the bathroom, he peeks around the corner "...I wonder if you're thinking of my daughter's beautiful hair when you stroke it or if you're thinking of him."

"And if I'm thinking of him?"

Colten frowns, hunching in front of me again. "Do you *want* me to have self-doubt?"

"No. But if you do, I don't want you to lie about it."

He falls to his knees and rests his head on my lap. "No doubts. No cold feet. I love you without a single hesitation. And I trust you with my life."

"And Reagan's?"

"Daddy!" Speaking of ...

Colten jumps to his feet. "Time to open gifts." He holds out his hand to take my good hand.

He's not answering me. That's ... my answer.

We open presents, and Reagan loves all the book

stuff I got her. This brings a smile to my face. And that brings one to Colten's.

"I want to use my sled."

"Button, it's nighttime. Tomorrow, you can use it."

"Tonight. Just once. *Please ...*"

Colten sighs. "Fine. Let's get your stuff on after I run upstairs and get my snow pants."

"I can help her," I say, following Reagan and her sled to the entry.

She pulls on her bib and jacket. I zip it and help her with her hat and gloves.

"Scarf too?"

She nods.

I wrap the scarf around her neck and tie it once, holding one tail with my teeth because I can't grip with my injured hand.

"*I ... can't ... b-breath ...*"

I pull tight. And tighter. And ...

"Too tight, Josie."

I pull a little tighter.

"*Pl-please st-stop!*"

"Let me get that since your hand is hurt." Colten takes the ends of the scarf from me and quickly loosens it. "I don't think you need a scarf. We won't be out there long."

Reagan touches her gloved hand to her neck.

"Are you going to watch us out the window?" he asks.

The girls couldn't breathe. I couldn't breathe. I did to them what was done to me.

"Josie?"

I shake my head, staring at Reagan. Then my attention shifts to Colten, and I nod.

"Go stand by the patio door and watch us sled."

Another slow nod. He's treating me like a child. I would object to this treatment, but I don't have my wits about me enough to build a case for myself. So I turn and shuffle my feet to the patio door.

I wasn't going to strangle her. I was just ... fuck. I don't know.

The power of the mind is incredible. Even the best scientists in the world have only touched the surface of its capabilities. If you tell someone something enough, they start to believe it, regardless of its truth. It becomes their new truth.

Winston Jeffries is in my head, a voice whispering to me over and over again. How long before it becomes my truth?

I watch them sled a few times down the tiny hill in the backyard. For a man who thought he didn't want kids because he was afraid of being his father, Colten is the absolute opposite. He's engaged and patient. His love for Reagan shines brightly every second of every day. Occasionally, he glances at me. No smile.

It's sadness.

He loves me, but I'm unwell. He loves Reagan, but she is vulnerable around me because I can't be trusted. If Katy knew any of this, she would take her daughter and never let Colten see her again. That's what a good mom would do. And Katy is a good mom. She's everything I will never be, including the mother of Colten Mosley's child.

I turn away from the window and slide my socked feet along the hardwood floor toward the stairs.

Bang. Bang. Bang.

Reagan's mitten-covered fists drum against the glass. "Watch me on my tummy!" She's not ready to come inside, and he's not ready to let me be out of his sight.

He knows it wouldn't take me long to end my life. And he knows it wouldn't take me long to end hers. Not that I would. I wouldn't. Winston can scream in my head. He can rob me of every ounce of sleep from now until my last breath, but he won't convince me to hurt Reagan. I'm not him.

I'm not him. I'm not him. I'm not him ...

Reagan goes down the hill on her tummy and giggles when her face lands in a pile of snow. "Did you see me, Josie?"

I nod. Fabricate a smile. And wave both hands. That's what someone who isn't out of their fucking mind does, right?

Right? Who the hell am I asking? Is this it? Is this the prelude to the end? Nothing but a series of conversations with myself? Battle of the internal monologue?

I'm not going to die tonight, but I'm tired, so I go upstairs before anyone can knock on the window again and demand my attention. Managing a quick swipe of the toothbrush along my teeth first, I collapse onto the bed in my panties and one of Colten's hoodies. Sleep takes me within seconds while I hug my burned hand to my chest.

I don't know how long it takes, but when it happens, it's sheer panic and nausea. "NOOOOO!" I gasp, but I can't breathe. The pressure on my neck is unbearable. Panic ensues under the noose of my airway being crushed. This is it. This is how I die. It's like I'm drowning all over again, but I'm not. Someone is strangling me. When I peel open my eyes, my heart explodes. It's him.

Colten's strangling me. This is how he's protecting his daughter. I know it's for the best. I deserve this. It's what I've been preparing myself for since the day I should have died in the water. I don't hate him.

No ... I love him. I love him for loving me so completely. I love him for doing the right thing even when I didn't understand it. But this time ... I understand it. I'm trying so hard not to fight him, but my hands flail, hitting him.

Just let it happen ...

Fighting the instinct to survive is hard, and it feels so out of my control. I grab his arms, trying to pry them off my neck. I can't. He's stronger.

Stay strong. Finish the job. Focus on my eyes. I'm ready.

I cough. He's not gripping me hard enough. I shouldn't be able to get any air.

Again, I cough.

The hoodie slides over my head.

"Josie. Josie. Josie ... I've got you, baby. I've got you ... Breathe. Just breathe. You're safe. I've got you."

The pressure on my neck disappears, and air fills my lungs. The pounding of my heart overtakes all other sensations while he pulls me against his bare chest and kisses me over and over on my head, my cheeks, my lips.

"I'm sorry," he whispers. "I'm so very sorry."

My good hand touches my neck. "Why did you stop? I was ready."

He pulls back, confusion lining his forehead. "Stop what?"

"Strangling me."

"What? No ... no, Josie. I wasn't strangling you. You were having a nightmare. You woke up gasping and flailing, clawing at your neck like you couldn't breathe."

I sit up, tearing myself from his arms while swinging my legs over the side of the bed. Head bowed. Sweat along my brow. Confused.

"What is happening to me?" I whisper.

Colten crawls out of bed and disappears downstairs. A minute or so later, he returns with a glass of water. "I would never hurt you."

My gaze lifts to his while I take the glass of water. "What are we doing?" I ask, barely above a whisper.

"We're living." He sits next to me on the bed, taking my injured hand onto his lap and tracing the lines of the bandage. "And it's really fucking hard for you right now. If I could take this burden from you, I would. I feel like you're still drowning, and every day I'm trying to save you. Josie, I *have* to save you."

"Colten, I ..." Emotion clogs my throat. "I made Reagan's scarf too tight. I ..."

"It was an accident. She's fine."

"But what if—"

"She's fine," he repeats.

I feel so dead inside, so I hand him the half-empty glass and collapse onto my side, easing my legs onto the bed. "I'm tired."

"Then sleep, my love." He kisses my cheek. "Dream of me. Dream of being legally bound to me forever."

I attempt a smile because he's trying so hard to lighten the mood. I'm walking death, and that sucks for everyone around me.

CHAPTER
Twenty-Eight

IT'S A MIRACLE, and because of this miracle, I am a true believer today.

Today I'm marrying Josephine Watts. My heart feels full, overflowing really. Everything I didn't dare to imagine is here in this church.

A daughter.

The woman I've loved since I was ten.

Family.

Friends.

A future.

It's all right here.

"I'm proud of you, son," Josie's dad says to me as I straighten my tie in the mirror. "You've made something of yourself. You are a good man. And I can't imagine anyone better for my daughter." He blows out a long breath. "If your dad was here, he'd be proud of you too. He'd see that you are absolutely everything he never was. And I'm sad for you that he's not here because I think you would have been the dominant influence in his life that he needed. I think he would have been a better man because of the man you've become."

I don't want to think about my dad today. However, hearing Chief Watts say those words to me means a lot. He's reminding me why I always looked up to him over my own father. He *is* the better man.

"How are you feeling about the road ahead?" he asks. "Do you believe her? Do you believe she was that Winston Jeffries guy?"

"Yes." I turn. "I ..." I rub my forehead. "I don't know how it's possible to believe her, but I was there when she found those bodies. There is no other explanation. And here's the thing ... I will follow her down any rabbit hole, no matter how deep or how dark. If I didn't love her and trust her, I wouldn't be marrying her."

Chief Watts nods several times before grinning. "She's never been in better hands."

I don't know about that. If I was totally honest with him, I'd tell him I'm frightened out of my fucking mind that something is going to happen to her again on my watch. She's in this position because something happened to her on my watch.

"Daddy?" Reagan peeks her head into the room.

"Hey, Button, let me see you."

She closes the door behind her and runs to me.

I hunch down and hug her before holding her at arm's length. "I have never seen a more beautiful girl."

She twirls in a circle. God, I love this girl.

"Mommy went to get me a snack."

"A snack, huh?" I stand straight.

"Uh-huh. I'm going to see Josie now."

"Whoa, whoa, I don't want you running around here by yourself. It's not safe."

"Because of bad people?" she asks.

Isaac gives me a look. It's the don't-lie-to-her look.

"Yes. Unfortunately, sometimes there are bad people. Probably not here, today, but you should still be safe."

"But I want to see her."

"Do you know where she is?"

She nods.

"You can go see her, but I want you to stay with her until your mom comes back with your snack. Okay?"

Reagan nods, her curls and ribbons bouncing with each dramatic tip of her chin.

"Love you, Button. You look beautiful."

"Bye, Daddy!" She blows me a kiss with fishy lips.

This is the very best day of my life. Everything has come full circle.

"Do you think you and Josie will have kids together?"

I turn toward Isaac, hiding the confusion I feel from his question. Did she not tell her family that she can't have kids? Did she never tell her parents that she didn't want to have kids?

"I'm not sure it's what she wants. And I have Reagan. My life is complete. Anything else would just be extra. So ... one day at a time." I find a believable smile. I'd have a dozen babies with Josie because it would mean a dozen more pieces of Josie walking the earth, gracing my life with giggles and fishy kisses.

There's a knock at the door.

"Everyone dressed?" Savannah asks before opening the door a crack.

"You're not allowed to see the father of the bride before the wedding," Isaac says.

Savannah opens the door the rest of the way. "Is that so?"

Isaac saunters toward her, wrapping his arms around her waist, hands resting on her ass. If I said I'm not having a blow job flashback, I'd be lying.

"What's that look for?" Savannah asks me when he releases her.

I realize I'm cringing and quickly correct my expression. "Nothing. Just ..."

"Cold feet? Nerves? Your bride-to-be is stunning. Just ..." Savannah gets tears in her eyes. "And Reagan couldn't look more adorable. They're having a private moment right now."

I nod.

"She told Josie you said she needed to stay with her because there are bad people around. I certainly hope there aren't any here today."

"She what? She said that to Josie?"

Savannah nods.

"W-where are they?" My stomach twists into knots. I have a feeling. A terrible feeling.

"You can't see Josie before the wedding, silly."

I take long strides to the door. "Where are they?"

"Colten ..."

As soon as I open the door, my world explodes. That *feeling* comes to fruition in the form of my daughter standing before me with confusion on her face, a short bob, and her long hair banded and hanging from her fist.

I can't fucking breathe.

Reagan holds out her shaky hand with the hair. "J-Josie said I'm safe." She's on the verge of tears. "And s-she said she's j-ust a star."

I take the hair and pull her into my arms.

"She said t-to step backwards ... and I ... think she said there's a galaxy."

"I'm sorry, Button. Your hair will grow back." I hold her at arm's length again like I did when she showed me her dress. "Where is Josie?"

"What's going on?" Isaac asks.

Reagan shrugs. "Her room? I don't know. I unzipped her dress and came to give you my hair."

"Stay right here. Don't move." I kiss her forehead and take off running.

"Colten?" Savannah calls behind me.

When I throw open the door to the lounge just off the ladies' room, an unwelcome emptiness settles into my chest. She's not here. She's not in the building. I feel it. Fishing my phone from my pocket, I call her.

She doesn't answer.

"Colten, where are you going?" Katy asks as I pass her on my way out the door to the parking lot.

I don't answer her. I can't.

Josie is nowhere in sight. She rode here with her parents, and their vehicle is here.

"Josie!" I scream, running my fingers through my hair. She's gone.

Fuck ... I can't breathe or feel anything but my heart losing all control while I turn in a slow circle, my world spinning out of control.

She's gone.

"She's not answering her phone." Isaac says.

I grip my hair tighter and continue turning in a circle.

"Nerves. It's just nerves. She probably decided to walk around the block. She'll be back," he says.

Does he really believe that?

I don't.

She's gone. And I'm so fucking scared she's gone for good.

"Where are my keys?" I search my pockets.

"Probably inside with the rest of your stuff," Isaac says.

I run inside, grab my keys, and run back to my car, ignoring everyone saying my name along the way. They're concerned the bride has cold feet. I'm worried her entire body could be cold if I don't find her soon.

"Just hold on, baby ... please." I speed out of the

parking lot, scouring the area. I can't file a missing person's report, but I can call Rains.

"Hey, I'm trimming my beard just for your wedding. Why are you calling me?"

"I need a favor."

"What's wrong? Your voice is shaking. Colten?"

I clear my throat, the thick pain of reality shrinking my airway. "Josie's missing. And I need to find her."

"It's probably cold feet. Give her a bit. She'll show back up."

"No. You don't understand. She's not having second thoughts about marrying me. She's ..." I pinch the bridge of my nose, waiting at a stoplight. "She's suicidal. If I don't find her soon, we won't find her alive."

He doesn't answer for several seconds.

"Are you—"

"I'll get her picture out to everyone. Colten, what hap—"

"Thanks." I disconnect the call.

Over the next three hours, I look everywhere. Rains gives me updates.

Nothing.

Her parents give me updates.

My mom waits at my house.

My brother waits at the church, even after the guests go home.

Her brother waits at her house.

"Colten," Mom whispers my name when I open the back door and shrug out of my jacket, yanking at my tie to loosen it.

"We'll find her."

I shake my head.

"Yes. We'll—"

"NO!" I pound my fists on the kitchen counter.

She jumps.

Then I swipe my arms along the granite, knocking everything to the ground. "FUCK!" My fist lands into the glass cabinet door, then the next, and the next. Blood runs down my arm. "SHE'S DEAD. SHE'S DEAD!" I grab a chair and hurl it through the patio door. "FUCK YOU, WINSTON JEFFRIES!"

"C-Colten ..." Mom sobs, trying to approach me before I break something else.

When my gaze meets hers, I see it. The perfect reflection of my pain. Even if I stopped loving my father, she did not. He selfishly took his life, leaving her with nothing but a million unanswered questions.

"Colten." She takes a cautious step toward me while I pant with the intensity of a rabid animal. When she wraps a towel around my fist, my torso curls inward.

"Noooo ..." I sob.

She hugs me when I fall to my knees. No more promising everything will be alright. Nothing will ever feel right again.

He won. And I lost.

CHAPTER
Twenty-Nine

"ARE YOU AFRAID OF DYING?" Josie asked while we sat in the grass fishing in the pond by the playing fields.

We were thirteen. I didn't think about my mortality as often as Josie did.

"I mean ... I don't want to die."

"Duh. But are you afraid of it? Like a car accident or a tornado? Cancer? Kids get cancer too. Murder ... oh murder would be the worst, especially if it were slow. Like someone tortured you."

"If you're asking if I'm afraid of being tortured, then the answer is yes."

We sat in silence for a few minutes, neither one of us getting a single bite.

"Can you imagine wanting to die? Remember last year when they found that kid hanging from the swing set at North Elementary? The janitor found him in the morning?"

I nodded.

"He wanted to die. That's why he hung himself. A fifteen-year-old who wanted to die. My dad said it's a tragedy, but lots of kids commit suicide."

Another nod.

Just another day in the life of being Josephine Watts' best friend. Death. Death. And more death. Maybe I would have been more scared of it had we not talked about it so much.

"I can't imagine wanting to die." She blows out a long breath. "I suppose that's good, right?"

"Sure."

"But what if you lost everything. Like what if a tornado hit our neighborhood and my parents and Benji died. And you and your family died. And I lived. Maybe I would want to hang myself from the swing set too."

I finished reeling in my line and cast it again.

"Or what if you had cancer and you felt bad all the time. And you knew you were going to die eventually. Would you just get it over with? It might save family a lot of sadness. They wouldn't have to watch you slowly die."

I shrugged. "I don't know."

"You never think about that? You've never thought about how you would kill yourself if you needed to do it?"

"Nope." I had no idea that my dad would one day

drive my mind there. He would anger me and embarrass me to the point of thinking about how I would kill myself.

"At first, I thought I would use a gun because it would be quick. Then I thought about it a little more and realized someone would find me and have to clean up the mess. Now, I'd probably do it in a way that nobody ever found me. They'd never have to see me dead. And they could remember me when I was happy and wanted to live. Doesn't that sound like the best way to go?"

"Or …" I chuckled. "You could *not* kill yourself. I like that idea best. Don't kill yourself."

"Because you would miss me?" She nudged my arm.

I grinned. "Maybe."

Undoubtedly.

My young brain had quite the imagination, but it couldn't imagine a world without Josephine Watts, my best friend.

"I'd tie bricks around my feet and jump off a bridge into the river. I wouldn't leave a note. Maybe my family would wonder if somewhere I was still alive. They'd have hope. Hope is good. It's better than knowing for sure that you will never see someone again."

I didn't know. Josie's mind worked different than mine and everyone else I knew. Not different bad, just … different.

"Would you cry if I died?"

I lifted a shoulder. "I don't know. I don't like to cry. Would you want me to cry?"

"Nah. Just sit in my tree and eat a whole candy bar by yourself. Maybe talk to me. I think it's cool when people talk to the dead like they can hear them. Do you believe in ghosts?"

And just like that ... we jumped to another interesting conversation.

"Oh my gosh!" She shot up as I tugged on my fishing pole. "You caught one, Colten! You did it! Don't let it go! It's a big one." She helped me hold my fishing pole as I reeled it in. "If you lose it, you'll never catch one like it again."

I kinda thought the same thing about Josephine Watts.

CHAPTER Thirty

"ONCE THE SNOWSTORM LETS UP, we'll go out again," Isaac says a week later.

A week after our wedding day.

A week after Josie lost her battle.

A week after I knew she was gone forever.

"You won't find her." I stare at my untouched plate of food.

Savannah and Mom think I need my strength. I lost it a week ago. I'm the only one facing reality.

The Chicago PD are still looking. Signs have been posted. Her picture's been all over the news and internet.

"Son, we'll find her," Isaac says.

Her body. He means they'll find her body. I think he knows she's gone. They need a body for closure. Should I tell him and Savannah that they won't find her body, which means they can carry this "hope" with them forever? Should I tell them that Josie has been planning her death (even if unknowingly) for decades?

Savannah wipes a tear from her cheek and smiles at her hopeful husband. She, too, knows. My mom keeps to herself. This has resurrected all the memories of my dad hanging himself. At least he left his body in plain sight, which made closure a little easier.

I don't know which is worse: their hope or my certainty.

My phone chimes with a FaceTime from Reagan. I take a deep breath and search for a little smile. "Hey, Button."

"Hi, Daddy. Did you find Josie?" She has a smile for me. And a cute, short hairdo. Josie was right. She's adorable in short hair. "Mommy said she's been sharing her picture and looking for her. I look for her too when I'm at school."

My little girl knows how to hit me in the feels; her words make my eyes burn with unshed tears.

"That's ..." I swallow hard. "That's nice of you and Mommy. Thank you."

"I'm not mad that she cut my hair. Mommy said Josie wasn't well. She said she was sad about something that happened a long time ago."

I nod slowly. "Yeah. That's right."

"Well, she'll get better. And when I see her again, I'm going to show her my hair and tell her that I'm not mad. And I'm going to tell her that Mommy has read me three of the books Josie gave me for Christmas.

And yesterday I took the bag she gave me to the library, and it held eight books!"

"Oh yeah?" I hold my phone away for a second while I stand and head to the stairs, wiping the corners of my eyes with the heel of my hand. "That's great."

There's a tiny but mighty thread I'm holding on to, and her name is Reagan Annabel Mosley.

"Mommy said I need to say goodbye. Can I spend the night with you this weekend? I want to go sledding."

"Reagan, I told you Sean and I will take you," Katy says in the background.

"But I want Daddy to do it."

"Of course, Button. We can go sledding this weekend."

"Maybe we'll find Josie. Maybe she's sledding. I feel better when I'm sledding."

"Reagan ..." Katy takes the iPad away from her and frowns at the camera. "I'm sorry, Colten. She just doesn't understand."

"Bye, Daddy!"

"Bye." I ease my head side to side and rub the back of my neck. "It's fine. I'm glad she doesn't understand."

"How are her parents doing? How is your mom doing? God, I'm sure she's thinking about your dad a lot."

I nod. "Yeah, I'm sure she is. Josie's parents are playing the part. They're going through the motions. Not giving up hope."

"I don't think any of us should give up hope, Colten."

"I think everyone needs to do what's right for them. If that's hope, then I won't take that away. But I knew Josie better than anyone, and that's left me with a lot … a lot of love, a lot of memories, and a lot of emotions. Hope isn't one of them."

Katy frowns. "I'm keeping hope. I think Reagan needs it."

I try to smile. "Agreed." Reagan needs hope. She needs fairy tales. She needs Santa Claus and the Easter Bunny. I need something different.

"I BOOKED MY FLIGHT." Mom peeks her head into my bedroom. "Home just in time for Valentine's Day by myself."

I smile, glancing up from my notebook, back against the headboard, legs stretched long. "You could stay. I could be your valentine."

She grins, taking a seat on the end of my bed. "Actually, Chad promised to take me to dinner anywhere I want to go since Philip will be out of town."

"Go big."

She chuckles. "I plan on it."

It's been nearly five weeks since the wedding. I work. I spend time with my mom and Reagan, and I send updates to Josie's parents. It's always the same update: nothing.

Rains thinks we might find her in the spring when the snow thaws or when Lake Michigan starts to thaw. It's been frigidly cold. And what he means is we'll find her body.

We won't.

Maybe we were only kids when Josie said she'd die in a way that nobody would find her, but I have no doubt that adult Josie with her vast knowledge would keep that promise. Everything's in limbo. She's a missing person.

No funeral.

Her house sits empty.

Her parents can't collect life insurance until a body has been discovered and one of her colleagues signs a death certificate. Most likely, they'll see the money in seven years. That's how long it takes to collect life insurance on a missing person.

Nobody needs the money.

Nobody needs her house.

We never got the chance to say our vows, so dealing with her possessions is up to her parents.

"Writing me a love letter?" Mom asks, nodding to my notebook and extra fine tipped Sharpie in my hand.

"Do you want me to write you one?"

She shrugs. "It would be nice. I've never been given a love letter."

That's sad. It's sad she married an asshole. I suppose had she not, I wouldn't be here which means Reagan wouldn't exist. So I back up the mental train and let myself be a little grateful that my mom did marry that asshole.

I find a blank sheet and scribble a few things before tearing it from the spiral bound book and handing it to her.

She reads it, tears instantly filling her eyes.

Dear Mom,

Thank you for loving me more than any other human has ever loved me.

Your favorite son,

Colten

While she wipes a few tears she laughs. "I won't show Chad."

I shrug. "He's a big boy. He can take the truth."

She shakes her head. "I do. I love you so far beyond words, it's ... unimaginable." Her hand rests on my foot. "I feel your grief. I feel the hollowness of your heart. I feel your fractured soul. I feel *you*. God, I wish I could take it all away. I wish I could bring her back and make her better. A mother wants many things for her children, but I wanted you to experience love. The kind I never had. And I knew it was Josie. I knew it from the time you were young kids, and I've known it every day since."

Pulling in a long breath, she releases it slowly. "You will be okay. You will go on to do great things like you did when you let her go the first time."

Let her go.

Is that what I'm doing?

I'm not sure I ever really let her go the first time.

For seventeen years, I held on to hope. And she came back into my life. It was a goddamn miracle.

Mom folds the note I gave her in half. "I know you weren't writing me a love letter. What are you writing? If I can ask?"

I toss her the notebook. "I'm writing down all of my memories of her." I shrug as Mom glances through the pages. "I think some people are afraid of moving on because they don't want to forget. I'll admit, I don't *want* to move on without her, but I have a job, a daughter, a mother, and a brother. I have a life even if it's a life with a Josephine Watts-sized hole in it. And whether I want it to or not, life is moving forward. Some days I feel tied to a treadmill. I don't want to move on, but I don't have a choice." I take the notebook back when she hands it to me. "In forty ... fifty years, I might need some of these memories. I don't want them to fade to the point that I don't recall them."

Mom moves to the side of the bed and bends down to hug me. "You're everything your father wasn't. You are a good man and just ... a good human."

CHAPTER
Thirty-One

March.

April.

May.

"You came." Savannah smiles and hugs me.

"Of course." I peer at the crowd seated in the botanical garden for Josie's celebration of life while Savannah whispers, "We're not giving up on a miracle." She releases me and squeezes my hand. "Friends and family need this. We'll have a different kind of celebration when she's home again."

I hide my reaction behind a neutral expression. It's been two months since I've seen Savannah and Isaac. The last time, they visited to go through some things at Josie's house. I was under the impression that they had accepted what I've said all along ... Josie's dead.

"Okay." That's it. That's my best response. "Um ... I

didn't expect to see so many people here." I narrow my eyes and survey the crowd. There are people from school that I haven't seen since senior year. People who were not friends of Josie's. It's ... weird.

"They're here for you too. A lot of people wanted to pay their respects to you after your father died. Now they can do it for both your father and Josie."

Yep. So weird.

"Would you like to speak? I put your name on the program, but if you can't do it, we'll just skip over you."

Maybe this wasn't a good idea after all. I clear my throat. "Sure." I'm not doing it for Josie. This would drive her crazy. She hated being the center of attention, except with me. She wanted to be my center of attention. And she was ... just my everything. I'm doing this for her parents, to help give them closure I'm not sure they're really looking for yet.

I take a seat in the front row. A collage of photos resides on wood stands lining both sides of the podium. Josie's parents were married in this very spot. Two years later, Savannah was raped on their anniversary. There's too much to wrap my head around in this surreal moment.

Josie's dad speaks first. I tune him out. Then her mom speaks, causing everyone to reach for tissues. Except me. I'm too busy thinking about my life with Josie. Thinking about what I'm going to say.

"Next, we're going to hear from Colten Mosley, Josie's fiancé," Savannah says through sniffles.

Am I her fiancé if she's dead?

I give Savannah a hug while she steps away from the podium.

I'm not the best at winging it, but they didn't leave me with much choice.

Clearing my throat, my gaze slides over the faces of the crowd. "The day we moved into the house across the street from the Watts, my dad told me he met Chief Watts. And then he told me there was a boy named Joe who was my age. I was ecstatic because I hated being the new kid starting school with no friends. I had the whole summer to become Joe's best bud. Then I discovered Joe was Josephine. And ..." I smile, shaking my head. "I was really conflicted. She was a girl. That was disappointing. It was also the day my life changed in ways I never could have imagined.

"Josie poured me a glass of milk and offered me the best chocolate chip cookie I had ever tasted. Then she spent the next eight years threading herself through my heart one stitch at a time. She held me together when my world fell apart around me. Our love was unlike any love I have ever experienced. Unlike any love I have ever seen or any love written with words ... or even in the stars. It's not a father's love. It's not a son's love. It's not even a husband's love. It's that feeling you get when everything is dark, and you can't even see yourself. Then ..." My voice cracks, and I pull in a shaky breath. "She slides her hand into mine and squeezes it." I shake my head, glancing at the smattering of puffy clouds in the blue sky. "And just like that ... I felt *seen*." Closing my eyes, I picture her. That slow growing smile of hers. That knowing smile.

I see you.

When I open my eyes, I release a long breath. "I believe wherever my beautiful Josephine is right now, she's at peace. And making whatever world she's in a better place. That's what she does. She makes everything ... better."

I weave my way between the rows of chairs instead of taking a seat in the front row again. Then I get into my car and drive to the Watts' house.

Through the backyard.

Into the woods.

Up the tree.

Swinging my legs from "our" branch, I laugh. Then I laugh a little more, a little harder. "Tessa Hart was at your celebration of life. Remember her? The placeholder? Actually, there was a surprising number of people from our class, which means nobody moves away from Des Moines unless they are awesome like us. It also means you had more friends than you ever imagined because *you* were awesome. And everything." The smile slides off my face. "Josie ... I'm sorry. I'm so fucking sorry I couldn't fix it. Fix *you*. I'm sorry I only saw you and not him. Had I let myself focus on him, I would have seen you dying long before you took your own life."

Fuck the tears. I set them free.

Everything hurts from my burning eyes to my aching heart. The cold void of nothingness in my soul has never been as chilling as it is right now. It's taken me months to make it here. *Home.* And now that I'm here where she used to be *everywhere*, her absence feels like it's crushing my fucking heart.

I sniffle, tipping my chin to let more tears find their way to the earth below. "Is this how you felt? Alone? Like the best part of you was gone? Stolen?" Nodding slowly, I swallow past the lump in my throat. "Maybe you ..." I grit my teeth when more tears blur my vision. "Maybe you were him ... but he wasn't you. Josie ... He. Wasn't. You." And with that, I pull out a candy bar and eat it all by myself.

CHAPTER
Thirty-Two

"I don't want to wear that." Reagan scrunches her little nose at me while I hold up her T-ball shirt.

"It's your team's tee. You have to wear it. Everyone else will be wearing theirs."

"Mom said I don't have to be like other kids."

I sit on the end of her bed, chuckling. "That's correct. You are unique. No one is like you. This shirt will not change that. It will make it, so the rest of your team recognizes you as one of the team members. When you're on the field, you need to know if the person standing by a base is the one running on your team or a player from the other team trying to get you out."

With her arms crossed, she huffs. "Fine." She holds up her arms and lets me pull her shirt over her head. "I'm sad mommy won't be at the game."

"She is too. But she'll be at your next game. Now, grab your shoes and I'll get your bag. We don't want to be late." My hands cup her face a second before I give her a big smooch on the cheek. "I love you, Button. Let's go have some fun."

As soon as we get to the ball fields, Reagan bolts toward her team.

"Your glove!"

She turns and stomps her way back to me as if it's my fault she forgot her glove.

"What do you say?"

She mumbles a thank you before breaking into a full sprint again.

"I don't want to play!"

I glance over at the girl throwing a fit in the minivan next to my car.

"I don't like T-ball. It's stupid."

"Find a better word than stupid if you expect me to listen to your little rant," her mom says, grabbing her glove before tossing the girl over her shoulder.

I don't expect that, so I snort a laugh and cover my mouth when she glances in my direction. The daughter pulls her mom's blond ponytail.

The mom ignores her, closing the sliding door and locking the minivan like she's a pro at getting things done with a young girl held hostage over her shoulder.

"I don't know a better word than stupid," the girl says, yanking the ponytail a little harder.

"Then tough luck, little duck."

Tough luck, Mr. Duck.

Following the echo of her words, I make my way to the field where the kids are warming up. A few seconds after I take a seat on the bottom bleacher, that mom takes a seat on the same bleacher a good four feet from me.

She gives me a smile. "Which one is yours?"

I nod toward Reagan. "The one chasing butterflies."

She laughs. "At least she wants to be here."

"Sort of. She didn't want to wear the shirt because her mom told her she doesn't have to be like everyone else."

"Ha. Well, I agree with your wife. But I also feel your pain of trying to get a strong-willed child dressed and to the game on time."

"Well, her mom and I never married, so that might be why I was caught off guard. We should communicate better."

"Oh, sorry. That was a poor assumption on my part."

"Nope." I shake my head. "Totally logical assumption."

She stretches out her hand. "I'm Layla."

I shake her hand. "Colten. And the butterfly chaser is Reagan."

Layla laughs again. "The sack of potatoes I had over my shoulder is Nora."

Several other parents climb the bleachers behind us.

I smile and nod at them.

"Nora's dad was a high school girls' softball coach, so she's determined to never touch any ball that's hit with a bat."

I chuckle. "As the son of a high school boys' basketball coach, I can honestly say I feel Nora's defiance."

"Oh, no … don't tell me that."

I shrug. "Sorry. Nora's dad might want to lower his expectations in this sport."

Layla keeps her gaze on the girls. "Unfortunately, that will be pretty easy. He passed away last summer."

"Well …" I, too, keep my gaze on the girls. "Crap. I just … yeah. Sorry. I stuck my foot in my mouth."

"No. Really. It's fine. I didn't know Reagan's mom isn't your wife. Some assumptions are natural and fair. Joe had cancer. Battled it for nearly ten years."

Joe. Of course, his name was Joe.

"My family and his thinks I need to date. Move on. Blah, blah, blah." Layla laughs. "But some people you don't move on from. I fear my brain knows he's never coming back, but my heart doesn't reason the same way." She tips her chin and blows out a long breath. "Wow … that was a lot to share with a stranger. Cleary, I needed to get that off my chest, and family isn't the best sounding board. I'm uh…" she makes a popping sound with her lips "…just going to shut up now."

I don't respond because Reagan is first up to bat.

"You've got this, Button!"

Reagan whips her head in my direction.

I cringe. "Oops. I guess I need to call her by her name in public."

Layla laughs, but it's subdued. I should respond to her. But what do I say?

Reagan gets to second base but out at third. She scuffs her feet along the dirt toward the bench, pouting like a champ.

"Nice job. Chin up. Just have fun." Reagan doesn't respond to my pep talk.

A good ten minutes pass while we cheer on the teams. Then one of the girls trips and skins up her knee, so the game is paused.

"I lost my fiancée last January," I say. Through the corner of my eye, I see Layla turn toward me, but I keep my gaze on the dirt by my black sneakers. "I met her when we were nine. And you're right, the brain and the heart don't speak the same language. I don't trust my brain, so I've been writing down things about her, about us, in a notebook because I don't want to forget the good stuff."

"The good stuff ..." Layla echoes. "Yes. I like that. I think I need a notebook too."

"Do you have other kids?" I ask.

Layla's fingers curl along the edge of the metal bleacher while the rest of her body stiffens.

"Don't answer that. In fact, I'm just going to go sit up there before I do any more damage today." I point behind us and start to stand.

Layla reaches for my arm, snagging my wrist. She smiles. It's filled with pain, a desperate kind of pain. I recognize it too well.

"Don't go anywhere. You're stuck with me now, at

least until the end of this game."

I ease back onto the bleacher, and she releases my wrist.

"Six months before Joe died, we used some of his pre-chemo frozen sperm because he wanted to see Nora become a big sister before he died." As tears fill her eyes, she turns away from me. "Go, Nora!"

Nora hits a single, and we clap for her.

Layla clears her throat, managing to keep her tears at bay. "I lost the baby a week before he died, but I didn't tell him. I wore baggy clothes and kept it to myself. Nora didn't know either. I couldn't imagine letting him leave this world with that kind of grief. It gave him peace of mind knowing that after he died, we would have something to look forward to."

I give her words a little space before whispering, "I'm sorry."

We manage to make it through the rest of the game without oversharing anything else.

Reagan runs toward me. "Can we go for ice cream?"

I nod behind her. "Depends. Are you going to get your bag and your glove?"

She gives me her annoyed eye roll and pivots to get her belongings.

"Can we go for ice cream?" Nora runs toward Layla.

Layla laughs. "Is that what your coach told you to say?"

"No."

"Now can we go for ice cream?" Reagan returns with her bag and glove.

"We're going for ice cream too," Nora says.

Reagan frowns. "Is ice cream only for the team that won?"

I shrug. "I don't know. What do you think? Do you deserve ice cream too?"

Her little lips do their fishy pucker. "I think so."

"Good game, Reagan," Layla says. "Tell your dad you definitely deserve ice cream. Oh, and did you and Nora get to meet?"

Reagan shakes her head.

"Well, this is Nora."

The girls share a quick hi.

"There's an ice cream truck a block north of here. We can walk together," Layla suggests.

"Okay," Reagan answers for us.

I grin and shake my head. "Sounds like a good idea. Thanks."

Reagan and Nora walk in front of us, chatting like they've been friends forever. It reminds me of the instant friendship I made with Josie.

Layla and I don't say anything right away. Then she sighs. "Are you as afraid as I am to say anything? I mean, the weather is probably a safe topic."

On a chuckle, I nod. "It's hot. Too hot. Too soon."

"Agreed," Layla says. "We're on the schedule to get a pool next month. It was a promise Joe made to Nora. She's a little dolphin."

"You're getting a pool?" Reagan nearly squeals.

I find myself shaking my head at her again. "How is it you pay no attention to me when I'm talking to you, but the second I'm *not* talking to you, you hear everything?"

Layla giggles.

"My dad died, but he promised me a pool before he died," Nora says.

Six-year-olds talking about death makes me think of a young Josie. So matter-of-fact.

"My dad's Josie maybe died too. The police are still looking for her, but she might be dead. She was sick."

"My dad was sick too," Nora says.

Layla and I share uncomfortable smiles. What can we say? Kids process things differently.

"Look, Mom!" Nora says, pointing to a fire engine.

Layla nods, offering her daughter a tiny smile. "Her dad was a fire fighter."

"My dad's a detective," Reagan says.

"What's a detective?" Nora asks as we approach the food truck.

"He finds bad people and puts them in jail," Reagan says.

Nora nods, seemingly good with that explanation or just too distracted by the ice cream.

"Detective, huh?" Layla says.

"Yeah. Homicide."

"Oh, you put the really bad people behind bars."

"I try."

We order ice cream and eat it on the short walk back to the ball fields.

"Can Reagan come swim in my pool?" Nora asks when Layla opens the minivan door.

"We don't have a pool yet."

"When we do."

Layla glances up at me.

"She gets plenty of trips to the pool. She has a pool pass."

"Well..." Layla shrugs "...we could exchange numbers. Nora doesn't have that many friends in the neighborhood. She'd love to have someone to play with in her pool."

"Yeah, Dad!" Reagan's not giving me a choice.

"Sure." I bring up my contact info and share it with Layla. "Reagan's at her mom's house more than mine. So if you message me when she's at her mom's, I'll give Katy your info if that's okay."

"Perfect." Layla sets her phone on the seat and pulls a wipe out of a plastic tube. "Wipe your sticky hands before you get in the minivan." She glances over her shoulder at me. "Help yourself to a wipe if you don't want sticky hands in your car."

Reagan holds up her sticky fingers and wiggles them.

I frown at her before smiling at Layla. "Thanks."

When both girls are in the vehicles, I head to the driver's side of my car.

"Colten, thanks for being the sounding board I didn't know I needed today."

I smile. "My pleasure."

"Maybe we'll see you when the pool goes in."

I nod. "Maybe. Enjoy the rest of your weekend. It was nice meeting you."

"IF YOUR WIFE DIES, will you find another wife?"

"I'm sixteen. I have a girlfriend, not a wife," I said to Josie while we washed my truck in the driveway.

"Jennifer is your girlfriend?" She stopped her motions and stood ramrod straight while the sponge dripped water and suds down her leg.

I shrugged.

"You're an asshole. Do you hear me?"

I was thankful that her parents had gone to dinner, my parents were seeing a counselor, and Chad was glued to the screen playing games because I had a feeling it was about to get bad.

"You had your hand up my shirt and your tongue down my throat last Friday night. And now Jennifer is your girlfriend?"

I glanced around to see if any of the neighbors were outside and within earshot.

"You can't be my girlfriend."

Josie hurled the sponge at my head then grabbed the hose nozzle and turned it onto the hardest stream, spraying every inch of my body. I just stood there with my eyes closed, letting her do her thing. I liked her thing. All of her wild emotions and her willingness to let me stay in her dad's good graces by not telling him about us. Had he really known what we did when no one was looking, she would have had a 4:00 p.m. curfew, and I wouldn't have been allowed on their property past the driveway.

When I didn't give her the satisfaction of reacting, she charged at me, shoving my chest, pitching a fit. I loved it.

"Tell me she's not your girlfriend or so help me, I'm going to end you, Mosley." She continued to shove my chest until we were in the garage.

I grabbed her face and kissed her.

Again, she shoved me. After several seconds of her huffing and puffing her anger, hands balled into tight fists, she threw herself at me.

We kissed for a long time. She had a point to make, or so she thought. I knew the score. I knew what we were even if nobody else did. And maybe I should have said as much, but I enjoyed her attacking me like that. I liked the chase. And then I liked letting her catch me, letting her win.

When she released my mouth and rubbed her lips

together, I couldn't hide my grin. It was a silent victory lap.

"Now I'm wet," she said.

I waggled my eyebrows. "Is that so?"

Her cheeks flamed in shades of red. "Pervert."

"Jennifer doesn't think I'm a pervert."

"If you mention her name again, I'm going to tell my dad that you felt me up last week."

I took a step closer, peering down at her with the usual look I gave her to call her bluff.

"Fine." She sighed. "I'm not going to tell him that, but you will never see these," she pointed to her tits, "again."

I grinned. "Well, why didn't you say that to begin with? Jennifer? Jennifer who?"

Josie's addictive smile swelled until I felt it punch me in the chest. She rolled her eyes and sauntered toward my truck, plucking the sponge from the ground and dunking it into the five-gallon bucket of soapy water. "Now, answer my question. If something happens to your wife, will you find another? Or will your heart only belong to your first love?"

"Well, I told you I'm not getting married."

"No. You said you weren't having kids. Not the same thing."

I used the brush to scrub the tires. I didn't like talking about my future like Josie wasn't going to be part of it. I knew she didn't want marriage and a family, but I guess I kinda wished she'd at least want me.

"I don't know, Josie. I'm pretty sure I'm supposed to

be focusing on college and baseball, not first and second wives. If you got married and lost your husband, would you remarry?"

"I'm not getting married, but hypothetically, sure. I'd remarry. Nobody wants to be lonely, right?"

I chuckled. "Apparently you're okay with it since you don't plan on getting married."

"Doesn't mean I won't date or maybe cohabitate with a man."

"Cohabitate?"

"It means—"

"Yes, Josie. I know what it means. It just seemed like a new dorky low, even for you."

"Says the dumb jock who plays piano all the time."

"I'm not dumb."

"Well, I'm not a dork."

"Why are you asking me about my imaginary second marriage?"

"Because Mrs. Leach is getting married again. Her husband died less than a year ago. So I have to wonder if she really loved him, since she not only found another man, but she's marrying him. Or ... is marriage like a comfort food?"

"Mrs. Leach, the advanced chemistry teacher?"

Josie nodded before tossing the sponge aside and grabbing the hose again to rinse the back of my truck.

"Uh. I didn't know her husband died."

"Where have you been?"

"Playing baseball, hating my dad, and dealing with you."

"Me? Pfft ... whatever. Anyway, I think she's getting remarried because she has two kids and could use some help around the house."

"Or maybe she loves the new guy."

"Well, duh. I'm sure she does. I bet we can love more than one person. Don't you?"

Nope. I loved Josephine Watts. My heart was constructed cell by cell in the womb to one day seek her out and love her forever. "I don't know, Josie," I said instead of my knee-jerk response. "My parents haven't exactly been role models for marriage or love for that matter."

"Well, Mrs. Leach is pretty cool. I think she's my favorite teacher. And if she can move on so quickly and remarry after losing her husband, I think you can too."

I bit my tongue. Really, what was the point of that conversation and my *second* wife?

CHAPTER
Thirty-Four

Thought I'd steal a page out of this journal to write you a letter. Today I met a woman. It's not what you think, so just cool your afterlife jets, okay? She lost her husband to cancer last summer, and she has a daughter who is Reagan's age. We chatted during the T-ball game. She said so many things that resonated with me. It made me feel like I was supposed to meet her.

I'm not the only person in the world who feels like love is a one-and-done. At the same time, I recalled the time when we were sixteen and you wanted to discuss my imaginary second wife. Some days are confusing, like today. Am I living the life you would want me to live? Would you hate that those words are even going through *my head? I don't know what to think right now. I'm too busy missing you. I'm really good at it, but I don't let anyone else see it.*

Anyway, the woman today, her name is Layla (in case you want to secretly hate her in the afterlife), and she made me think. She said her family is pushing her to move on and date. I hope my mom never pushes me to move on, but I fear she will even though she never did after my dad died. I guess I'm struggling with figuring out my new normal.

If it weren't for Reagan, I would have gone with you. I would have left this life. But you knew that, didn't you?

What am I even doing? Writing to you as if your spirit is looking over my shoulder reading this. I need something. I need direction. I keep looking over my shoulder for you, but you're not there. You'll never be there again.

I need my friend. I need "a" friend.

CHAPTER
Thirty-Five

A WEEK LATER, I meet Sean and Katy at Reagan's T-ball game. While grabbing a drink at the concession stand, someone taps me on the back.

I glance over my shoulder. "Oh, hey, Layla. Nora have a game today too?"

"No, I just like the popcorn at the concession stand." She slides her fingers into the back pockets of her shorts.

I grin. "Sorry. Stupid question."

She gestures with a head tilt to the right. "On that field. They're just warming up. You?"

"Same. No game. I just come for the overpriced sports drinks. The blue one is my favorite."

Layla snorts. "The blue is the best."

"Hi. What can I get you?" the volunteer parent behind the counter asks.

"Two blue sports drinks and a popcorn," Layla jumps in and says.

Before I can protest, she throws down a twenty and winks at me. "Let me buy you a drink. It's the least I can do after vomiting my life's tragedies on you last weekend."

I take the blue sports drink and twist off the cap. "It's unnecessary but thank you."

"My pleasure." She takes her change, popcorn, and the blue drink. "Besides, now I can tell my family that I bought a guy a drink, and it will get them off my back for a bit."

I laugh a little because it's a joke. Right? She's not flirting with me. She said she doesn't think she'll move on from her husband. And I'm not moving on from Josie ... probably ever.

"Listen, the pools not in yet, but Nora has been asking to have Reagan over to play. I guess they really bonded over ice cream. Would Reagan like to go with us to the children's museum? I get free tickets."

"Free tickets, huh?" I sip my drink.

"Yes. I work there. I'm their information technology manager."

I nod. "Okay. I'm going to pretend that I know what that means."

She laughs. "Think computer geek and just leave it at that."

"Got it. Well, I'm sure she'd love to go, but I'll need to check with her mom."

"Great. You've got my number. Just shoot me a text after the game."

"Okay. Well..." I nod toward Reagan's field "...I'd better get back before I miss her home run."

"Oh definitely. Bye, Colten." She winks at me again. Winks.

That's flirting. Right? Or am I reading into it? She's still grieving the loss of her husband. And she knows it's only been five months since Josie died. Yeah, I'm reading into it.

"Reagan made a friend last week. I saw her mom at the concession stand. She invited Reagan to the children's museum after the game. I said I'd check with you and text her," I say to Katy, taking a seat on the bench.

"I'm sure she'd love that," Katy says. "What do you know about her parents? Are we comfortable with them taking our daughter to the museum?"

"It's just the mom. Her husband died last summer. She works at the museum."

"Oh, she's a widow. Is she nice?"

I watch Reagan staring at the sky in the outfield instead of paying attention the game. "What does 'oh, she's a widow' mean?"

"Nothing. Does she know you're single?"

"Yes. She invited Reagan to play with Nora. She didn't ask me on a date."

"I know, but everything has a beginning."

"I'm not beginning anything. And neither is she."

"Katy, it's a playdate," Sean says.

I like Sean. Always have. He's a no-nonsense kind of guy. Works long hours in construction. Adores my daughter. But doesn't act pussy whipped by his wife.

"I'm just saying, you're quickly going to find that Reagan is ... for lack of a better term ... a chick magnet. She'll make lots of friends who have single moms. And single moms love single dads, especially widowers who work in law enforcement."

"Jesus Christ ..." Sean mumbles. "Let the guy properly grieve and figure out his own shit in his own time."

I nod. "Yes, what he said."

Katy nudges Sean's shin with her foot. "Stop. I'm just helping him out, so he doesn't get into a sticky situation."

"He's a homicide detective. I think he's good in sticky situations."

Really, I think I'm on the verge of a bromance with Sean. He just ... gets me.

After the game, Reagan gives an enthusiastic yes to going to the museum with Nora, so I shoot Layla a text.

"I think you should go with her." Katy says. "In all seriousness, it might be too early to send our daughter off with someone you met a week ago for all of two seconds."

I give her a tight grin and a slight nod.

THE GIRLS JUMP from one exhibit to the next with Layla and I close behind them. This feels normal, like something I should be doing. It also feels wrong. I should be here with Josie.

"Say it," Layla says.

I glance over at her. "Say what?"

"All the things going through your head."

"What makes you think anything is going through my head?"

"Because I keep thinking, what if someone I know sees me with you? Will they think I have a boyfriend? Will they think I've moved on? Will they tell anyone? And then I think, what would Joe think? Then, of course, my mind wanders into really depressing territory. Joe died. He will never think anything again. So the real question is, what am I thinking? And when I can't answer that question because I really don't know what to think or what to feel, I wonder what you're thinking. You lost your fiancée more recently than I lost my husband."

My cheeks puff with a big breath before I slowly release it. "You are further along than I am. I'm still stuck in the 'I wish she were here' phase. I guess that makes me terrible company. Who wants to hang out with someone who is wishing they were with someone else?"

"You're right. It's early for you. I still have times when I'd give anything for Joe to be here to see something or experience something with me. But he's been gone long enough that I no longer have moments when I think it's nothing but a bad dream. I'm fully aware that he's gone. I'm consciously moving forward, not merely drifting along. Does that make sense?"

"I think so," I nod slowly.

"So now my brain has started to wander into other directions, somewhat prompted by my family urging me to date. And while this is not a date or anything at all like that, you are a man, and what we're doing feels weird even though we're not doing anything."

I don't respond right away, so an awkward silence fills the air around us while we stare at the girls doing a water race.

"That was the dumbest thing a human has ever said." Layla snorts, covering her face with her hands. "Kill me now."

I chuckle and shake my hand. "You forget I hear a lot of terrible alibis, so you have a ways to go before you're saying the dumbest thing ever. I should have responded right away, but I was letting your words settle, maybe resonate."

"Well..." her hands drop from her face "...that's very kind of you to spin it like that."

"Not kind. Just honest. And if I'm being completely honest with you, I have an unfair advantage at this ... whatever this is."

"An unfair advantage?" She lifts an eyebrow at me.

"When Josie and I were younger, we had a very unusual relationship. We had an on-and-off-again relationship like no other. Then her dad, who I admired and liked more than my own dad, asked me to never be more than friends with her. So when we *were* being more than friends, we had to keep it a secret. And sometimes I dated other people and so did she. It's hard to explain. It sounds crazy when I hear myself say it. But I got used to being around other girls even while I knew my heart belonged to Josie and she knew it too. I guess I can be here, not feeling guilty because I know where my heart is."

Layla hums and nods several times. "I like that. I felt that too. I think I still do, but I feel like there comes a point when you start to feel guilty or maybe a little broken because your heart is what gives you life, and giving so much of it to someone who is no longer in this life feels like ..."

"A waste?"

Her nose wrinkles. "It sounds so terrible, but I read it in a book about grieving, and it stuck with me."

I watch Reagan and think of Josie. She's not her daughter, but I swear she reminds me of her. The curiosity. The smile. The way she embraces her uniqueness. Not trying to fit in, just trying to make her own space in the world.

"I think losing the love of your life is the biggest self-reflection ever," I say.

"It's the me without you."

I nod. "Yes. And I think it's possible to reach a silent acquiescence and truly move on. While I don't want to ever forget, I agree it would be nice if my heart would someday let go ... be fully invested again in this life."

Layla gives me a smile I can't decipher, but it feels like a good one. "We should be friends. Do you have room in your life for another friend? Because you say all the right things at the right time."

I chuckle. I asked if she had other kids, bringing up the memories of a lost child. I'd hardly call that right timing. Still, I feel the same. I feel a little understood. "Friends sounds good."

She winks.

What's with the winks? Maybe it's payback for all the times I winked at Josie while hugging another girl.

CHAPTER
Thirty-Six

"We found a body," Rains says as soon as I step into my office.

I turn slowly. "Hers?" I whisper.

"Don't know yet."

I brush past him.

"You can breathe down their necks all you want, but it won't expedite anything. Mosley, let them do their job. She was one of theirs. They'll want to know just as quickly as you."

"They let her go. She wasn't one of theirs," I mumble, but I doubt he hears me before I step into the elevator.

At the county medical examiner's office, I flash my badge and make my way to the morgue. As soon as I see Dr. Cornwell in the hallway, he shakes his head.

"I don't know yet. We're waiting on dental records."

It's not her. I don't know why I rushed down here. I knew it then, and I know it now. She left this life in a way that her body will never be found. Still, my foolish heart likes to torture me.

"Why do you need dental records?"

He frowns. "Are you really asking me that?"

"She had tattoos."

"I'm aware. But the decedent doesn't have skin or organs if you get the gist."

I swallow a little bile.

It's not her. It's not her.

"How long will it take?"

He pushes through the door to the locker room, and I follow him. "As long as it takes."

"You owe her this."

He laughs while donning PPE. "She'd hate you pestering me, and you know it."

"I hope you take a little responsibility for what happened. You took her life from her."

"Here we go ... I'm impressed it's taken you this long to confront me, Detective. Had Dr. Watts been of sound mind, dealing with a subordinate who was experiencing what she was experiencing, she would have done the same thing I did. Josephine wasn't just gifted; she took her job seriously. She was a professional and understood the need for rules and protocol. What happened to her was tragic, but it wasn't anyone's fault."

"Is that how you sleep at night?"

He glances up at me. "It's been nearly six months. I

grieved her when I had to let her go and again when she went missing. I grieved her for the same reason you're grieving her. We cared about her, and we couldn't fix her."

Fix her ...

He rests his hand on my shoulder before opening the door. "She left her mark on the world, and it was a good one. Honor her by moving on and living a good life, Detective. It's what she would have wanted."

I swallow hard. She's still so close to me. It's a suffocating grief.

"Oh, the body is not hers," Cornwell says.

I turn. "How do you know?"

"There's a gold crown."

"Then why didn't you tell that to Rains?"

He shrugs. "I wanted to check in on you. Josephine would have wanted me to check in on you. Good news. You're going to be fine." He closes the door.

THE FOLLOWING WEEKEND, Reagan and I meet Layla and Nora for a Cubs game.

Dinner.

A pool party for the grand opening of their pool.

Coffee just with Layla early on a Wednesday morning before either of us has to be to work.

T-ball.

Movies.

More swimming.

Layla is the sister I never had. She's not Josie, but she's a good friend. And she makes good chocolate chip cookies. I'm not saying better than Savannah, but still ... really good.

Everything feels easy when I'm with Layla. If I'm having a good day, she's eager to hear all about it. But if I have a bad day, she's ready with funny memes and long lists of how my life could be worse. I find myself comparing her to Josie, and that sometimes bothers me. Layla is just my friend. Josie was my everything. There is no comparison, so I don't know why my brain insists on trying to make one.

"Can I be honest with you?" Layla swings the bat in the batting cage and misses.

"Elbow up," I say. "Have you been lying to me?"

She chuckles. "Not exactly." She tosses the bat aside and exits the cage.

"You're not done." I narrow my eyes.

"I am." She sighs. "I hate baseball. And softball. Volleyball. Football. Basically anything that involves a ball. I danced in high school. But mostly, I sat in front of a huge computer and programmed weird stuff. I'm a geek. I like books. Art museums. And the ballet. I *love* the ballet." She gives me a little cringe. "Can we still be friends?"

I blink several times. "Did Joe know you hated baseball?"

"Yes, but he married me anyway. That's why I'm hoping you can still be my friend."

After another long pause, I nod. "I play the piano. Do you play an instrument?"

"No."

I frown. "I've never been to a ballet. But I'd go with you because that's what friends do."

Her smile doubles in a matter of a second. "I'll get us tickets. Do you want to take the girls, or is it just a friend's night out?"

"Depends if I have Reagan."

"Okay. I'm going to just get two tickets and a sitter for Nora."

I have a moment. It's the first real moment I've had in the weeks that I've been friends with Layla. We've been a foursome except for morning coffee, which was rushed because we had to get to work. The ballet feels like a date. But I'm not dating. And neither is she. So why am I hesitant?

"Is that okay?" She eyes me suspiciously.

"Um ... yeah. Sounds great. Fair warning, my job is a fun spoiler, so I might cancel at the last minute or have to leave in the middle of the ballet if some asshole decides to kill someone."

"Got it." Again, she winks.

CHAPTER
Thirty-Seven

"You look mighty handsome," Mom says on our FaceTime call while I tie a red tie that I never wear to work. Still ... black suit. "Thought you said it's not a date."

"It's not. But I think I should wear a suit to the ballet."

"The ballet? That's where you're going? Colten, I think that's a date. Bowling is something friends do. The ballet is romantic."

I narrow my eyes at the screen. "It is? Why?"

"For starters, you're in a suit. That in and of itself says romance."

"I wear suits for work."

"But has this woman seen you in a suit?"

"Yes. We had coffee before work one morning, and I was wearing a suit."

"Fine. Then let's move on to the music. It's romantic."

"Not all music is romantic. Trust me, I know a thing or two about music."

"Are you in denial that this woman might like you more than a friend?"

I check my hair one more time. "No. The reason we're friends is because we both lost people we loved, and we don't have a desire to find a replacement."

"Need I remind you that you thought Josie was a boy, and you said you were only going to be her friend until school started. Look how that turned out."

"Yeah, look how that turned out."

"Colten ..."

"It's not a date. Now, I have to get going so I'm not late to the ballet with my *friend,* Layla."

"Layla? You didn't tell me her name. That's a beautiful name. Is she as pretty as her name?"

"Mom ..." I frown at the phone screen.

"Just tell me you know it's okay to feel something more than friendship for another woman. Josie would have wanted it for you."

I sigh. "It's funny how everyone seems to know what Josie would have wanted more than me ... her best friend. Nobody knew Josie better than I knew her."

"Fine. So you tell me. Would she have wanted you to find love again?"

"No."

"What?" Mom sounds shocked by my answer. "Liar."

"I'm not lying. I'm not saying she wouldn't have said that's what she wanted. But the one thing that seemed to have flown under everyone's radar was how much she loved me. How much she wanted me. How much she hated every girl I ever dated. She'd want me to die a lonely man." I lie. I lie because I don't like the truth.

"Well, Mrs. Leach is pretty cool. I think she's my favorite teacher. And if she can move on so quickly and remarry after losing her husband, I think you can too."

I wanted her to believe we would never find another love like ours. We weren't the Leaches.

"I don't know if I believe that, Colten. She wasn't selfish like that."

"Well, it's a moot point anyway. I'm not ready to date. Don't know if I'll ever be ready to date, but tonight I'm going to the ballet with a friend who knows what I'm going through."

Mom nods. "I'm happy for you. Have a nice evening. I love you."

"Love you too. Night, Mom."

On my way to pick up Layla, it hits me ... picking her up seems like a date.

It's not a date.

There's no turning back now. I've spent so much of my life with the wrong women all the while thinking about Josie. Loving her was as much a curse as it was a gift. Still, I'd do it all over again.

When I pull into Layla's driveway, I'm a little relieved that she's waiting for me outside. I don't even get my car in *Park* before she heads straight toward the passenger door in her red dress that matches my tie. Total coincidence. Red lipstick. And her hair is in loose blond waves. She is pretty.

But she's not Josie.

"Hey, handsome. Nice tie." She closes the door and fastens her seat belt.

"Thanks. You look nice too."

If it were a date, I'd up the nice to pretty.

No ... no, I wouldn't.

You look pretty.

I'd use another word like beautiful or lovely.

"What are the chances that you could run by CVS so I can grab some lozenges? My allergies are acting up, and I know I'm going to get that crazy tickle in my throat during the performance and make a scene with my coughing if I don't have a lozenge."

"Sure. We can do that."

When we get to CVS, I park and follow her inside.

"You could have waited in the car. It will only take me a minute."

"It's fine. I might grab some gum or something myself." I follow her to the aisle with the lozenges.

"They don't have cherry. I'm going to have to go with lemon eucalyptus. Not great, but it will do." She grabs the package.

I turn to head toward the front of the store with her right behind me.

"Oops, sorry." I nearly run into a lady with a walker.

She glances up.

She. Glances. Up.

And I ... I ... can't breathe. I'm so fucking afraid to even blink. This ... this isn't possible.

"Hi," she says in a weak voice I barely recognize.

If it weren't for her eyes and the tattoos on her arms, I wouldn't recognize her. She's so ... *so* incredibly frail. In one breath, she's resurrected, only to look like she's withering away. Loose skin. Hollow-eyed. Haggard.

It takes my brain a moment to decide if this is real.

"Colten?" I barely register Layla's voice.

I don't have one. Single. Word.

My heart has been ejected from my chest and shoved into my throat.

Josie's gaze slides to my right. To Layla.

"We don't want to be late," Layla says.

I didn't think it was possible for Josie to look any sadder, but with the downcast of her eyes, she says, "Nice seeing you." She barely has a voice. Did she lose it?

"Josie, did you find—" A guy stops behind her, midsentence, eyes on me.

I can't tell if he recognizes me. I don't know him. But the way he gently rests his hand on Josie's bony shoulder tells me he knows who I am. Is it just me? So fucking lost in the dark? I don't know if this is a dream or a nightmare.

Again, Josie's gaze drifts to Layla. "You l-look …
pretty."

Emotion punches me so hard, my eyes can barely
see past the burning tears in them. "Fuck you … Josie."
My words break into pieces as I barely get them out in
a whisper.

As I take a step forward.

As I take her into my arms.

As I support her when her knees wobble beneath
her.

As my lips press to her thinning hair.

I don't even have to blink for the tears to release.

She doesn't wrap her arms around me. Maybe she
can't.

It wasn't a mistake. It wasn't by chance. I met Layla
so that our path would bring us to this exact CVS phar-
macy at six o'clock on this very Saturday night. So I
would find my Artemis.

Josie was wrong. She isn't a star. She *is* the galaxy.

CHAPTER
Thirty-Eight

REAGAN UNZIPS MY DRESS. I turn and press my palms to her face. She's fighting tears. So am I. We are strong for each other.

"I love you. Okay?"

Her lower lip quivers. She's so brave. She will get Colten through this life. Of that, I have no doubt.

When she gives me a tiny nod, I press my lips to her forehead. It's warm, as it should be. She has so much life in her. "Bye, beautiful girl."

A quick change, an Uber, a stop at home, and a long drive across town later, I arrive at Felix Trevino's house. It's a traditional, stone front two-story with a white mailbox that matches the snow and a neatly shoveled drive. Before I ring the doorbell, I kick some snow off my boots.

More than one dog barks before the door opens a crack. "Josie?"

I rub my hands together to keep warm. "Are you going to invite me in or leave me out here to freeze to death?"

Felix shoos the dogs away and opens the door. "I've never seen you with short hair."

I step inside and remove my boots while the dogs sniff me. "I've never seen you with no hair."

He frowns. "There wasn't much left, so I shaved it."

"Happy New Year, by the way. It's been a while."

"Uh ... yeah. To what do I owe the honor?"

I shuffle my socked feet over his hardwood floor, snooping around his main level. "Is your wife home?"

"She's out of town for a week."

"Well, isn't that perfect," I murmur.

"Josie, I'm not trying to be rude, but are you going to tell me what you're doing here? Are you looking for something?"

I turn, just inside his kitchen. "No. Sorry. Just checking the place out. You've done quite well for yourself. I read that you're chief of cardiology, and you married the hospital administrator's daughter. Well done. Glad I could help." I offer him an exaggerated smile despite my heart bleeding out in my chest.

This is my wedding day. I'm supposed to be marrying the only man I've ever loved. Instead, I'm here, cashing in on a favor owed to me.

Felix turns a little paler than he already was.

"It's payback time."

Felix's mom died while he was a first-year resident under me, the chief resident. He spiraled downhill with alcohol and drugs. I got him help instead of getting him kicked out of the program. I covered his ass on multiple occasions. He knows he owes his career to my grace.

"What do you need? A job? I heard you were out of a job. Is it true that you knew the whereabouts of those girls' bodies?"

"It's true."

"And you think you were one of them in another life?" He gives me an unblinking expression like there's a right answer to his question.

I'm about to fail the test. "No." I smile.

Felix relaxes a fraction. Relief washes over his face.

"I was the killer. I was Winston Jeffries."

He's well over six feet, but Felix's back straightening with my answer puts him another inch or so taller. "What's the favor?" He clears his throat. His words are rushed like I stopped by for a quick cup of sugar that he can quickly give me before sending me on my merry way. Debt fulfilled.

"I need you to kill me."

Felix's lips part a fraction while he blinks slowly. Then he chuckles. "What?"

"If it makes you feel better, I also want you to bring me back to life."

His brow furrows, head inching side to side. "Have you lost your mind?"

"Yes. But I'd like it back. And I'm hoping if that happens, it will be mine and only mine."

"Josie ..." He scratches the back of his smooth head and chuckles again. "I don't understand. But I think you've got the wrong guy for whatever job you need help with. Have you looked into counseling?"

"I didn't save any counselor's career. Just yours."

"So payback for me is life in prison? For what? Why the hell would you want to die again? You realize the stats on resuscitation aren't exactly in your favor, right?"

"Yes, I know. But here's the thing, I see dead little girls. I see him—me—poisoning them. Sadly, with the passing of time, these visions or recollections have only gotten worse. To the point that I don't fully trust myself. Some days I have trouble separating the two lives. If I can't erase these memories, then I can't do this."

"Do what?"

"Live."

He laces his hands behind his neck and bows his head. "Jesus, Josie."

"I talked to a parapsychologist in California. She's had a slew of lives. She said my only hope is that I die again, and someone brings me back to life so whatever new near-death experience I have will erase the last one. I have to try."

Glancing at me, he lets his hands fall from his

neck, flopping at his side. "Surely you know there are grave risks."

"Death. Yes. I'm well aware."

"*If* you're resuscitated, you could be in a coma."

"I know. I'm going to go over all of this with you."

A manic laugh bubbles from his chest while he turns and paces the kitchen. "You'll go over all of this with me. Great. That's a relief. I feel much better now."

"Do you want to know where I was a little over an hour ago?"

"Not really. I don't want to know where you are right now, but I do because you're standing in my kitchen after having not seen you in years."

"I was in a wedding dress. Today is my wedding day. *Was* my wedding day. I cut off the flower girl's hair in a ponytail, told her to give it to her dad, the groom, and then I left. I left knowing there is an extremely high probability I won't ever see him or any of my family and friends again."

Felix stops his pacing and stares at me, maybe to gauge the sincerity of my words. Maybe he's stopped pacing because my words are shaky, and my eyes are filled with tears.

"This is my only chance," I whisper, blotting the corners of my eyes. "If I can't get rid of these memories, I can't go on living."

Felix deflates on a deep sigh. "What are you expecting from me?"

Drawing in a shaky breath, I hug my arms to my

chest and pad my way to the wall of windows facing his backyard. "I need you to suffocate me."

"Jesus Christ ..."

Ignoring his reaction, I continue. "You will tie me up, so I can't fight you."

"No ... no. No. No. Do you know what the chances are of saving your life after asphyxiation?"

"Slim, but I drowned, and they brought me back."

His eyebrows shoot up his forehead. "Great. Let me rephrase it then. Do you know what the chances are of me resuscitating you after being asphyxiated for a second time in your fragile little life?"

"Felix, I'm most likely going to die. Look at it this way. If you knew that your wife's heart was going to stop beating, would you rather it happen when she's alone or when you're right next to her with a defibrillator, oxygen, and medication to restart it regardless of the statistical chances of bringing her back?"

He frowns. "What happens if you don't make it? Or what happens if I restart your heart, but you're in a coma? What happens if—"

"Again, I'll go over all of this with you."

"This is too much." He shakes his head.

"You owe me."

"Not this."

"Look around, Felix. The house. Your family. Your job. Hell, probably even those two dogs. You have this life because of *me*. And for the record, I was never planning on asking you for a single thing. But I'm in a dire situation, the way you were in a dire situation. I need you to step the fuck up and help me. I need you to take a little risk the way I took a risk covering your ass."

He rests a hand on his hip, head bowed. "You are not a good person."

"But I want to be," I whisper. Again, I tear up. "I want to sleep and dream like a normal person. I want to smile because I'm happy not because I'm hiding the pain. I want a job. I want love. I want what you have. I want what I gave you."

I hate this.

I am not this person.

Desperation squeezes every last ounce of humanity from my soul. Maybe I shouldn't have come here. Maybe I should have just ... ended everything for good.

"I have a storage unit with electricity."

My gaze lifts to Felix's. I was right. He was worth saving.

CHAPTER
Thirty-Nine

"I DON'T UNDERSTAND," Colten whispers against my head. "Help me understand."

"This might not be the best place for a reunion," Felix says.

"Colten ... I'll uh ... grab a cab home," the pretty woman in a red dress says.

He doesn't respond. He doesn't move.

Pressed to his chest, I make eye contact with her. She offers a sad smile, touches his arm, giving it a tiny squeeze, and clicks her heels toward the exit.

Colten doesn't stop her. Not a single word of acknowledgment.

He moved on. In his mind, I died, and he moved on. And now a pretty lady in a red dress is broken-hearted because she thinks I'm back from the dead? I can't walk unassisted. I'm skin and bones.

Colten should let me go and follow the red dress woman. She's beautiful and vibrant. She has life in her eyes. I am the echo of death. Alive, but just barely. And it feels like years since I've seen him. I'm still making sense of what I know and what I've been told.

"I don't know who you are, but you can leave," Colten says to Felix.

Oh, Colten ...

With what little strength I can muster, I push against Colten's chest, forcing him to lighten his grip. Taking a cautious step backward, I rest my hands on my walker. He's so handsome in his suit. Tan from the summer's sun, not pale like me. My heart hasn't stopped galloping since my eyes landed on him. I can't imagine a day when my heart can control itself around Colten Mosley. And I can't imagine a day when seeing him with a beautiful woman doesn't sting. Is it just not in the cards for us?

Colten uses one hand to wipe his face.

"I'm glad you're good." I push my way past him. I need conditioner and toothpaste. Felix said he'd get it for me, but I wanted out of the house. I wanted to do something on my own.

"Are you joking?" Colten asks, following me less than a step back. "I thought you were dead!"

"I was," I murmur, choosing the sensitive toothpaste. My teeth have been terribly sensitive lately.

Damn ... the woman in the red dress was so pretty. Such soft skin. So blond. So opposite of me.

My brain won't shut off. Did he kiss her? Have they

had sex? Does she know about me? How did he meet her? Is she like Tessa or nicer than Tessa? And why is my brain comparing red dress lady to high school slut?

"Josephine Eleanor Watts, you left me on our wedding day. I haven't seen you in nearly six months. I spoke at your memorial service or 'celebration of life.' I've grieved you. Your family and friends have grieved you. Yet you're shopping for toothpaste at a fucking CVS like it's no big deal?" He turns toward Felix. "Who the hell are you, and why are you still here?"

"I'm uh ... her ride. Felix. Dr. Trevino. She's living with me. And uh ... my wife. We're helping her rehabilitate."

"Rehabilitate from what? She looks emaciated. Whatever you're doing, it's not working."

"Oh, no. She looks so much better than she did a few months ago."

While they sort through things, I make my way to the shampoo aisle. My hair is disgusting. I need a good conditioner. It's grown out too much. I'm not sure why I ever cut my hair, but I wouldn't mind it shorter again like in the video.

"Josie, let's go. We're going home," Colten says.

"Where do I live?"

"With me."

"I do?"

Colten eyes me like he's sad, like he's trying to figure me out. A puzzle he can't quite solve. I know how he feels. I've been trying to figure myself out for nearly three months.

"Yes," he whispers. "Don't you remember?"

I hand my items to Felix so I can push my walker. Colten snags them from him before I baby step my way to the checkout. "The woman in red is pretty. You always liked the pretty g-girls," I trip over my words. It's so much better than it was even just weeks ago. But it's not perfect. I don't know if anything about me will ever be perfect. Colten scans my items at the self-checkout and taps his credit card to the machine.

"She can't walk that fast," Felix says as I try to catch up to Colten because he has my toothpaste and conditioner.

Colten turns and shoves the bag into Felix's chest. "Take this, and take the walker." He scoops me up in his arms.

"She won't learn to do it on her own if you do it for her," Felix says.

"Shut up, Dr. Whoever The Fuck You Are."

He has no idea what Felix has done for me, but I don't try to explain it now. I'm too busy staring at the side of his face. I want to touch it. I want to kiss it. And that makes me want to cry because I think he's let part of his heart go to another woman. And I'm ... still so broken.

"She needs to come home with me." Felix doesn't back away from Colten. He's invested in my recovery, and for that, I will always be grateful.

"Nope." Colten nods for Felix to open the passenger door of the car.

Felix eyes me.

I give him a slight nod. "I'll get a ride home later."

"No. No you won't," Colten says while setting me on my feet to get into the car.

I sit sideways first, with my legs outside of the door. "Felix is helping me."

Colten gives me a look. The emotion in his eyes tears my heart into tiny pieces. It's painful. He takes the bag and the walker from Felix and puts it into the back.

"You okay?" Felix asks.

I give him a slight nod. He hands me my purse. "My number is in the phone I got you."

I nod again.

"See you in a while, Josie."

Colten closes the trunk and scuffs his black dress shoes to me. On an infinitely deep sigh, he hunches in front of me, resting his hands on my legs. And he just … stares at me. His gaze slowly brushes along my face. I don't know what to say. My memories are so out of order; therefore, the emotions tied to them are scattered as well. I don't know how to explain this to him. I don't know where to begin.

I just know that my heart is crashing against my ribcage. And I swear I can hear his doing the same.

When he doesn't speak, I expect him to help my legs in the car. I expect him to ask me questions. He doesn't.

He drops his head in my lap. I lift my hands, staring at his head and holding my fingers above it for a few seconds, afraid to touch him because I don't know what's appropriate, how he's feeling, or anything about the lady in red. I draw in a shaky breath as tears flood my eyes. Even if my memories are fuzzy, my feelings are not. I've loved this man my whole life. My fingers find his hair, gently stroking it. His body shakes with silent sobs.

I blink.

All the tears race down my face onto him.

What did I do to us?

What did I do to him?

As quickly as he fell apart in my lap, he lifts my legs into the car, fastens my seat belt, and closes the door. When he doesn't appear on the driver's side right away, I glance behind me. His back is to the car, head bowed, fingers slowly running through his hair as he lifts his chin, gaze to the night sky for several seconds before he moves toward the driver's side.

We make the trip to his house in silence. He retrieves my walker and the bag while I open the car door.

"Need help?" he asks, appearing a little less agitated without Felix's presence.

I shake my head, swinging my legs out of the car and standing with the ease of a sloth. He moves with me, an inch at a time, into the house.

"Is it hard or strenuous to talk?"

"No. Just ... sometimes I can't find the right word. Or I say it wrong."

"Can you walk up the stairs?"

I shake my head.

"Hungry?"

Another headshake.

Again, he scoops me up and takes me to his bedroom, leaving me on the end of the bed while he gets my bag and walker.

I rest my hands on the edge and glance around the room. It's familiar. My mind goes straight to red dress woman. Has she been in this room? In this bed? Is it my business anymore?

Colten sets my walker next to the bed. Then he shrugs off his jacket and loosens his tie. I can't force my gaze to his. I feel too weak.

Too vulnerable.

Too inadequate.

I think my plan backfired. I should have stayed dead.

"Hey ..." He demands I look at him.

So I do, hoping I don't start crying again.

"That woman?" He unbuttons his white dress shirt. "She's a friend. That's it."

Pressing my lips together, I return a tiny nod, again letting my gaze slip to my lap.

When he emerges from his closet in a pair of jogging shorts, he turns on the TV, lifts my legs onto the bed, and fluffs the pillows before hooking his arm around my waist, spooning me to him.

I swallow hard. "I know you have questions."

He kisses my head. "You already answered the only one that matters for tonight."

I stretch my neck around to look at his face.

"You're alive," he says. "That's all I need to know until tomorrow."

My hand makes a slow ascent to his face, cupping his cheek. His eyes redden with more emotion while the pad of my thumb brushes his bottom lip.

He closes his eyes and leans into my touch. How did we get here?

I know, yet ... I don't think I will ever truly understand.

CHAPTER
Forty

I glance around the setup in the storage shed. The "borrowed" medical equipment. Crash cart. Bed. Medications. I hope if he's found out, being the son-in-law of the hospital administrator will help his case.

"Looks good."

He shakes his head. "It's not good. We need a vent."

"I told you, no ventilator. If I can't breathe on my own, you let me die. You know where to dispose of the body. Return everything, and pretend this didn't happen."

"Sure. Because I kill people on a daily basis. No big deal."

"You're a doctor. And you're human. It's probably not daily. I'd hope not. But you kill people," I mumble. The visions. The voices. The burden of accountability has been multiplying with each passing day. I haven't slept more than a few hours in the four days I've been at Felix's.

Nightmares.

Waking up with a racing heart.

Cold sweats.

And then I see Colten. I imagine him looking at his daughter with her short hair. I see all his fears come to fruition. And ... I start to hate myself even more.

"Josie?"

I shake my head, coming back to the present. "What?"

"I asked when we're doing this. I'd like to go to prison before my wife gets home, so that she thinks I just left her."

"You're not going to prison. And I need you to record me."

"I'm not recording this. No way."

I shake my head. "Not you suffocating me. I need to tell myself a few things in case this works."

"I'm not following."

I pat my pockets. "I don't have a phone. I destroyed it. We'll use your phone."

"We'll use an old video recorder that used to belong to my parents."

I frown. "Fine."

An hour later, Felix has the video recorder dug out of his attic, and I'm perched on the borrowed hospital bed recording a message for my post-suffocated self.

"Hi, Josephine. If you're watching this, then you're alive. Give Felix a huge hug."

Felix rolls his eyes while recording me.

"I hope you're okay. I'm recording this because I don't know what you'll remember. If my plan works, you won't remember why you had to die and be brought back to life. You had a near-death experience months ago. You remembered a previous life. And you might see news articles about you and claims about that previous life. Here's all you need to know. You were having terrible visions and nightmares. You lost your job. You couldn't sleep. Your life was miserable to the point that you didn't want to be in this life most days. You were going to marry Colten, but you didn't trust yourself. He has a daughter, and you never wanted to put him in a position to choose between being with you or being with her. I hope what I'm saying sounds unreal to you. I hope you can hear me but not feel it. I hope you're detached from that life. That was the purpose."

I think about what else I want to tell future me. I've got nothing. The chances of a future me is really slim. I nod to Felix to stop the video.

"If I'm in a coma, end it."

"You could be in a coma for a few days, maybe a week or two."

I nod. "Two weeks, not a day longer. You have a life. Your debt will more than be paid."

Deep worry lines cut across his forehead. I think they're nearly permanent by now. I know I'm asking something so much bigger than what I did for him. But I'm desperate.

"When?" he asks.

"After dinner."

His Adam's apple bobs before he nods.

"Let's eat."

Another nod.

We order food from my favorite restaurant. Dessert too. As he pours himself a glass of wine, I give him a look.

"I need your mind clear to save me," I say.

He laughs, pouring the wine to the very top of the glass. "I need to relax so I can go through with this. If I can't suffocate you, I can't resuscitate you."

I chew a bite of food before wiping my mouth. "I bet that's a phrase you've never said before now."

Felix frowns just before taking a long swig of his wine.

"You'll be good at this. Winston Jeffries used to drink heavily before poisoning the girls. I remembered that a few weeks ago. Never told anyone. But now I know why I've had no desire to drink. He was so messed-up. Everything's come in pieces to me. A puzzle. A heinous puzzle. Eventually, I stopped sharing the pieces with Colten because I saw it in his eyes. The doubt. I know it pained him to have those moments, but I didn't miss the subtle flinches, the extended looks when I interacted with his daughter. We got so good at pretending everything would be fine if we just kept ..."

"Pretending?"

I nod.

"Winston was abused by his mom. Always being compared to his sister. And I think his mom got so mad at him one time, she tried to drown him in the tub. She shaved his head because he didn't comb his hair. I never see her in the vision, but I *feel* his fear. One day I feel his anger, his wrath toward the girls, and the next day I feel his despair. Every inadequacy. Every inclination to end his own life."

I poke at the food on my plate, but I've lost my appetite. "That would have been the better choice. It would have saved so many lives." I glance up at Felix. "I've started to think that about myself. I often wonder if there's a switch that could flip, and I'd be more him than me. What if I go from imagining self-harm to harming someone else? An animal that needs to be put down."

"When does a killer become a killer?"

I nod. "I don't know, but it's always fascinated me. The conception of a killer. I used to fixate on mass shootings. I'd do so much research on the killers, trying to get inside of their heads to understand. My parents used to say understanding a killer would be impossible. Yet I felt like I could. Not like I wanted to kill anyone, just ... I understood. You know?"

Felix takes several more gulps of his wine. "I'm about to find out."

I reach for the bottle of wine.

Felix raises an eyebrow. "Shall I get you a glass?"

Bringing it to my nose, I take a slow whiff. Then ... I take a sip.

And another sip.

And eventually, I consume the rest of the bottle. A nice buzz. Felix can't kill me if his mind is clear, and I'm not sure I can die with one.

It's bizarre how methodical we are while we finish dinner and dessert. We clear the dining room table and wash the wine glasses. I put the silverware in the dishwasher while Felix takes out the trash. Then I take a shower, shaving everything but my head.

Floss.

Brush my teeth.

Dry my hair.

I trim my fingernails and toenails.

Deodorant.

Lotion on my legs.

Why? I have no idea. It feels necessary.

We drive in silence to the storage unit. I completely undress, and Felix doesn't question it for a second. He knows it's easier to use the defibrillator, perform any necessary procedures, or administer medications if I am naked.

I never prepared to die the first time. I know people do it. Suicidal people. Terminally ill people. Inmates on death row.

"I need to say this," Felix says, holding the bag in his hands while I sit on the edge of the hospital bed. "*If you survive death, you will likely have severe, permanent neurological damage. Language, behavior, mood,* and cognition disturbances. I don't know what kind of life you imagine, but the chances of you miraculously coming out of this without those issues is so close to zero, I can't put enough zeros after the decimal. I need ... really *need* to know you understand this. I need to know this is what you want. I need to know you are making this decision with a sound mind."

I think his buzz has worn off. Mine is still swirling in my head, but it doesn't numb my conscience to the words he's saying.

"If you weren't doing this for me, I would take my own life. And I'd do it in a way that no one would be around to save me. So please always, *always* remember that you didn't kill me. I'm already dead. And while I can't be *him* in this life any longer, I've loved my life. I love my family. I loved my job. And I love Colten to the very deepest parts of my soul. So for this life I love, this life I don't want to leave, I owe it one last chance. I owe it the greatest risk, no matter how tiny the chance might be. I am making this decision with a sound mind, even if slightly buzzed." I manage a small grin, but Felix struggles to find one of his own.

"No keeping a vegetable. Understood? Throw out the vegetable."

After a few seconds, Felix nods.

First, he inserts an IV and makes sure the crash cart and epinephrine are ready.

Then he walks behind me and ties my wrists together so I can't fight him. My heart jumps, gallops, takes off like a fighter plane. When he walks around to the front of me again, I blink, and several tears work their way out.

Felix isn't immune to the harsh reality either. His Adam's apple bounces over and over while he glances toward the ceiling to keep from blinking.

"Thank you," I whisper when I can't find a strong voice behind the emotion.

The adrenaline.

The fear.

I'm scared. I don't want to die. But I can't be him. I say this to myself over and over again. I wish it made it easier to let go, but it doesn't.

Felix stares at the bag in his hands. A gun would be easier and faster. Carbon monoxide would be more peaceful. A drug overdose would increase my chances of coming back. But this ... this is how *he* has to die. This is how he has to leave me. Of that, I am certain. Winston left that life by hanging. I'm not asking Felix to do that to me, but this will be close. Close enough.

When Felix lifts his gaze to mine, I nod once.

He puts the bag over my head and seals it with a tight grip and several firm twists. Felix's jaw clenches while he holds the bag in place and closes his eyes. I don't want to fight, but I do. I don't want to panic, but I do. I don't want to feel pain, but I do. My oxygen hungry retinas cause my vision to blur while my mind tries to change its mind. It's too late. There is no going back now. There is only ... darkness.

CHAPTER
Forty-One

"God, I missed you." Isabella jumps up from the sofa when I get home from work.

"I would have picked you up from the airport," I say when she hurls herself into my arms.

"I know, but I took an earlier flight, and I knew you were working." With her arms draped around my neck, she grins and gives me a slow kiss.

I need her kiss.

When she reaches for my tie, loosening it, I decide I need that too. I need her in every way. I need her body to distract my mind. I need her soft moans to spur some life back into my black soul.

Our clothes pile up at our feet, and we make it up three stairs before I'm inside of her.

"F-Felix ..." She giggles, wriggling away from me.

She gets up two more stairs before I hook her waist and take her from behind, her knees on one step, her hands two steps higher. This time she doesn't giggle. Her fingers dig into the runner rug, and she grunts with each thrust.

Fucking my wife like an animal on the stairs is a good way to not think about Josephine Watts in my storage unit ... in a coma.

"Oh god ... Felix ..." She wiggles her ass, doing the work for me as the sound of skin slapping fills the room.

I grip her hips and enjoy the view. Her long auburn hair splays along her face as she looks over her shoulder at me, mouth slightly agape with each tiny grunt.

Uh. Uh. Uh ...

They're little staccatos drowning the memory of Josephine trying to scream inside the plastic bag.

She gives me a tiny smirk and pulls away from me, running the rest of the way up the stairs. I chase her down the hallway and into the bedroom, where I pin her beneath me and wedge myself between her spread legs.

My tongue flicks her nipple, and she whispers, "Tie me up." She lifts her hips and grinds against me while stretching her arms above her head toward the bed posts in surrender.

My erection dies, her words a marksman with a direct hit. In all the years we've been together, I've tied her to the bed maybe ... twice? And tonight ... out of all fucking nights, she asks me to do it.

I crawl off her and drag my limp dick to the bathroom.

"Felix? Where are you going? What's wrong?"

"I haven't had dinner, and I need a shower."

"What? Are you serious? We didn't finish!"

I close the door, knowing she'll be opening it in a matter of seconds. What am I supposed to say? I grab my cock and stroke it over and over, thinking about my Isabella, my sexy wife. Her tits. Her pussy. When that doesn't work, I think about Heather, one of my nurses. She's twenty-four. A double D. And she's always wearing a fucking pink thong under her scrubs that I see every time she bends down to tie her shoes when she's not wearing her lab coat. I don't want to fuck her in real life. I'm a happily married man, but in a pinch, I think of her, and it always does the job.

Not tonight.

The tire is flat, and I don't have a spare.

"Felix." Isabella opens the door and traipses up behind me as I turn on the shower.

I cringe when I jump in before the water has a chance to warm up.

"Brr ..." She squeals, following me into the shower.

There's no escaping her hand reaching for my flat tire.

She frowns when I turn toward her.

"Sorry." I shrug. "Cold water." I squirt shampoo into my hair and work up a lather.

Isabella drops to her knees and pulls me into her mouth.

Nothing.

This is emasculating. She's been gone for over a week. She'll think I don't want her, or worse, that I'm cheating on her.

"Ouch!" She pulls away when I not-so-accidentally squirt body soap into her eye.

"Oh, Izzy ... I'm so sorry, honey." I help her to her feet and guide her face under one of the jets.

"Oh my god. It burns!"

"I'm *really* sorry." I hand her a washcloth.

She takes it and exits the shower.

"I'll be out in a minute. I can help rinse out your eye," I say, resting my forehead against the tile.

I suffocated a woman four days ago. By some miracle, I brought her back. But now she's in a coma in my fucking storage unit with stolen equipment from work. Losing my job is the least of my concerns right now. If someone found Josie, would I be arrested for ... attempted murder? I have no alibi. And there is not one good reason why she's in my storage unit. If the electricity goes out during the night, she'll freeze to death. If she wakes when I'm not there and is disoriented, she could try to leave on her own. What have I done?

Eleven more days. Josie has eleven more days to come out of her coma before I take her life for a second time and dispose of the body where no one will ever find it. And I have to do all of this while saving lives at work and trying to act like a normal husband who can properly fuck his wife.

Regardless, we are even. More than even. What I did for Josie was so far above and beyond what she did for me. There's no way to adequately measure it in one lifetime.

Tomorrow is the last day for Josie unless she wakes up before then. I've had a shit day at work because I can't stop thinking about burying a body for the first time in my life and hopefully the last. I can't stop thinking about what prison will be like.

On the way to my car, Izzy calls me. "I can read your mind. You want me to pick up dinner." I open the driver's door.

"Felix, I'm in our storage unit."

Fuck. Fuck. FUCK!

Isabella has been to our storage unit once in the seven years we've had it. ONCE!

"I'm on my way. I'll explain when I get there."

"Felix," she says with a shaky voice. "W-why is there an unconscious woman in our storage unit? In a hospital bed? T-tell me!"

"I'll be there in less than twenty minutes. Don't touch anything."

"Touch anything? What am I going to touch? The

unconscious woman? Felix, this is the woman that's been on the news and online. She's the missing woman! What the hell did you do?"

"Izzy, I *need* you to calm down. Stay put. Don't call anyone else. And just wait for me."

When I get to the unit, Izzy's standing at the end of the bed, arms hugged to herself. "Felix! What is she doing here? What have you done?"

I hold my finger to my lips, wishing she'd keep her voice down a bit. "Do you want a lie or the truth?"

She frowns.

I thought of a lot of things, but I didn't imagine having to tell Izzy without first being arrested. "When I was a first-year resident, Dr. Watts, Josie, was my chief resident. After my mom died, I struggled with addiction, and Josie saved my ass on more than one occasion. She saved my medical career. While you were gone, she showed up at our doorstep, out of the blue. You see, I owed her a favor after what she did for me. And so I had no choice."

"Why is she unconscious in our storage unit?" Izzy asks like she's on the verge of losing it.

"Shh ..." I cringe again. "Can you keep it down?" I say while checking Josie's vitals, her IV, feeding tube, and catheters. Over the next fifteen minutes, I proceed with the whole story, as unbelievable as it is. Then I show her Josie's video because I need her to believe that I'm not a true killer.

"Felix ..." Izzy whispers my name, dazed as she shuffles a few steps away from the bed.

Is she distancing herself from Josie or me?

Her fingertips touch her parted lips, gaze on Josie between slow blinks. "You c-can't kill her t-tomorrow," she stammers.

"That was her wish. It's been two weeks. We are, in fact, in a storage unit. It's winter. I have a full-time job. Her chances of waking up are slim. Her chances of waking up without neurological deficiencies are nearly zilch. I will follow her instructions. Return the equipment. And go on with my life. With our life."

Izzy's gaze flits to me. "We can't let her die. No. It's only been two weeks. She could wake up. You know this. And she might have minimal or no neurological deficiencies. It's not impossible."

Izzy's experience as an ICU nurse isn't helping this situation. I need her to feel helpless and reliant on me, not like a superhero.

"She has family ... a fiancé looking for her. What if we can save her? What if she doesn't remember her past life? Felix, what if we can do this?" She laughs. It's a shaky laugh before she releases a long breath.

I'm glad she's hopeful or relieved, but it's not realistic.

"I'm following her wishes. The way I'd follow a living will. It's the legal and ethical thing to do."

"Legal and ethical? Are you joking? We are in a *storage unit*. You have a former medical examiner in a coma because you tied a bag over her head. Her fiancé is a homicide detective. You stole thousands of dollars' worth of medical equipment, and now I'm either a witness who is going to report you or I'm an accessory."

I unbutton the top of my shirt with my sweaty hands. Her assessment has my heart quickening. Reality fills the room, stealing all the oxygen.

"I'm proud of you," Izzy says, donning a pair of blue gloves and rechecking everything I just checked, except she's also checking for bed sores. She's focusing more on the contents of the catheter bags. She's assessing Josie like a nurse would do if she were caring for someone's loved one ... to return them to their family—alive. "Most people don't seek the truth because it's too messy. Most people don't stretch their minds to make room for things they haven't experienced and can't see. I'm proud of you for listening to her. I'm proud of you for believing her."

"Who said I believed her?"

Izzy glances over at me while holding Josie's wrist, feeling her pulse. She traded in nursing to become an acupuncturist. "She's in our storage unit. You tied a bag over her head. You believed her."

"I owed her."

Izzy chuckles, resting Josie's wrist at her side. "Not this. Nobody owes anyone *this*."

She's right. I believed Josie.

"It could be months," I say just above a whisper. "We *have* to let her die."

Izzy doesn't look at me. She messes with Josie and her bedding, sliding her one way and then the other way. "The bed doesn't adjust."

"It's not plugged in."

She unplugs the crash cart and plugs in the bed to adjust Josie. "How did you get all of this here?"

"The janitor helped me load it into a moving van."

"Without question?" She glances over her shoulder.

I shrug. "I said it was going to one of the clinics."

"And how did you get it in here by yourself?"

"The bed? I paid Jonah to help me. I told him there was some renovation happening at the hospital, and we had to store some things until it was done."

She snorts. "The neighbor kid? And he believed you?"

"He's seventeen."

Crossing her arms, she stares at Josie. "You tied her hands behind her back ... that's why you had *issues* the night I came home, when I asked you to tie me to the bed."

When I don't answer, she glances over her shoulder at me.

I nod once.

"We're going to take care of her, Felix. We're not going to give up on her." Her head dips into a resolute nod.

"That's not what she wanted."

"She didn't want to inconvenience you any longer than possible."

"She asked me to kill her. I think fear of inconveniencing me went out the window at that point."

Izzy turns and wraps her arms around my neck.

"I'm going to work on her tomorrow. Acupuncture. I'm going to get some essential oils, objects with different textures. She needs to be moved, adjusted, bathed, talked to like she's not in a coma. Maybe a little music from time to time. Let's bring her back."

There's no use arguing with her, so I nod.

A MONTH PASSES. I start to lose hope even with Izzy feeling optimistic.

"Her brain is healing," she says.

She's braindead, but I don't say that.

Another month passes. It's official. I've kept the vegetable. I'd say Josie will be pissed off at me, but she won't. Not in this lifetime. I don't blame Josie for wanting to try, to exhaust every last effort. I would do the same thing to stay in this life with Izzy. But time is up.

"No," Izzy says when I come into the storage unit after work. She knows what I'm going to say.

"No one's immortal, Izzy. You've blown me away with your generosity, your kindness to a complete stranger. But—"

"She squeezed my hand today."

"Palmar grasp reflex. You know this."

She takes Josie's hand, running her finger along her lifeline.

"Izzy, I don't want her to wake up."

"Why would you say that?"

"You know why. She wouldn't be able to physically function. She'd be, at the very best, I'm talking truly miraculous best, mentally impaired. It's unlikely that she'd be able to speak."

"That's what therapy is for. Speech. Physical. Occupational. It will take time, but I believe she will recover."

"Time? You mean years? What are we supposed to do? Take her and dump her off at Colten's front doorstep? At her parents' front doorstep? Are we going to rehabilitate her? Izzy, you have to be realistic. The humane thing to do for her and everyone is to let her go."

"Would you let me go?"

"I would if that's what you wanted."

Izzy turns toward me, mouth slightly agape.

I shrug. "I think you forget about your years as a nurse. I think you forget what I see and do every day. And..." I smile "...I love that about you. I imagine us having kids and how lucky they will be to have you as their mother. I want that life, Izzy. I don't want to go to prison. I don't want anything to jeopardize our future. Maybe that's selfish of me, but when it comes to my life with you, I feel protective and selfish."

She holds out her arms while she makes her way to me. I embrace my world. And then ... it's as if the world stops for a breath. More like a blink.

Josie opens her eyes.

CHAPTER
Forty-Two

I WAKE UP ALONE. No Josie. For a few seconds, I rub my eyes. Was it real?

She's alive.

She uses a walker.

She's incredibly thin and frail.

She's. Alive!

I climb out of bed, grab a T-shirt, and go downstairs. She's nowhere in sight and neither is her walker. How did she get down the stairs ... with her walker? Did Felix pick her up? How did I sleep through everything? I run back up the stairs, and just as I head into my bedroom, I hear her.

"I'm in here."

I follow her voice to Reagan's room. She's perched on the end of Reagan's bed, staring at the cat mural.

"Who painted this?" she asks.

"I did." I bend down and kiss her head before sitting next to her.

"Did I know that?"

"Yes. You did."

"Huh ..." She continues to stare at it.

"Josie," I whisper, taking her hand in mine. "It's time. I need to know. Where have you been? What happened?"

"I'm not sure."

"What does that mean?"

"There's what I know and what I've been told. I've been trying to piece everything together, but it's been hard. I know I loved my job. I know you moved to Chicago, and it was the first time I had seen you in seventeen years. I know I was mad at you. I know you did a weird proposal over donuts. I know I said no. But I watched a video I made before I died, and I guess I was going to marry you, so I must have said yes at some point. The video version of me said that I had a near-death experience where I remembered a past life, and it was giving me horrible visions. I was suicidal. I was afraid of making you choose between your daughter and me. I must not have thought we could coincide in your life. Felix has filled in some more information as well. I have memories from before the first death, the shooting, but I think everything from after that until I woke up from the coma is gone."

"Josie ..." I stand, running my hands through my hair before turning toward her. "You were in a coma?"

She nods.

"Wh-how … for … Jesus … for how long? Why am I just now hearing about this? Why didn't your name come up when you were admitted to the hospital? I've been looking for you for months!"

She winces.

I feel instant regret. I'm angry, but not really at her. I'm confused. My chest aches, and I feel so lost and helpless.

"I didn't go to the hospital."

"What?" I shake my head. "That makes no sense."

"I told you what I know. Now this is what I've been told. I left you on our wedding day. I showed up at Felix's house. He was a first-year resident when I was chief resident. He had some issues, and I saved him and his career. I went to his house because I thought he owed me. I asked him to kill me. He restrained me and tied a bag around my head—"

I shake my head over and over before running to the bathroom and hurling. Not much comes out because my stomach is empty. Everything from the pit of it to the top of my throat aches and burns. I've seen truly horrible crime scenes and barely blinked at the carnage. But imagining someone restraining Josie and tying a plastic bag over her head … it's gutting me.

She left me on our wedding day… to die.

"I'm sorry," she whispers.

I stand and rinse my mouth in the sink. Pressing a towel to my lips, I glance at her in the mirror, standing with her walker in the doorway.

"I should leave."

I turn and clear my throat. "How long were you in a coma?"

"Two months. In a storage unit filled with equipment Felix *borrowed* from the hospital."

Two fucking months in a coma ... in a goddamn storage unit. And I thought she was dead.

"I was confused as to why Felix kept me alive that long. I thought I surely gave him instructions, but I couldn't remember. When I pressed him, he told me it was two weeks. His wife found me, and she refused to let me die. I think ..." Josie's gaze drops to the floor, eyes narrowed.

I turn, resting against the counter.

"I think ... sometimes ... that they should have let me die because I'm nearly four months post coma, and I look awful. And I can't walk without a walker. And my memory is slow some days. And piecing things together is painful. I'm trying to form these connections in my brain, and it's so very hard." She takes in a shaky breath. "It's statistically unlikely that I'll ever be what I was before the coma ... before I died a second time. Most days I wonder why. What is the point? Why did I want to stay in this world so badly?"

I run a hand through my hair. "For me. You wanted to stay for me. Because you know I love you. Because you know I need you."

Her head eases side to side. "You wanted me. But you didn't need me. You didn't *need* me when you broke my heart our senior year, even if you wanted me ... you didn't need me. And you didn't need me when we reconnected seventeen years later. I know this because you made it seventeen years without me, without making any effort to find me. You had other relationships. A career. A daughter. All without me. So I wanted to stay for me. I wanted to stay because you came back into my life, and I liked the version of me with you. I've always liked that version of myself. But now I'm barely a ghost of what I used to be. And I hate it. I hate that I allowed this to happen. I hate that I didn't have the courage to just let go. Let *you* go. Let this life go."

How can she be alive yet I hurt more than I did when I thought she was dead?

Something chimes from the bedroom. She turns and pushes her walker toward the bed, taking her phone off the nightstand and answering it. "Hello? No. I haven't done my exercises yet. No. I haven't—yeah, I know. I will. I know." She closes her eyes for a few seconds and blows out a long breath. "Fine. I'll meet you out front." Ending the call, she glances up at me. "I have to go. That was Izzy."

"Who's Izzy?"

"Felix's wife. I go to therapy four times a week, but I have exercises to do at home every day. Izzy feels very responsible for my recovery since she's the reason Felix didn't let me die."

"Sounds like I owe her a debt of gratitude."

"No." She frowns. "You don't. I'm not her. I'm not the woman you asked to marry you in a donut shop. I'm the car that needs to be sent to the junkyard because my parts are worth more than the whole of me. I'm nothing but a liability."

"Don't say that. Don't ever fucking say that again."

Pushing her walker toward the door, she mumbles, "Izzy's coming to get me. Give my apologies to your date from last night. Felix was right; I should have let him run my errands."

I follow her to the stairs. "It wasn't a date."

"Can you get my walker?" Josie holds the banister and lowers herself to the top step.

"I'll carry you."

"I can do it." She takes it one step at a time on her butt.

I watch her. I used to watch her cut into dead bodies and help solve cases. I used to watch students study her, envy her, want to be her. Now, she's scooting down my stairs on her butt. She wishes she would have stayed dead. Maybe she's right. Maybe that woman is gone. Still, I just ... fucking love her so much. Reason 683 why everything hurts right now.

"Are you going to tell your parents, or am I?"

She glances over her shoulder when she reaches the bottom stair and stands with the assistance of the banister.

"For that matter," I say, carrying her walker down the stairs, "when were you going to tell me? Never?"

"I'll call my parents." She frowns. "And the plan was to come back to you when I was functional again."

"And if you're never functional?"

She takes her walker and heads toward the front

door. "Then that will suck for me, but it doesn't have to suck for you." She opens the door. "Call the woman with the red dress. Apologize. And move on with your life like you were doing before you saw me at CVS."

"Stop. Just ... stop!" I ball my hands, ready to send one of them through the wall. I'm ready to crawl out of my skin. How can Josie be alive and it feel like a nightmare? Where is *my* Josie? "I told you she's a friend. That's it. I don't want to talk about her again. I want to know why after *six months* I found out you're alive by pure luck. Happenstance. I was supposed to be your husband. Your. Husband."

She stares at the floor. It's hard to read her. Is she numb to what I'm feeling?

"A serial killer. That's weird, right? I mean, I've had such a fascination with death. I was really good at my job. Dr. Cornwell used to say 'eerily' good. He said I thought like a killer when I worked on cases." She chuckles. "I suppose every soul has to find a new life. At least this life has been mostly worthwhile. Good deeds this time."

I deflate. She's unfocused, almost indifferent to the words I say to her. I want to hold her. I want her to hold me back. I want to feel her love. I need to feel missed. I need to feel *us*.

What happened to *us*?

"Izzy's here. Thanks for taking care of me. Please let me tell my parents first."

Taking care of her? Does she have any idea how much it's killing me to let her leave?

"I need the address," I say. "I have to go in to finish up a few reports, but I can pick you up by three."

"I'm staying with them for now. So if you pick me up, they'll just have to come get me again tomorrow."

My heart has been stuck in my throat since I saw her yesterday at the CVS. I hate that she's three feet from me. She's *alive*. Yet she doesn't get that she belongs with me.

"I'll pick you up at three. And I'll return you to their house tomorrow," I say.

And I'll drop you off the next day. Pick you up. Drop you off. Repeat. Repeat. Repeat.

"If you have plans later, don't let me disrupt them."

I LOVE YOU! Stop pushing me away!

Controlling every crushing emotion racking around inside of my chest, I give her a simple nod. "I'll see you at three."

"Okay. Have a good day." She steps outside and closes the door behind her.

"A good day," I whisper to myself, taking a seat on the stairs, resting my hands on my knees while shoving my fingers into my hair. "You're alive, baby. It's a fucking *amazing* day."

CHAPTER
Forty-Three

"How are you?" Izzy asks, backing out of Colten's driveway.

"Good. Why?"

She puts the car in *Drive* and gives me a quick sideways glance. "Well, yesterday your fiancé—who thought you were dead—saw you at a CVS. He had to be in shock. I can only imagine. Completely stunned. It's been six months. And Felix said he was there with another woman. You must have some feelings about all of this. What did Colten say when you got back to his house? Is he serious with the other woman? What are your feelings at the moment?"

"Colten was ... in shock. I think. As for my feelings? I feel bad. And I feel guilty. And I still feel confused. Insecure. Frustrated. Brokenhearted. You name the emotion and I'm feeling it. Angry ... I'm definitely angry."

"At Colten?"

"No. I'm angry at myself for not ending my life, for not thinking this through. It's good that I don't have memories of Winston Jeffries. It's bad that I'm crippled. It's bad that Colten knows I'm alive, and he feels responsible for me ... just when he was moving on. And now I have to tell my parents before he tells them. I'm mad at myself for thinking that my existence in this world was necessary."

"Josie, I don't know if anyone's existence in the world is necessary. It's life. The good, the bad, and the ugly."

I can't stop thinking about the woman in red. "She's beautiful," I say. "The woman. They were clearly going someplace nice. They were way too dressed up for 'just friends.' In his head, I died. And I *did* die. Do I think six months is a little early to be dating someone new?" I shrug. "I don't know. My memory is so messed-up. I'm having trouble sensing time. Six weeks. Six months. Six years. It's all about the same to me."

"How did it make you feel when you saw the other woman? Were you angry then?"

"I was surprised to see *him*. She was an afterthought. And I think ..." I sigh. "I think it brought back memories of all the times he was with some other girl when we were younger. I got so used to being silently jealous and irra-tionally angry. I never felt good enough for him, and it had nothing to do with him. Colten never made me feel anything short of the most special person in the room. But *I* felt different than the other girls. He was so talented, and everyone adored him. It was easy to want him yet feel inadequate, like he deserved someone better than me."

"That's sad, Josie."

I nod. "It was sad. Inadequacy is a soul-robbing emotion. It was then, and it is now. When we were younger, it took me a while to feel like he wasn't being my friend or my boyfriend because I was the default girl next door or the chief's daughter. And no sooner did I let that feeling of inadequacy fall away, he let me go. Seventeen years passed, and we were back in each other's lives. I didn't need anyone to tell me that I hated him. I remember all too well. I also didn't need anyone to tell me that I still love him. I remember that all too well. So this second chance at being with him gets trampled by, yet again, something else that spirals me back into that soul-robbing feeling of inadequacy. Fuck my life. Really ... just fuck my life."

"Are you saying he's no longer interested? No longer in love with you?"

"He loves me," I whisper. "He's hardwired to love me. I know this. But sometimes we're hardwired to do things that aren't in our best interest. Some would say addiction like alcoholism is something hardwired within people. So sure ... Colten loves me. He'd leave the pretty girl from last night to be with me. But who am I? I'll tell you. I'm a mutated version of my original self. I'm a salvaged vehicle. I don't know if I'll ever be mentally the same. Or physically the same. He's …"

I laugh despite the pain. "Colten is so sexy. In his prime. Virile. And deserving of a woman who …" I shrug. "A woman who looks like a gift from God in a red dress with magnificent heels and long flowing hair. He doesn't need, nor does he deserve, someone who can't climb the stairs. She has sexy shoes. I have a walker. Which one do you think gives a guy an erection?"

"I highly doubt he saw you last night and thought, 'There's the love of my life. Finally, I can get a proper erection.'"

I snort, staring out my window at the congested sidewalks. It feels inappropriate given the events of the last twenty-four hours—or the last year for that matter. But I can't help it. It feels good.

"He was hours, minutes, from promising to love you through sickness and health. You are getting better, Josie. You will continue to improve. Do you know how many times Felix has said you're a miracle?"

I scoff. "It's a miracle that I survived death twice. I am not miraculously using a walker. Not miraculously piecing together memories or thoughts. Not miraculously trying to find myself again. All of that is nothing short of a tragedy that could have been avoided had I just left my wedding and left this world for good. He just …" My voice fades into a whisper. "He deserves the red dress and heels."

THAT STRONG, wide-shouldered, handsome, virile man comes to the door at three. I watch out the front window like I'm fourteen and my dad is letting me go on my first date.

"I'm proud of you for remembering our address," Izzy says, sneaking up behind me.

"I didn't. Colten is a detective. Felix introduced himself."

"For someone who doesn't feel adequate, you didn't hesitate to pack an overnight bag." Izzy picks up said overnight bag.

Pushing my walker toward the door, I frown. "I told you; he's hardwired to love me. He thinks I belong with him. It's going to take a while for him to see that I no longer fit. That I can't give him what he deserves ... what he wants even if he can't see it clearly now."

Izzy reaches for the door handle. "What if he can see it now?" She opens the door and smiles. "You must be Detective Mosley. You met my husband, Felix, last night. I'm Isabelle." She holds out her hand.

Colten, in all of his sexiness, offers his hand. "Nice to meet you. Thank you for all you've done and are doing for Josie. I owe you a huge debt of gratitude."

Oh, Colten ...

She hands Colten my bag. "It's been our pleasure. She's a miraculous human, this one here." Izzy winks at me while I maneuver my walker out the door.

"Bye, Izzy," I clip before she can sing my praises for another second.

"See you in the morning."

"I'll drop her off," Colten says. "We should talk about her therapy."

"Absolutely," Izzy says. "Have a good night."

The boy who used to race me on our bikes or to my favorite tree is now waiting for me to slide into his car so he can take my *walker* and put it in the back of his vehicle. I'm not eighty. I'm thirty-six.

When he gets into the driver's seat, he eyes me with a smile so big it's almost clownish. "It's good to see you."

I can't quite match his smile. This isn't the happily ever after I dreamed of having with Colten Mosley. It's not happy. It's not even forever. It's simply after. After I did something I should not have done.

"That's my line," I say for lack of a better response.

Colten slides his hand to the back of my head and leans over the console, not letting his smile waver for a second before pressing a soft kiss to my cheek. He hasn't kissed me on the lips yet. Maybe he's conflicted —as he should be if he found someone else. That's not true. He shouldn't be conflicted. He should simply choose her.

I died. I should have stayed dead.

"Stop," he says, fastening his seat belt and backing out of the driveway.

"Stop what?"

"Thinking whatever you're thinking that's feeding your self-doubt."

"I'm not doubting myself." I stare at my hands folded in my lap. "I have no doubt that I made a mistake. I have no doubt that I shouldn't be here. I have no doubt that I may never be mentally or physically normal again."

"Josie ..." He rests his hand on mine.

I can't look at him. He symbolizes everything I will never be. It's a more debilitating pain than reteaching my body to function properly again.

When we get to his house, I shake my head over and over. "No. Stop. Why did you tell them? I'm not ready." Panic overtakes my whole body, shocking my heart into an irregular rhythm.

My parents' car is in his driveway.

"I didn't tell them. I asked them to come today. It was a big ask with no explanation. They did it for me."

My head continues to shake. "You had no right. I said I'd tell them on my own time."

He kills the engine, gets out of the car, and comes around to my side. As soon as he opens the door, he rests his arms on the roof and sighs slowly while closing his eyes for a brief moment. "If it were Reagan, I'd want to know. If you were my daughter, I'd want to know without hesitation. I'd have a hard time forgiving anyone and everyone who kept it from me. Josie, we all lived through your tragedy. We've been grieving you for months. It's cruel to let them grieve for another day ... for another second."

When I unbuckle my seat belt, Colten retrieves my walker. He lets me step out of the car on my own, in my own time. Then he leads me to his front door.

I take a deep breath as he opens it.

"Oh thank goodness. We've been dying to find out the surprise—" My mom's words die like they stepped off a cliff when she comes around the corner and sees me. Her hand slowly covers her mouth, eyes unblinking while they fill with tears.

"What's the surprise—" My dad turns the corner right behind her.

I force a smile while wiping a few tears from my own face. "Hi."

My mom's gaze inches along my body, stopping at my hands gripping the walker. "Josie," she exhales while her hand falls from her mouth and tears cover her cheeks.

Before I can take another step forward, my parents rush toward me, sandwiching me between them, casting my walker aside.

"Oh my god …" My mom cries. "You're a-alive …"

My dad doesn't speak. I don't think he can speak without breaking down. When their hold on me finally loosens, I grip my dad's arm, reaching for my walker with my other hand.

He catches me, scooping me up into his arms like he did when I was a little girl.

I wrap my arms around his neck and smile. "I can walk … with a little help."

He drops his forehead on my shoulder and just …

breathes. It's reminiscent of Colten having a moment when he put me in his car at the CVS.

Disbelief.

Shock.

Utter speechlessness.

I give him the moment, as does my mom and Colten. Nobody says a word for a few seconds.

Canting my head toward his, I rest my cheek on it and whisper, "I missed you too."

His head makes a slight nod without lifting it from my shoulder. When he sets me back on my feet, sniffling to keep his emotions in check, Colten has my walker waiting for me.

"Well..." I glance up at the three of them "...I'm sure you have questions." I smile.

Over the next hour, I tell them what I know, what I've been told, how Colten discovered me, and what Felix and Izzy have been doing for me.

"You'll come home," Mom says with a sharp nod.

"Yes," Dad seconds.

Colten stiffens on the sofa beside me.

"I have therapy."

"We have therapists in Des Moines," Mom says. "There's no need for you to be a burden on Felix and Izzy anymore."

I open my mouth to argue, but I can't. She's right. I don't want to be a burden on anyone.

Colten clears his throat and sits up straight before leaning forward to rest his hands on his knees. "She should stay with me. I'll hire help for when I'm at work."

Who's going to take care of me? I hate this conversation. I hate how helpless I feel. I hate that I'm now this decision that has to be made.

"Or I can live in my own house. Everything is on one floor. I can pay for rides to therapy. I can have groceries delivered, or I can set up a meal service while I'm recovering."

There's a collective no. My parents and Colten eye each other as though I'm not in the same room.

My mom moves from the chair to the sofa, taking ahold of my hand. "Come home, just temporarily. Stay a few weeks. A month? Stay until you're feeling more confident."

Colten readjusts in his spot again. "Why is everyone acting like I can't do this?"

"You have work," Mom says to him.

"I said I'd hire someone."

"And you have a daughter," Dad adds.

Colten gives my dad a look. I think he's used to him being his ally.

"I'll come home," I say, giving my parents a sad smile and slight nod. I'm thirty-six and moving back home so my parents can take care of me. It's a new low.

Colten stands and walks out of the room.

"Colten?" my mom calls after him.

He goes upstairs without a word.

Mom squeezes my hand. "He'll be fine. This is just a lot right now. Give him time, and he'll see this is for the best. When you get better, you'll be able to move back to Chicago. Go back to work. Get married. We just want to help you get your life back." She hugs me. "Josephine ... you're alive," she whispers in my ear, her voice cracking beneath the weight of the day.

"I'm alive," I whisper back, not feeling the same level of gratitude or relief.

"WE COULD GO FISHING next weekend. That would help with strength and coordination of your arms, Jo," Dad says while we eat dinner.

Colten hasn't said more than a few words to anyone since the food arrived, and he came back downstairs with us. Even now, his head is bowed toward his plate while he picks at his food.

Just as I start to speak, Colten's phone vibrates.

"Hey." He listens for a few seconds. "Yeah, sorry. I was going to call you. What time is her game? Okay. Yeah, I'll be there. Thanks, see you tomorrow." He ends his call.

"T-ball game?" my dad asks.

Colten nods, taking another bite of food.

"I'd love to see her. Can I go?" I ask.

Colten glances over at me. He doesn't say anything at first, so I shrug.

"It's fine. I don't have to go. I should probably go to my house and sort through things before I go back with my parents."

"You can go. She'd love to see you. I haven't told her that you're …"

"Alive?" I assume that's what he's trying to say.

"She thinks you're missing. That's all."

I nod.

After dinner, my parents decide to head to my house. "You should stay with us since you can't take the stairs," Mom says.

"I carried her last night," Colten says.

"Yes, but that's silly when she can sleep in her own bed."

I know my mom doesn't mean to disregard all of Colten's suggestions. She misses me. I guess they all miss me. Why don't I feel more missed and less of a burden?

"I thought my bed was her bed," he mumbles. I'm not sure she even hears him as he grabs my overnight bag from the bottom of the stairs where he set it when we arrived.

My dad takes the bag while my mom holds open the door.

I smile at them. "I'll meet you outside in a minute."

They nod and shut the door behind them.

"You brought them here. And I'm grateful, truly. But you can't expect them to say hi and leave like it's no big deal. Would you do that to Reagan?"

Colten slides his hands in his front pockets and inches his head side to side. He's incredibly quiet. I don't know how to make this better. Make this, whatever *this* is, go away. There's no roadmap for this.

"Do you want to pick me up tomorrow, or should I meet you at the park?"

"I'll pick you up at ten." He stares at the floor between us.

"Sounds good."

There's an awkward silence.

"Good night," I say, opening the door barely an inch before he steps behind me.

His hands rest on my shoulders, and his lips press to the top of my head, staying there for several long seconds. I draw in a shaky breath and blink back my tears. I just want to be in his arms. I want to be me before all of *this*. I want to have him chase me up the stairs and jump on the bed as I try to get away from him, giggling and taunting him before he captures me.

Before we lose our clothes.

Before he loses himself inside of me, and I lose myself so completely to him.

"Good night," he whispers before taking a step away.

The loss of his touch feels like an unwelcome chill.

CHAPTER
Forty-Four

I'VE STOPPED TRYING to hold it together. Josie's going back to Des Moines. My heart is nothing more than pea gravel on a playground, getting trampled without a second thought.

Before my fist makes contact with Josie's door, Isaac opens it. Josie smiles at me for a brief second, then she frowns. "Don't say anything about my hat. Izzy let me sit at her vanity to do my hair. I don't have a seat. So … it's a mess."

"You look pretty," I say.

Her gaze shoots to mine. I offer a tiny smile that feels forced because I don't know if references to our past matter anymore.

"Thanks," she says softly.

"See you after a bit," Isaac says.

She doesn't wait for me. Not my help. Not even for

me to offer her help. It's hard to see her fight for independence when I know she's feeling so helpless. I don't know where I fit with her right now. She's leaving Chicago, so that feels like a strong sign that I don't fit anywhere in her life at the moment.

"How's her team doing?" Josie asks on the way to Reagan's game. She asks a lot of questions that have nothing to do with us. Anything to fill the void, I suppose. That painful silence.

"We can go over the gravel or take the long way on the sidewalk. I can carry you," I say when she steps out of the car.

"I'll take the sidewalk. You can take the gravel. I don't want you to miss any of her game."

"We have time." I lock the car, and we take the long way to her field.

"Hey."

I glance up. "Hey," I reply to Layla.

"I was going to check in on you, but I didn't want to pry." Her gaze ping-pongs between Josie and me.

I'm a dick. I should have called her or messaged her. My brain has been spinning for the last two days. How do I explain Josie coming back from the dead? "I should have messaged you. Sorry." I nod toward Josie. "Layla, this is Josie. Josie this is Layla. Her daughter Nora and Reagan are friends."

Layla's eyes narrow just a fraction, maybe to see the ghost I'm introducing to her.

"Nice to meet you, Layla." Josie stabilizes herself

and shakes Layla's hand. "My apologies for interrupting your date the other night. I feel bad."

Date.

It wasn't a date. I told her that.

Layla slowly shakes her head. "It's ... uh ... don't apologize. I got a ride home. It's ... fine."

She doesn't correct Josie and say that it wasn't a date. Was I stupid? Naive? Was it a date?

"Well, you two can chat more without me, but I'd better keep moving since it will take me a bit to get to the right field." Josie smiles at Layla but doesn't give me so much as a quick glance.

"Nice ... meeting you." Confusion masks Layla's face while Josie hobbles down the sidewalk.

"I'm really sorry," I say again. "She just ..."

Layla tucks her hands into the back pockets of her jean shorts, head cocked to the side.

"She went missing. We thought she was dead. So the other night ..."

Layla's eyebrows crawl up her forehead. "Oh my god ..."

I nod while she shakes her head. "That ... I mean ... you must have thought you were seeing a ghost."

"Something like that."

"I'm happy for you. I hope she's going to be okay." Layla glances in Josie's direction, as do I.

"Me too," I whisper. "Tell Nora I said hi. Okay?"

Layla nods. "Of course. She still wants to have Reagan over to swim."

"Sure. Just ... call me." I say before jogging to catch up to Josie.

"Hey, sorry about that. Do you want me to grab you anything from the concession stand?"

Josie continues to push her walker down the sidewalk and shakes her head. "Nope. I stopped being a fan of concession stands when I saw you making out with Tessa behind one."

"Well, I'm pretty sure I can get you some popcorn or candy without making out with anyone."

"You sure?"

Layla.

I step in front of Josie a few feet from the bleachers, forcing her to stop. "Look at me."

After huffing a breath, she lifts her gaze.

"Layla invited me to the ballet. That's where we were going that night. We were *friends.* She lost her husband a year ago, so we had something in common, or so I thought."

Josie frowns, but I ignore it.

"We met at a game. The girls bonded. It's that simple. I didn't make out with her behind a concession stand. I didn't ask her to homecoming. I haven't had sex with her. We haven't kissed. We haven't held hands. We've been *friends.*"

"I don't care." She pushes past me.

I drop my shoulders and glance at the sky, looking for help, looking for answers.

"Josie!" Reagan comes barreling toward her, dropping her glove onto the ground while her team continues to warm up. I'm so glad I called Katy this morning, explaining things so she could give Reagan a heads-up.

"Easy," I say to Reagan as she hugs Josie.

"Cute hair. When did you decide to cut it?" Josie asks.

Reagan releases her and steps back. "You cut it, silly. Don't you remember?"

"Reagan—" I try to interrupt, but Reagan ignores me.

"On your wedding day. You put it in a ponytail and cut it off. Then you told me to give it to my dad. Then ..." Reagan's smile vanishes. "You disappeared."

Josie remembers none of that. I can tell from the loss of all color in her face.

"Reagan, you need to get back to your team. The game's about to begin." I shoo her toward the field.

"Hey, Josie. So good to see you," Katy steps down from the bleachers, followed by Sean, and hugs Josie.

"I'm ..." Josie shakes her head. "I'm *so* very sorry."

"Sorry for what?" Katy squints at Josie and then at me.

"I ... I shouldn't be here." Josie tries to push her walker over the gravel toward the parking lot.

"What did I say?" Katy presses her hand to her chest.

"Nothing. Just ... nothing." I take long strides toward Josie and grab her just as her walker catches, and she starts to tumble over it.

Pulling her into my chest, I rest my hand on the back of her head while she cries.

"I'm sorry ... I'm so s-sorry ..."

"Shh ..." I kiss her head. "There's nothing to be sorry for."

"I c-cut her h-hair. Who does th-that?" She shakes in my arms.

"We'll tell Reagan something came up, and you'll call her later. Okay?" Sean says from behind me as he bends down to pick up Josie's walker.

I give him my best thank-you smile and a slight nod. Resisting the urge to pick her up, I keep Josie hugged to me and help her to the car while Sean follows us with the walker.

Josie slumps against the door while I drive toward home. "Take me to my house," she says, her words void of life.

When we get to her house, she opens the door before I have her walker out. She stands on shaky legs, holding tightly to the door to keep upright. "Layla is beautiful and normal. She's not a monster. She would never cut Reagan's hair. She would never leave you at the altar. I'm giving you a pass, Colten. Just ... take it."

"Shut up, Josie. Just shut the fuck up." I grab her face and kiss her.

Taste her.

Inhale her.

With her lips pressed to mine, I come to life for the first time since our wedding day. The gaping hole she left in my heart fills with her touch, expanding my chest, healing it one slow breath, one slow beat at a time. When I release her mouth, I whisper over her lips, "You died for *this* life. You died to give up that life, to forget it. So please … *please* let it go. Be who you are, not who you think you were. Be mine. Not his."

"I'm broken," she whispers in a shaky voice.

"Baby, we're all a little broken. I'll take *you* chipped, cracked, or shattered into a million little pieces."

CHAPTER
Forty-Five

Josie wouldn't go with me to homecoming our senior year. Over the summer, I got a fake ID, started drinking on the weekends, and dove headfirst into self-destruction. She also didn't tell anyone. Not my parents. Not hers.

I never knew why she kept my secrets yet refused to do something as simple as go to homecoming with me. Either she liked me, or she didn't.

Nothing was that simplistic with Josie. I should have known that, but I was too self-absorbed in my own miserable life to see her—really see her.

"Jason is a dick. Why would you go with him to homecoming?" I leaned my back against the lockers while Josie swapped out her books before her calculus class.

"Because he asked me."

"So you'll go out with any guy who asks you out as long he isn't me?"

She slammed her locker door shut and glared at me. "I want to graduate. I want to have a clean record to get into college. I want a future that doesn't involve addiction. And before you decided to let your dad win, I thought I wanted you." She took off down the hallway.

"What's that supposed to mean? Let my dad win?"

"Colten, I have to get to class."

"What's that supposed to mean?" I grabbed her arm to stop her.

She sighed. "Let go of me. I don't have time for this."

"Time for this? You mean time for me. No time to talk to me. No time to go to homecoming with me because you no longer want me? Really? We've come this far and you're done? We're done?"

"I'm going to class. I don't know what you're doing." She took several steps and turned her head, resting her chin on her shoulder while her dark eyes lifted to mine. "Do you, Colten? Do you know what you're doing?"

I let her go. I had a way of letting her go when I knew she was right, and I was too stubborn to admit it.

So Josie went to homecoming with Jason, and I spent the evening drinking under the bleachers. Alcohol on school property. Not my finest hour.

When I felt adequately buzzed, I sauntered toward the school entrance and waited for Josie and Jason to leave the dance. They were kind enough to not keep me waiting too long. An hour before the dance ended, Josie pushed through the doorway, giggling like Jason was somehow entertaining her. She looked pretty in her white dress and hair pulled back with ringlets around her face. Her nails were painted light pink like the color of her lip gloss.

I didn't go to homecoming with Josie because my dad wanted me to go to the dance since it was my senior year. Fuck him. I wasn't going to the dance *because* he thought I should go.

"Josie ..." Her name slurred from my lips as I stumbled toward her. "Did you have fun with Jason?" I asked as if Jason wasn't standing right next to her.

"Have you been drinking?" she asked, but she knew the answer.

I held up my fingers and tried to measure an inch. "A wee bit."

"How are you getting home?"

I patted my pocket, then my other pocket, then my back pocket before I felt my keys. "My truck."

"You can't drive."

"Well, you wouldn't go with me, so I had to drive myself." I laughed and shrugged, finding it nearly impossible to hold still because everything around me seemed to be moving.

"Dude, you're going to get suspended. Just call your parents."

"*Dude* ... I didn't ask for your fucking opinion. I didn't ask for you to take *my* girl to homecoming, and

I'm sure as shit not going to call my parents because you said I should."

"Colten ..." Josie reached for my arm.

"Uh uh uh ... don't touch me. We're not allowed to touch because you didn't say yes to me. And I told your dad I wouldn't date you or kiss you. Maybe even screw you. I can't remember for sure." I scratched my chin.

"God ... you're a mess. Give me your keys."

"Can't. Gotta go. Don't fuck him, Josie. I heard he has crabs."

"Fuck you, man. I don't have crabs." Jason took a step toward me, but I was bigger and stronger, and he knew it. Even slightly inebriated, I could have knocked him flat on his ass.

"Just ... let me handle this." Josie stepped between us.

"Handle?" I smirked "Are you going to *handle* me?" I grabbed her hand and pressed it to my cock. I wasn't even hard.

"Back the fuck off!" Jason shoved me.

I laughed, stumbling backward. "Josie's my girl. Did you know that? She's mine. She's been mine since we were nine." I laughed some more. "That rhymes. Mine since we were nine. Ha! I'm a poet, and I don't even know it." I turned, still chuckling at myself.

"Colten!" Josie chased me, but I pulled away every time she tried to grab my arm. "You are not driving!"

"Are you handling me again?" I clucked my tongue. "Don't tell Jason."

"Colten."

"Josie," I parroted.

Then she was gone.

I turned.

"Josie?"

She wasn't in sight, and neither was Jason. It took me several attempts to not only fish my keys out of my back pocket, but to get them into the door of my truck to unlock it. More time was wasted trying to poke the key into the ignition. The truck sputtered to life, and I shoved it in *Drive* before speeding out of the parking lot. I barely made it to the stop sign before bright cherry lights flashed. Someone snitched.

"ARE you trying to blow your whole goddamn future? If so, congratulations, Son, you're hitting it out of the park," my dad lectured on the way home from the police station. "If it weren't for Chief Watts stepping in, this would be on your record. You'd be in jail overnight. And god only knows what kind of fine we'd have to pay. When are you going to start thinking about someone besides yourself? You could have killed someone. You could have killed Josie. Did you think about that? What if she would have been out on the road and you crashed into her car? Do you think the chief would have saved you? No. He would have let your pathetic, careless, irresponsible ass rot in prison."

Even though the alcohol was the reason for my situation, I was oddly happy that I had it in my system.

I wasn't nearly as buzzed as earlier, but it kept me from losing it with my father and his self-righteous lecture. God ... could he taste the utter hypocrisy in his words?

When we reached the house, I marched past my mom to my room, ignoring her tear-stained cheeks and forlorn expression. Yes, I was a disappointment. Yes, all the men in her life were fuckups and disappointments. She was partially responsible. She allowed it to happen. She was too damn forgiving ... of all of us.

When I heard my parents arguing about me, I opened my window, hopped onto the lower roof, and shimmied my way off the edge of it, body dangling for a second before letting go and dropping to the ground. It should have surprised me that Josie was standing two feet away from me, still in her white dress, arms crossed, but it didn't. "Did you turn me in?" I grumbled, walking down the street.

"Yes."

I whipped around because I didn't really mean it. I didn't really believe she turned me in. "Are you fucking kidding me?"

"No." She shoved my chest. "No, I'm not *fucking* kidding you, you stupid asshole." Josie cut through the neighbor's yard and wormed her way to the woods, but not to her favorite tree. I wasn't sure where she was going. I don't think she knew either. "You could have killed someone!"

"You could have killed Josie."

I stopped next to a tree, slumping beside it and sinking to my ass, knees bent, head bowed. "I hate my life," I murmured. "I hate it so much there are days I don't want to be here."

Josie clung to denial when it came to me. She never really believed I wanted to end my life, maybe because she didn't know what to do with that potential reality. For the most part, she protected me.

She protected me from her dad.

My parents.

Officials at school.

Other kids.

Everyone ... but myself.

I was my own worst enemy, my biggest threat.

"Don't say that," she whispered.

"It's the truth."

"It's not. You just ... you just need to get through this year. Go to college. Get away from your dad. Things won't seem as bad. High school is like a prison. Just hold it together for one year, Colten. Not even ... more like eight months."

I stared at her shiny black shoes, and I thought she might wear them and that dress if she died, if some asshole like me killed her in a drunk driving accident. Then I wondered if they put shoes on dead people when they dressed them up for visitations and funerals. It was very Josephine Watts of me to wonder morbid shit like that. She'd clearly rubbed off on me.

My gaze worked its way up her legs. She had the best legs. Her dress. Her kissable lips. Her pretty hair. Under the wedge of moonlight finding its way between the trees, she looked ethereal.

Unexpected emotion caught in my throat, making my chest ache and my stomach roil with regret—or maybe it was too much beer. "I feel so b-broken." My words cracked under the weight of guilt, under the weight of her perfect existence in my fucked-up world. It was an awful feeling to know that you were not good enough for someone, yet you selfishly wanted them against all sound judgment.

Josie stepped closer, forcing my legs out straight while she straddled my lap. Her hands slid around my neck, and she kissed my forehead, my nose, my cheeks. I didn't deserve her. How did she not see that?

Her next words ripped a sob from my chest, and I hated her and loved her in equal parts for saying them. "We're all a little broken. I'll take you chipped, cracked, or shattered into a million little pieces. You're my Colten. And I'm your Artemis."

CHAPTER
Forty-Six

"Hɪ," Colten says as soon as I answer. He says it before I answer with my own greeting.

"Hi." I can't help my smile while sitting in a chair, doing my physical therapy exercises before bed.

"How have you been?"

I chuckle. "I left Chicago yesterday."

"And I already miss you."

I don't know how to respond. Of course, I want to scream the words, "I miss you too!" But I don't because I feel like we've reversed roles. I'm the one feeling like I need to let him go for his own good. Only, I can't find the actual words to say it to him.

"I called my mom and told her you're alive. She's dying to come see you. Don't be surprised if she calls you. I gave her your new number."

"I'd love to talk to her."

He doesn't say anything for several seconds. Have we already exhausted the small talk?

"Listen, Josie ... what Reagan said to you—"

And here it is.

"Is it true?" I ask. "Did I cut off her ponytail before leaving you at the altar?"

"You didn't leave me at the altar. We didn't make it to the altar."

"Colten ..."

He sighs. "Yes. It's true. She wasn't mad. Nobody was mad. We were concerned. That's all."

"I ..." My eyes close while I lift a bent knee. I'm slowly getting stronger ... physically. Mentally, I'm struggling with who I was and what I did to get rid of the images of another lifetime. "I'm sorry."

"I told you, Reagan's not—"

"That's not what I mean. I'm sorry for thinking this insane plan I concocted would work."

"But it did."

I laugh. "I can't walk unassisted. I had a speech issue for several months. I don't have a job. Everyone I loved thought I was dead. And now that I'm alive, those same people, who spent months grieving and moving on, have to figure out how to take care of me like a child. I've caused so much pain only to now be a burden."

"You're not a burden."

"My dad is sixty-six, and he's going to have to carry me to my bedroom if he's uncomfortable with me sleeping on the sofa."

"That's why you should have stayed with me."

Switching legs, I grimace because I'm pushing myself through another set of leg lifts. I don't want to be dependent on anyone. "We can be friends. You know that, right? We were friends before we were more than friends. In fact, we spent our childhood being friends and then more than friends and back to friends again. If you move on, I won't be mad. I'll be happy for you. And that would be something new. I was never really happy for you when you had other girlfriends. This time would be different. I swear."

"Can you just say that you love me too? Can you do that?"

I press my hand to my face and rub my eyes. "It's late. I should go."

"I don't want to be friends, Josie."

"Have a good week."

"Josie—"

I end the call.

"You can't avoid him forever," Mom says a week later after I've religiously ignored Colten's calls and texts.

"I'm afraid of giving him false hope," I say on our way home from therapy. Today, I practiced using a cane instead of a walker. Now I feel eighty instead of ninety.

"False hope? Why would you give him false hope? He's your fiancé."

"Yeah ..." I whisper while my blank gaze affixes to nothing in particular out the window.

"Josie, what's going on with you? You're alive. I feel like I'm the one who's been given a second chance at life. It's something so much greater than a miracle. Why are you so sad? Did Colten do something?"

With a tiny headshake, I release a slow breath. "It's ... hard to explain. When I was with Felix and Izzy, before anyone else knew I was alive, I felt the tiny improvements in my health. We celebrated every milestone. The world looked different. With Colten, I don't see that version of myself. I don't see everything I am or everything I've become. I see everything I'm not and maybe never will be. When I'm with him, I miss the old Josie, and I know there's no way he doesn't miss her too.

"I didn't ..." Wiping a tear, I try to swallow past the thick pain in my throat. "I didn't think this through."

"Josephine Eleanor Watts, that boy loves you. I'm not sure I've ever seen so much as a glimpse of anything but love and adoration gleaming across his face with your presence or just the mention of your name."

I think about her words. And I'm not denying that he loves me, but that doesn't mean that he wouldn't be better off without me. "He met someone."

"What?" Mom pulls into the garage and shuts off the engine.

"When we told you what happened? How we saw each other at the CVS? What we didn't tell you was that he was there with another woman. A beautiful woman in a red dress. I saw her again at Reagan's T-ball game. They met there, at a game for Reagan and her daughter. She lost her husband a year ago. And they became friends."

"Well, yeah ... *friends.* So what?"

Glancing over at her, I offer a smile that doesn't feel right on my face. "They were dressed up for the ballet. Just the two of them. I'm not stupid. I know where things were headed whether Colten would ever admit it or not. And I'm not mad. I died. He deserved to move on. And if it's her or someone else, my point is ... Colten *did* move on. He took those first steps which means he can live without me. And I think he should live without me. I want this for him. Eighteen years ago, he thought he knew what was best for us, for me. And maybe it was or maybe it wasn't, but we survived. I went to school and landed my dream job. He served his country and fathered a beautiful little girl. We can have a future without it being *ours*." Those words hurt. They hurt so much my heart feels like a ball of sandpaper working its way up my throat.

"Were they ..." Mom clears her throat.

"He said nothing had happened between them."

"Do you believe him?"

I nod. "But I don't believe nothing would have happened had we not run into each other at the CVS."

"Did you ask Becca when she called?"

"Mom ..." I shake my head. "She was too busy crying. I didn't think it was a good time to ask her about Colten's dating life. And I saw what I saw. Maybe he never told her about Layla."

"Who's Layla?"

"The other woman."

"Josie, don't say it like that. That makes it sound scandalous."

I open my door, sliding out my new cane to stand. "It's not scandalous. It's life. His life. I just want him to have everything." It takes me a second to shift my balance to using the cane instead of the walker. "I am his past. The past is something, but the future is everything."

CHAPTER
Forty-Seven

"EARTH TO DETECTIVE MOSLEY," Rains says.

I jerk my head in his direction.

"They found a gun in the dumpster." He nods behind him as we canvass the entire block after the three bodies have been removed from the alley.

"Okay."

"Gang related?"

"What?"

He chuckles. "Sorry, am I disturbing you with work. Where are you?"

I shake my head. "Nowhere. Here. I'm ... I'm fine. Sorry. Let's check the cameras at the convenience store."

Rains follows my lead. "She'll come around, man. You just have to give her some time."

"She wants me to move on. That's not coming around. That's the kiss of death."

"Give her time."

"Time?" I shoot him a look, squinting one eye. "It's been over six months. That's half a year she's been alive when I thought she was dead. She didn't come knock on my front door. I saw her at a CVS. And the look on her face..." I shake my head "...it was guilt. Not surprise. Not excitement. It was guilt. An 'oops, didn't think I'd run into you' look. She said she was trying to get better before coming to see me or her family, but that's bullshit. If you love someone, you don't let them exist, thinking you're dead, for even a second if you have a choice. And she had a choice."

"Okay, you're mad. That's probably a good thing. Josie, in her physically impaired state, will naturally get the most attention and sympathy, but you've been through hell too, and repressing those feelings is not good."

"Are you giving me therapy?" I open the door to the convenience store.

Rains offers me a wink. "I'm a man of many talents. That'll be a hundred and twenty dollars."

OVER THE NEXT TWO WEEKS, I start to spiral out of control. When I'm not working, I'm drinking. Katy and Sean took Reagan on vacation, so I don't have her to distract me from thoughts of Josie. I need a distraction that doesn't involve beer.

No such luck.

It's just me and my thoughts of Josie.

Me and my anger.

Me and my resentment.

It's her refusing to reply to my texts, refusing to answer my calls. It's me and my irrational behavior like now as I call Savannah at 10:00 p.m.

"Colten?"

I take another swig of beer from my sofa with the TV on mute: Cubs vs Dodgers. "Is Josie there?"

"She's in bed. I know she's not taking your calls or responding to your messages. We're trying to convince her that she needs to just talk to you. But ... she's struggling."

She's struggling?

"How are you, honey?"

"Me?" I chuckle. "I'm uh ... great. Yeah. Never been better. How are you and Isaac? I bet it's nice having Josie back. It was nice when I had her back, but now I don't. I don't have her anymore."

"Colten ..."

"But it's good. I've been hanging out with my friends." I glance at the bottle in my hand. "My buds. Budweiser. Bud Light. His cousin Michelob."

"You sound a little ... over-served."

"Do I?" I finish the last ounce or two of the bottle. "Huh. I didn't realize that. Is she asleep or just in bed? Did Isaac carry her to bed? I carried her to bed when she was staying with me. But ... she's not with me. She doesn't want to be with me."

"Colten, she needs time. Give her time. She'll come back to you. She always comes back to you."

"She didn't come back to me. She died. Came back to life, but not back to me. Doesn't it piss you off, even a little, that I found her by accident? We all thought she was dead. Nope. She wasn't dead. She was living with essentially two strangers. She was eating pizza and watching Netflix while all of us thought she was dead. You don't feel even a little hurt by that?"

She doesn't respond. I glance at my phone. She's still on the line.

"She wants me to move on with my life. Did she tell you that? Maybe you and Isaac should move on too. You know? Let Dr. Felix and his wife be her new parents, her new family. I mean ... they probably love her more than you guys do."

"Colten ..."

"I won't keep you. I just wanted to talk to her, but maybe I'll never talk to her again. I deserve it, right? I broke up with her before graduation. I was a dick. I didn't tell you and Isaac how much I loved her. I didn't tell my dad to fuck off. I let her go. This is payback. A nice little 'fuck you, Colten.'"

"Listen ..." She sniffles.

Shit. I've made her cry.

"I'm trying to hold on. It's that simple. I have a million feelings about the events of the past six months. I've had my moments of elation, relief, confusion, frustration, even anger. But at the end of the day, I'm just *so* grateful that she's alive. Every day I see her fighting depression. Every day I watch her work her butt off to walk on her own. To get stronger. Watching my independent girl hobble around with a cane breaks my heart. I spend every waking second putting on a brave face for her. So instead of drinking away your feelings, come visit her. Show her that you are committed to her no matter how much of a martyr she's trying to be right now."

"She doesn't want to see me."

"So what? Don't come for her; come for you."

I try to think over her words, but I can't think right now. "Night, Savannah."

CHAPTER
Forty-Eight

"I DON'T NEED A LIFE JACKET."

Dad chuckles, casting his line from his fishing boat while I reel in my line. "You keep saying that."

"And you keep ignoring me."

"I'm not ignoring you. I said you don't have to wear one when you can walk up the stairs by yourself."

"I did!" I angrily recast my line.

"Five. You walked up five steps. We have twelve."

I set my pole aside and whip off my life jacket, tossing it into the water.

"Christ ... what are you? Five?" he grumbles, quickly reeling in his line while glancing over his shoulder to the shore. "Oh good. Maybe he can talk some sense into you."

I follow his gaze to Colten strutting his way toward the dock.

345

What is he doing here?

A dozen emotions collide and tangle somewhere between my head and my heart. Then ... I rock forward and summersault out of the boat. The whoosh of water fills my ears. I feel weightless for the first time in a long time.

Peaceful.

Serene.

My nerves relax, letting go of every ounce of stress. I'm alive and unburdened. I'm unafraid.

In the next second, I'm yanked from my cocoon. An arm hooks under mine, dragging me to the surface. "JOSIE!" Colten's voice booms as he pulls me like a tugboat. His free arm and legs frantically working to take me to the dock.

"Stop," I say.

"Josie!" Dad's voice sounds from the opposite direction. He's in the water as well, right behind us.

"Stop," I repeat, but no one listens.

Dad bypasses us and climbs up the dock. I kick and wiggle.

"Josie, it's okay. We've got you," Dad says while Colten passes me off to him and he plucks me from the water. A hooked fish. His biggest catch of the day.

"What are you two doing?" I bat away Dad's hands and sit up on the edge of the dock with my feet dangling over the edge.

"Are you trying to kill yourself? What the hell was that?" Dad asks just as Colten lifts himself onto the dock, clothes drenched.

I slowly shake my head. "I ... no. No ..." I continue shaking my head. "I wanted in the water. Not ..." They thought I was trying to drown myself? "I just wanted to be in the water."

Both men wear panicked expressions. Pure torture.

"Jesus, Jo ..." Dad runs a hand through his hair before trying to wring out his clothes. "Watch her," he says to Colten. "I have to go get my boat and take it to the loading dock. Bring her home, please."

Colten nods while trudging to the end of the dock next to me.

"What are you doing here?"

He scrubs his hands over his face, letting them flop to his sides, tugging his shoulders down a couple inches. "Why did you do that?" He ignores my question. There's a world of anguish in his words.

Why did I try to kill myself?

"I told you. I wanted in the water."

"You can't swim."

"I can swim."

"You use a walker. I doubt you can swim."

"I'll have you know I don't use a walker anymore. And I most certainly can swim."

"I'm tired of pulling your lifeless body out of the water."

I wince, and instantaneous regret covers his face. Resting my hands on the side of the dock, I hang my head. "You shouldn't have saved me the first time," I whisper. "And I wasn't drowning this time, but even if I were ..."

"I should have let you drown? Let you die?"

I nod.

"That's ..." He turns his back to me, stabbing his fingers into his hair. "That's fantastic, Josie. So fucking fantastic! I save you, but you don't want that. I try to marry you, but that wasn't right either. I find you, but now I'm not supposed to want you." He turns back to me, letting his hands slide to the back of his neck. "Whatever I did to you eighteen years ago? It's over. Debt paid. Time served. I let you go, but I didn't fucking let you believe I died. I didn't let you mourn me for months. And I sure as hell didn't hide from you. Just say it. You were never coming back to me."

I shake my head, tears in my eyes. "I was," I whisper.

"NO!"

I jump.

Colten's shaking. Hands fisted. Jaw clenched. "I don't believe you. I don't trust you. And I don't feel your love anymore."

I visibly jerk my head, his words kicking my chest, cracking ribs, and bruising my heart. "Colten ..." I blink, letting go of my tears.

"You keep pushing and pushing and pushing ... just ... *pushing* me away. And I'm exhausted. I feel like a fool for coming back." He laughs a little, shaking his head. "I did this when we were young. I was the boomerang that always came back to you when you held out your hand. I willingly, anxiously came back every single time because I knew you always wanted me. I knew the game. The hoops. The secret. It was simply *us*.

"But I don't see us anymore. I don't feel your open arms. I no longer know the game. All I feel is unrequited love. The darkest fucking hole. And I'm so very sorry that you've had these terrible things happen to you. But if you can't let it be me who helps you through this, then I'm done. I'm done waiting. I'm done hoping. I'm just … done."

Curling my lower lip between my teeth to keep it from quivering, I swallow as many of these suffocating emotions as I can. Colten blurs on the other side of my tears.

He scoops me up, his motions almost robotic. And he carries me to his vehicle. No words are exchanged. He doesn't even look me in the eye. Nothing between us has ever felt this final. When we get to my parents' house, he disappears inside the house, leaving me without anything to assist me to walk into the house. My dad's truck is still gone. He must have returned the boat to the marina. And Mom is grocery shopping.

I guess Colten could have left me on the dock. Still, this feels like a silent, although gigantic, fuck you.

When nobody comes to get me or bring me my cane, I open the door and find my wobbly legs. Taking a deep breath, I move one foot forward. My hands fly out to the side, but there's nothing to grip. Still, I'm still on my feet.

Another step.

And another step.

My legs tremble. Unsteady. Unsure.

I use the rail to climb the four steps to the front door. Three more jelly-legged steps to the door. Grabbing the handle, I press my other hand flat to the door and catch my breath. Sweat beads along my brow. When I open the door, I don't hear anything. I follow the wall, using it to steady myself to the stairs.

It's a mountain. My Everest.

One.

Two.

Three.

By the seventh stair, I ease to my knees, resting my forearms two steps above the one at my knees—head bowed, breathing labored. After a few seconds, I lift my head and climb to my feet again.

Eight. Nine.

Ten.

Eleven.

Oh dear god ... I'm dying.

Twelve!

I cling to the banister, resting my forehead on it. When the floor creaks, I glance up. Colten's a few feet away, a duffle bag slung over his shoulder, wet clothes exchanged for dry ones. He must have been here before he came to the lake. He was going to stay, but not now. He's leaving.

Leaving me.

Forever.

His eyes are red. I see the boy I fell in love with. I see the teenager who hated life as much as I do right now. I see every *us* we've ever been. With each blink, it gets harder to breathe.

The only thing more unimaginable than dying is living without Colten Mosley.

Today I don't want to die.

And I know ... I *know* that tomorrow and every tomorrow after I will not want to live without him.

His throat bobs once while he walks down the short hallway toward me, chin tipped to avoid looking at me any longer. "Tell your parents goodbye for me."

When he reaches me, lifting his foot to descend the stairs, my hand closes around his wrist. Colten's gaze slides to that hand.

"I can't do it," I whisper, waiting for him to look at me. When he does, I feel every drop of emotion trickle down my face. "I can't live without you." I sniffle and choke on my next words. Pulling in a shaky breath, I let my hand slide from his wrist to his hand, lacing our fingers. "I don't need anyone ... except you."

Colten's gaze sweeps across my face a beat before he kisses me. It feels new. He feels new. It took twenty-seven years for me to fully open up my heart to him. It took twenty-seven years for me to feel worthy of his love. I think it's taken twenty-seven years and two deaths to love myself.

Who we are is not what we've become. It's a beautiful reflection of everything we've always been. I've always been his, and he's always been mine.

Colten wraps his arms around my waist and walks me backward into my bedroom, kicking the door shut behind us. Our kiss breaks long enough for him to peel off our clothes. In a naked embrace, he lays me on the bed, settling between my bent knees, pushing into me while my eyes drift shut. This feeling ... it's perfection.

"Open your eyes, beautiful."

On a deep inhale, I gaze at him.

He grins, slowly moving inside of me, one hand planted next to my head while his other hand slides between us, making my breath hitch from its touch. "We're enough. You and I. We are—"

I lift my head and kiss him, dragging his lower lip between my teeth before whispering. "We are everything."

He pauses for a moment. Something serious steals his expression. Whatever it is tugs at my heart. And I hate that for even a single second, he had a reason to doubt my love.

"I love you," I say.

He nods slowly.

My fingers feather up his back and frame his face. "I *love* you," I repeat.

"Say it again," he murmurs, kissing down my neck.

"I love you ..."

"Again." He flicks my nipple with his tongue.

"I love you ..." My words mingle with a soft moan.

"Again." He slides out of me and lowers his body, his tongue dipping into my navel.

"I ... love you." I squirm, anticipating his next move.

"Again." He descends a few more inches, one hand

cupping my inner thigh while his other hand squeezes my breast.

"Oh god ..." My head rolls to the side, and my fingers thread through his hair.

He swipes his tongue between my spread legs and mumbles. "That works too."

"LET'S GO, baby, before your parents get home." Colten forces me to sit up. He pulls my wet tee down over my head and threads my legs into my shorts, minus my panties.

"What are you doing?" I'm drunk.

Drunk on sex.

Drunk on him.

Drunk on life.

"You'll see." He hurriedly carries me down the stairs and to his car.

"Colten ..." I fasten my seat belt while he backs out of the driveway.

He doesn't answer me.

I don't protest. I'm too busy watching him. Studying his features. Resurrecting dreams of our future and piecing them together with superglue. Occasionally, he gives me a quick sideways glance and grins. It's so mischievous and handsome.

"We're fishing again?" I say when he pulls up to the dock in the secluded cove where we were a little over an hour earlier.

Colten says nothing. Instead, he plucks me from the car and carries me to the water's edge.

Off with my shirt and my shorts.

"Colten ..." I glance around, buck naked.

"Can you stand?"

I nod.

He releases me and removes his clothes. Then he scoops me up again and carries me into the water. I stiffen as the cool water covers my body.

"What are we doing?" I giggle.

"You wanted in the water. So I'm giving you the water." His lips find mine, sharing a slow kiss before he releases me. "I'll give you everything, as long as you promise to stay."

Live. As long as I promise to live.

I straighten my body. Arms relaxed. Legs supple. Ears in the water bestowing peace again. I gaze up at the fluffy clouds outlined in blue and then close my eyes and float.

Exist.

Draw breath from this life.

Draw strength from the only person who has always set me free. And I always ... *always* find my way back to him.

I find my way home.

Epilogue

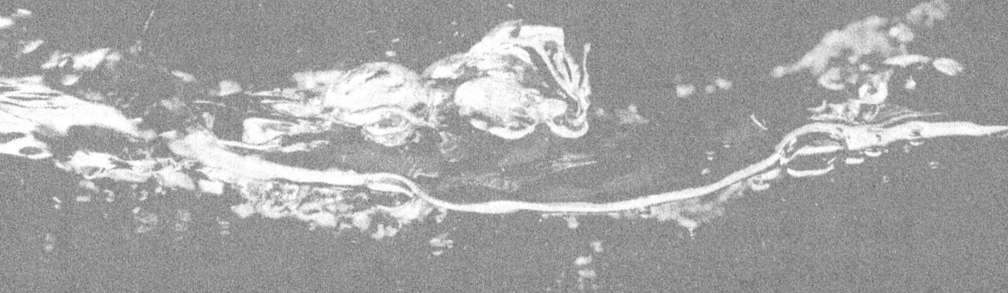

A year later…

"I'm not going to lie. I'm a little intimidated," Dr. Gellhaus says on my first day as Deputy Medical Examiner for Johnson County in Iowa City.

I laugh, taking a seat at the conference table to go over the one case for the day.

One case.

She already determined the other three don't require autopsies.

Things are a little slower here than in Chicago.

"Intimidated?" I question my superior.

"Yes." She sits across from me. "Dr. Cornwell was my mentor as well. But he never called me the best. He never said he learned anything from me. He never called me special."

I feel an invisible fist clenching my heart. It's been a long year of recovery. I wasn't sure I'd get here. And I never imagined here would be anywhere but Chicago.

When Katy and Sean decided to move to Iowa City, Colten didn't think twice. He insisted we follow Reagan, even though it's only a four-hour drive. I was on the cusp of begging Dr. Cornwell for my old job. The timing was undeniably perfect.

"I'm flattered." I smile, a little unsure of myself. Will I bring the same level of expertise now that so much has changed in my life?

"Have you taught before?"

I shake my head. This new job includes a clinical professor position at the University of Iowa.

"You have a gift, Dr. Watts. Go share it," Dr. Cornwell said when I visited with him just before the move.

"I'm sure you saw a lot in Chicago. Lots of stories to share."

A tiny smile curls my lips. She has no idea.

SIX HOURS LATER, I'm home. Home before five on a Monday. I might like this new job.

"Mommy's home. How's my baby?" I deposit my bag inside the back door and hunch down to nuzzle my nose into Artemis's neck, taking a deep inhale. She's the reason I don't mind short workdays. I get to be with her before Colten's off work. We get our special girl time. "Let's take a walk before Daddy gets home. What do you think?"

Her fluffy golden retriever tail whips side to side while she licks my face.

After an hour walk, I shower, make dinner, and wait for Colten. His new detective position is nearly as sleepy as my new job, but that means he has time to coach Reagan's rec softball team. It means we eat dinner together nearly every night. It means we get sunset bike rides and lots of time to fish on the weekends.

I rarely think about Winston Jeffries. Colten was right. I was him, but he isn't me. I'm the quirky girl who fell for the popular boy. I'm still fascinated by death. I love climbing trees and finding a shady spot to read. And ... I love being kissed by Colten Mosley. The best things never change.

"Tell me you're going to be under my naked body without telling me you're going to be under my naked body," Colten says from the deck door behind me while I sip sweet tea and read my book, occasionally gazing into the trees of our wooded lot.

I grin, setting my drink and book aside before standing.

His gaze roves along my body covered in a thin, flowing cotton sundress. Nothing underneath but my naked body.

"What makes you think you're going to be on top, Coach Mosley?"

Colten smirks.

I love that he leaves the house in a suit and tie and returns in jogging shorts and a tee.

"Did you walk her?" He leans down to scratch Artemis's head.

"I did."

"Dinner smells amazing."

I grin. "It does."

His teeth scrape along his bottom lip while his gaze takes another trip along my body. "Will it keep warm for a bit?"

I saunter toward him. "It will. But I'm hungry now."

Colten's hands snake around my waist then to my butt while he pulls me flush against him. "I am too, but not for food." His fingers gather the thin cotton of my dress, hiking it up my legs.

"Tough luck, Mr. Duck. Food first."

He buries his face in my neck, his hands finding bare skin along my backside. I'd be lying if I said my heart isn't racing, my knees aren't weak, my need isn't just as impatient and real as his.

"You're not even going to ask me about my first day?"

Colten pauses his motions, kisses my neck, and begrudgingly releases me. "How was your first day?" He adjusts his erection and blows out a long breath that ends in the best smile.

I match his grin and brush past him to the kitchen. "There was one case. It took me less than an hour." I pull dinner out of the oven. "I had a meeting at the university to discuss this fall's schedule. I made three new friends. And I think my associate professor has a crush on me. He's pretty cute, so we might have to break up for a bit while I let him be my boyfriend for a few months. Don't worry; we'll probably get back together."

Colten fills water glasses from the fridge dispenser. "That's cool. I ran into Tessa Hart. Remember her? She's recently divorced and hasn't let herself go one bit. Tits for days. She asked if I was married. And since you won't marry me, I told her the truth. I have her number. I'm thinking of meeting her for a drink this Friday."

After setting the Cornish hens onto the stovetop, I slowly turn and tug the oven mitts from my hands. "She's a placeholder, and you know it."

Colten smirks. "My, my ... all these years later and you still go a little feral at just the mention of her name."

"Tits for days? Really?" I narrow my eyes.

He sets the waters on the table and turns, offering me a one-shouldered shrug. "How *cute* is your assistant professor?"

I slide my arms around his waist and tip my head back to look at him. "They can't compete with *us*."

His palms cup my face, fingers teasing my short hair while he grins. Has it always been this simple? Did we get caught up in materialistic dreams, the mind games of success, and the expectations of everyone else, when the grandest thing we can possibly experience in life is love?

"Indeed. There is no competing with *us*. We are more than pieces of a life ... more than memories of a life ... we are ..."

I grin. "Everything."

The End

Acknowledgments

Jenn, I shall start with you because I feel like we start and end every day together. You were a true sounding board for this story on more than one occasion. If readers don't like it, I think we should share the blame. ;) Either way, you are the amazing talent behind my teasers, book design, formatting, newsletters, and a million other things. I love our friendship. You are The World's Best Assistant!

To my publicist, Nina, her daughter "That," and the rest of the magical team at Valentine PR, it's always a pleasure to work with you. Thanks for the forks!

To my editor and agent, Max, thank you for always believing in me. That sounds so generic, but after thirty books together, it's fitting.

An enormous thank-you to the rest of my editing team: Monique, Amy, Leslie, Kambra, Bethany, Shabby, Sian, and Shauna. I feel like every book gets messier just like my thoughts, and you swoop in to save the day.

Thank you to my ARC teams, Instagram team, bloggers, social media influencers, and EVERY

SINGLE READER who took a chance on this story. It's an honor to write for you—a dream.

Finally, thank you to my family and close friends for a lifetime of love and support. I'm blessed beyond words.

ALSO BY
Jewel E. Ann

Standalone Novels

Idle Bloom

Undeniably You

Naked Love

Only Trick

Perfectly Adequate

Look The Part

When Life Happened

A Place Without You

Jersey Six

Scarlet Stone

Not What I Expected

For Lucy

What Lovers Do

ABOUT THE
Author

Jewel is a free-spirited romance junkie with a quirky sense of humor.

With 10 years of flossing lectures under her belt, she took early retirement from her dental hygiene career to stay home with her three awesome boys and manage the family business.

After her best friend of nearly 30 years suggested a few books from the Contemporary Romance genre, Jewel was hooked. Devouring two and three books a week but still craving more, she decided to practice sustainable reading, AKA writing.

When she's not donning her cape and saving the planet one tree at a time, she enjoys yoga with friends, good food with family, rock climbing with her kids, watching How I Met Your Mother reruns, and of course...heart-wrenching, tear-jerking, panty-scorching novels.

www.jeweleann.com